Taming the Stallion

Dorothy Callahan

Published by
Crimson Romance
an imprint of F+W Media, Inc.
10151 Carver Road, Suite 200
Blue Ash, Ohio 45242

www.crimsonromance.com

ISBN 10: 1-4405-6345-4
ISBN 13: 978-1-4405-6345-4
eISBN 10: 1-4405-6346-2
eISBN 13: 978-1-4405-6346-1

Dedication

This book goes out to anyone who has ever loved an animal, for those who work daily with animals, and for those whose driving force is to make a better life for an animal in need. You are the souls of the planet, and every life you touch is grateful for your intervention.

Acknowledgments

The road to publication has been a very long one, and I have made some wonderful friends along the way. Enormous thanks to my mom and wonderful husband for the constant encouragement to keep going and their steadfast belief in my work. Thanks to Sheria and Lisa, for dropping everything for last-minute critiquing, and friends and family for the outpouring of love and support. Special thanks to Officer Ploof, for the ride-along, and Alice and Gillian for the community outreach that I never expected. And lastly, for Jennifer and Barb at Crimson Romance, for turning my dream into a reality. I wouldn't be here without all of you in my lives. Thank you, from the bottom of my heart.

Prologue

That Fateful Morning

Of all the backstabbing, spineless, ungrateful actions a man could do, this one took the cake. Moonlight filtered through the rectangular stable windows, outlining the young colt and the beefy gutless coward saddling him, right there in the center aisle. Ashton didn't need to look to the right to know High Eminence's stall was empty.

Of course he was stealing High Eminence.

Why *wouldn't* he steal Emin?

Still, Ashton Lyre had a stable to run, an empire to uphold, and his honor to defend. He crept forward, not knowing if this most-unwanted guest was armed, and positive he could not cross the wide span of rubber-topped concrete to his office and his sidearm without being spotted.

Just as the cretin looped the cinch and began to tighten it, Ashton stepped forward. "Need help, pal?"

Horror and something akin to fury raged in those eyes, and the thief yanked hard on the cinch, making Emin's head jerk up in shock.

"Don't. Don't do this," Ashton pleaded with the thief. "He's just a colt."

Belying his size, this wretched monster of a human darted across the aisle and grabbed a shovel. A menacing snarl curled his lips as he ran near, swinging.

Emin panicked and danced away, his hooves clunking on the rubber tiles as Ashton jumped back from his foe. Large eerie shadows spilled from the young Standardbred across the dark corridor, making it harder for Ashton to see his adversary.

He managed to block the shovel.

With his head.

Blinding light flashed behind his eyes, and moisture, damp and sweet-smelling, oozed down his temple.

His foeman swore—as if he had the right—and sprung into the saddle. He spurred the horse hard and blasted past. One lucky grab told Ashton he'd managed to loosen a foot from a stirrup, but it wouldn't be enough.

No, not today.

Not for this man.

The black-clad horse thief thundered down the corridors of Starstruck Stables, his knowledge of the layout as damning as the spurs he dug into the sulky racer's sides.

High Eminence was broke to saddle as well as his jog cart, and his speed lent those freshly shod hooves wings. Ashton knew he'd have the proverbial snowball's chance of catching up to him. Despite the flaring pain spurting behind his eyes and pulsing through his head like a stress squeeze toy, Ashton reached for the nearest stall and fumbled with the latch.

Typhoon.

Not the fastest horse in the barn. In fact, Typhoon had been relegated to stud these past three years.

Damn.

He didn't have time to stumble in the dark, hoping to find a horse half capable of keeping up, when he knew the only one that could was Emin's sire, Ralphie.

But Ralphie was dead.

No thanks to *him.*

Double damn.

He had to get him. Stop him. Had to.

He guided the stallion into the aisle and swung up, barebacked. He kicked Ty's sides and yelled, "Yah!"

A female squeak of shock issued forth ahead of him; he followed the sounds of receding hoof beats and saw Raylie sitting at the bottom of the loft's ladder. By the way she was sprawled and the anger radiating from her as she glared at the intruder, he could tell she didn't fall off the ladder.

She'd been pushed.

If he hurt one hair on her head…

"Stay here." Good God, did he just snarl at her as he galloped past? But he loved Raylie and he couldn't bear the thought of losing her.

Not now.

Not when he'd just found her.

And now their suspect was getting away.

He called the man by name; demanded his return. It made no difference. Cool predawn air misted over his skin as he charged through the stable door and blasted across his rolling pastures, following the crushed grass wake of his fastest sulky racer.

He'd never catch up to Emin.

Not on this old ride.

Hooves thundered behind him, and he chanced a glance over his shoulder. God, he hoped it wasn't another accomplice.

An *armed* accomplice.

How many of his horses were out tonight for a midnight run?

Inky blackness faded to the east as the hint of morning breached the horizon, sending the fields into a surreal realm he had never known. Ty's breathing pulsed, his hooves pounded, his mane whipped. When was the last time he had run so hard?

In fact, when was the last time Ashton had?

Still, he never lost his sense of balance, even a few years later, and at five a.m. Wan yellow light sprinkled across the fields, making the dew glitter like so many ocean swells.

Emin veered around an oak tree, and Ashton heard a "Yah," as the horse was directed straight into the fence.

He braced for the sound of splitting wood and splintering bones.

Emin ran straight on through.

No crash.

When Ashton guided Ty around the oak, he noticed the slats lying on the ground. Outraged, he screamed out a string of obscenities he was glad Raylie wasn't around to hear.

The rider at Ashton's back drew nearer, following their obvious wake. He leaned closer over the brown neck, making himself a smaller target should the other rider have a gun. Ty took the cue and stretched lower, his gallop turning faster.

They veered for the road, onto the asphalt of modern suburbia. Emin faltered on the pavement, his youth and training leaving him unprepared for the hard sensation thundering under his hooves, giving Ty a chance to draw nearer. Down flower-laden streets they went, until the gurgling of a diesel engine and the snake-like red glow of taillights dominated the road.

Oh my God, it was a trailer.

Starstruck's gooseneck trailer.

And the horse was racing right toward it.

Ashton reached out, to stop him, to catch him, maybe even to save him, but Emin was still a length in the lead. He urged Ty faster, although he knew what was about to happen. He ran even, but instead of grabbing clothing, he reached as far as he could and snatched the bridle.

Someone revved the chugging engine, touched the brake. The lights blared red.

And then High Eminence did exactly what Ashton knew he would do.

*

Eleven days earlier
Ashton's hands shook as he flipped open his cell phone. The numbers wavered through his unshed tears, but he managed to press 9-1-1.

"9-1-1. What's your emergency?"

His mouth bounced wordlessly as he tried to form words around his tight throat. "I…I need to report two murders."

"Where?"

He gave her his name and street address.

Then, "Do you know the victims?"

"Yes." He gripped the phone tight in his hand, tried to swallow.

"First victim's name, please."

"Ralphie."

"Last name?"

Man, she was annoyingly professional amidst his despair. He hedged. "Wing."

"Age of first victim?"

"Twenty."

"Your relationship to the victim?"

That one caught him off-guard. *Adopter? Owner?* "Guardian."

"Sir, I'm dispatching police and ambulance to your address. Do you know who could have done this?"

He stared into the stall as a few of his stable hands drew near, horror and shock freezing their expressions as they stared at the two dead horses.

They were too young and innocent to commit this atrocity. "No."

He sensed her nod on the other end. "Name of the second victim?"

Not so easy. "Um…Monarch."

"Monarch?"

"Yes." He bit his lip.

"Last name?"

Ashton leaned back. "He doesn't have one."

She paused. "Age?"

"Five."

"Weight?"

Weight? She didn't ask that a minute ago. Ashton shook his head, tore off his Stetson and wiped his brow with his forearm. "About four-hundred fifty-five…kilograms."

"*Kilograms?*"

Silence.

"That's, like, over a thousand pounds. Are these people or just animals?"

Slamming his hat back on, Ashton bit out the one retort people would never expect from a tycoon. "They're not 'just animals' to me. These two horses are worth over four million dollars, and yesterday they were fine, and today they're—"

"Sir, sir," she interrupted. "I appreciate your loss. But animals are property. Not only are they out of the police's jurisdiction, but you can't murder personal belongings."

No one ever understood how much his horses meant to him. Especially the two that he stared at right now. "Ma'am, someone killed them. Cold-hearted. I need help. I need cops. Evidence collected. Fingerprints, something!"

He heard her take a deep breath. "Sir, I'm going to give you the phone number of the local humane society."

Shoulders dropped as he closed his eyes. "No, not them. I want *cops.*"

"They have Peace Officers. They have all the same legal powers as the police."

"Wannabees," he muttered. He'd never had problems with the local law enforcement, of course. His horses were probably the best tended animals on the planet. But he'd always heard about confiscations, zealots, gunshot dogs from trigger-happy raids on drug houses. The last thing he wanted was someone coming in here, criticizing every nuance of his business.—*Half cup too much grain. Fifteen minutes too long exercising. Forty-five seconds too long in the sun without shelter.* Good God, it would be enough to drive him crazy.

He crushed the brim of his hat at the thought.

"Do you have a pen, sir?"

He trudged across the aisle to his glass-walled office and grabbed paper and ink. "Yeah, I'm ready."

She recited the exchange. Ashton mumbled a platitude and hung up.

Young Henry waited outside the door, scared and pale. The kid didn't deserve to be exposed to death like this, even if he did want to go to vet school in three years. Ashton pulled open the door and stood there. He felt wrapped in cotton, heavy, slow, and every noise seemed muffled, hard to hear. Hard to see.

"Sir? What should we do?"

Gone. Two of them. Just like that. He rubbed his eyes, trying to get the scratchy gauze out of them.

Tentative, Henry whispered, "Sir?"

He took a deep breath, looked around and almost didn't recognize the place. "Don't touch anything. Watch the rest of them like a hawk. Make sure they're all acting normal." He flipped open his cell and began dialing the number he just wrote down. "We're going to have the monkey squad here soon."

He feared they would drive him bananas.

Chapter 1

She felt it straight down to her bones. Maybe it stemmed from working so closely with Mother Nature's creatures, or maybe it was because of her years of job experience, or maybe even Angie watched out for her from the Great Beyond and still took care of her to this day, but Raylie knew the dreams were about to manifest into existence.

Soon.

Dead horses.

Of late, they were always about dead horses.

Raylie clenched her eyes shut and inhaled deeply, trying to erase the dream images that had plagued her these last two weeks as she turned her key in the black STAFF ONLY door. Cheddar spun and barked as he dashed around the empty lobby of the waking humane society, greeting each of her co-workers with his usual early morning vigor.

At least one of them liked Mondays.

That was only because Cheddar hadn't written a single report in the whole twenty-four months of his life. And, of course, he remained blissfully devoid of prophetic dreams.

The community corkboard showed a Thoroughbred mare for sale—a new posting. Two omens. Tomorrow, perhaps. Maybe even today. Not good.

These days Raylie needed the extra motivation; after all, with Jim two months from retirement, and a juicy field chief spot opening up, Raylie needed all the arrests she could get. With the promotion she could pay off Angie's house and move into the restored one provided by the shelter. Then, and only then, would she be able to move on with her life.

"Hey, Ray."

The sound of hooves clomping inside drew her attention. She turned and smiled at the woman—in clogs, not horseshoes—walking past on the gray ceramic tiled floor, carrying an armful of donated towels. Omen Number Three. "Hi, Jen." Raylie pulled open the door to the lit hallway and Cheddar raced on ahead.

Only on Mondays did Raylie enter through the main lobby, instead of the staff entrance around back where her office was. She glanced around at the many furry faces, spurring herself to save more of the wee beasties, like Flotsam, the black kitty tossed into a dumpster, now up for adoption. Or Barnum, the English Bulldog, left behind when the owners moved out. Or even Miranda, the lop rabbit, whose owners went to jail for thirty days for setting her free in the local park.

Many new homes were found here. But never enough.

Raylie grimaced as she followed her orange and white linebacker down the hallway, reminding herself she couldn't save all of them. She saved *him*, of course, her first month on the job. Twelve weeks old, half-starved, chewing on a tuna can. He'd been timid and fearful, with cuts on his soft pink mouth from the sharp edges.

Her excitable Pit Bull now spun in front of the Cruelty Department door, stepping on his leash over and over, tripping himself in his eagerness.

One warning bark—barely knee-high—issued from behind the door. Little footprints danced in the fluorescent crack.

"You want 'im? You want 'im?"

Happy toes clicked on the linoleum as Snort gave one more warning bark.

"Go get 'im." Ray whipped open the door.

A fawn Pug leaped up at Cheddar, and her linebacker skidded to his shoulder in submission. "Coward," she muttered.

Snort postured over him, a burbling growl in his throat as Cheddar exposed his groin and looked away.

"Snot," she said as she brushed past.

"Snort," Leann, the department's secretary, corrected automatically. As usual, she was early to work and ready to save lives.

Ray grinned as the aroma of hazelnut teased her. "Snort, Snot. What's an 'r' between friends?" She blew an air-kiss to the caged canary as she gave him fresh food and water. The bird had been found starving in a home after the owner died and was a new shelter resident. "He finally seems to be putting on weight. I thought we were going to lose him."

"He sang for a minute yesterday. Should be ready for adoption soon." Leann was already listening to the phone messages as Ray glanced at the inbox on her adjacent desk. Hopefully she'd get to the paperwork tomorrow. Mondays were usually too busy, and the notes that Leann had already filled out were piling up on the corner. Leann glanced up. "You look like shit," she said with her usual inter-friend tact.

Raylie pointed to her head as she poured herself a cup of motivation. "Hair gel shower. Someone dumped a litter of kittens in my backyard." She gave her a rueful glance. "Coaxed the last one out of the tree at three a.m."

Leann considered her. "I think I'll make you a badge…," she made a circle with her hands, "… 'Defender of All Things Furry.'" Receiver to her ear, Leann smirked. Her black hair and dark eyes were far softer than her words. Everything about Leann, in fact, was gentle, from her long lashes to her fabrics. Even her soft curls sensibly bounced along her shoulders to frame her face. Although probably ten years older than Ray, she could pass for a college student. Leann frowned and wrote something down, announced, "Dead cat," then pushed a button for the next message.

Knowing she had a few minutes to spare, Raylie gathered up the guinea pig with a cast on its rear leg and snuggled him close. She slipped some fresh parsley from the office fridge under his nose and watched him tear into it. She leaned against her chunky wooden desk and watched Leann do her thing. "Had the dream again."

"Second hang-up," Leann muttered, but then she looked up, and her shoulders dropped. "Again? That's what, like ten times? I swear you're psychic."

"Am not. Besides, it changed this time."

Leann cradled the receiver, giving Raylie her full attention. "More than the clean fluffy stalls?"

"Yeah." She returned the pig to his cage. "I was getting a lot of details this time. Weird. Like waxed hooves. Glossy coats. Braided manes. Really healthy."

"Show horses."

She sipped her coffee, held her eyes. "Yeah." She glanced into the corner. "And I could smell…"

"Horse dookie?" Her lips twitched.

"No. Money."

That one word made Leann sit tall in her chair. "Your dream smelled like money? Girl, sign me up."

She merely shook her head. "It was really unsettling."

"What's unsettling is how many animals you're trying to cram in here. But, yeah, it is hard to arrest someone whose horses are sparking clean."

"They need me," Raylie said, smiling at the turtle recovering from shell rot. "And, besides, what better place to have them heal than in the Cruelty Department? Isn't that why we're here? To help animals?"

"*Those* animals." Leann pointed out the window and smiled, then her expression turned playful. "This is why your dreams are so funky. That, and all those horse races you've been going to. You got to cut back."

Leann didn't know this, but once Derrick died, Raylie hadn't taken a single step near the beasts, unless her job demanded it.

Even then, she was so incredibly tense she usually gave herself a headache.

"Dang it, there goes my fun." She drew some antibiotics into an oral syringe, went to the rabbit cage and squirted the strawberry-flavored goop into the New Zealand's mouth. She checked the wound from the cuterebra and said, "Looks like it's healed. Hopefully he'll get an *indoor* home this time, away from botflies."

Leann's tongue poked out of her mouth. "Maggots are so gross." But then she brightened. "Oh, I need your phone number. You promised me you'd fill in for bowling, and my sister's still off her foot." Then Leann multitasked, shoving her a pad and pen and returning to her messages. The girl was good, Ray had to admit. 'Course, she was the first receptionist to run the department when it was created seven years back. Had it running like a hound on a coon's scent by the time Raylie applied two years ago.

Grumbling, she scrawled the word "Me" and her phone number under her shelter's logo. She hated bowling. "Why am I doing this, again?"

"Because you promised." Then that gentle smile dropped, and Leann started scribbling down the latest phone message.

Here it comes.

When Ray leaned forward, Leann shielded the note. One deep breath later, she pushed the SAVE button and looked up. With a reluctant flourish, she tore the report from the pad. "Looks like your dream is now your eight a.m. nightmare."

And there it was. Raylie swore a horse just kicked her in the gut. "Oh, God, why?"

Leann stuck out the paper. "Two Standardbreds found dead at Starstruck Stables."

The headache surged to life.

Damn it, she hadn't even tensed up yet.

*

After taking a few minutes to digest the bad news—and breathe away her headache—Raylie sipped her coffee and flipped through her day's work with the other hand. Dead cat, dog without shelter, two dead horses—a shiver of cold raced down her back as her pulse thrummed loud in one ear. Johanssen's house again.

She moaned, tipped back her head. "How many this time?"

Eyes closed, Leann shook her head and said, "At least thirty cats. Phone guy reported her. Turned out one of them ate the cord."

With a derisive snort, Ray said, "Probably the only food in the house."

"Yeah, guess they didn't like the marbles she fed them last time. Too hard to chew."

Futility roared within her. "You know, I didn't spend my life wanting to save animals only to have the same situation *in the same house* play out over and over again. When're we gonna get a sympathetic judge? Every six months we're yanking fifty cats out of there." Her jaw hardened; she pinned her cup to her desk. She always knew she wanted to be an animal cop, because she always wanted to get the bad guys who hurt the innocent animals. As a child, though, she never realized that that meant dealing with dead and dying pets and some of the skuzziest people on the planet.

Cops had it a lot easier. They could always do traffic.

"I know, I know." Fingers laced over her hip, Leann leaned back and said, "Know what else I think?"

Jaded. That's how she felt right now. Jaded. "I should have been a vet?"

She smiled. "You're stalling. No pun intended."

Ray groaned. "Horse. Stall. I get it." Splayed fingers raked through her hair, and she wondered if that made her horns better or worse. "Starstruck. I'll go there first."

Surprise made Leann's perfect eyebrows arch high. "You're choosing a dead animal over a savable one?"

Faux pas number one. A small shrug moved one shoulder. "It's the dream, Leann. I got to check this out. The last two times it happened were headline arrests."

A resigned nod was Leann's only response. Then she said, "Yeah, I guess you're right. Ham Head is still behind bars, so who am I to argue?" A small wry smile tooled around on Leann's face. "I used to jump, you know. Standardbreds aren't cheap, especially his."

Mid-sip, she stopped. "His?"

"Ashton's. FYI, he's a hottie. And somehow still single."

She shook her head, palms out, stepped back. "I'm devoting myself to animals and my job. Animals I understand. People, never. Even animal people don't get me. Like how I can own one pet but tend to fifteen. Or remember which foster pet gets what meds at what dose and when. But people? All they want to know is when I'm going to start dating again." She felt her thumb rub up along her ring finger. Her empty ring finger. Empty eighteen months now. "So, what are you getting at?"

Evasive, Leann shrugged. "Just said he's a single hottie."

Raylie swallowed, felt her anger claw its way up her back. "You know what I say about hot men: Jump 'em, pump 'em, dump 'em. They can't sustain." Except—all her friends *married* the guys they dumped…after they went crawling back. Raylie would be smarter than them.

With another wry smile Leann said, "Girlfriend, I'd bet you Mole Asses that Ashton knows his way around a woman's body."

Ignoring what owning a horse would do to her frayed nerves, Raylie countered, "Yeah? Why would you think that?"

A dreamy look swaddled Leann's eyes as she said, "I've seen that way that man moves. He almost swaggers. Not a girl in the stable wouldn't kill to know *that* man in a carnal way." The look she sent Raylie revealed all.

"Right. Hot men like that are too stuck on themselves to take care of their women." She almost crushed her cup into a puddle of foam and java, wishing she had been able to dump Derrick when he turned toxic.

But that would have meant abandoning Angie, something she never could have done, and he knew it, damn his wretched soul.

The phone rang, and Leann grabbed it, a head shake with eye rolls tossed in for effect. "Pause for Paws Cruelty, can you hold, please?" She nodded and pushed HOLD. Without looking up, she said, "Two words: Great. Catch." Pushed a button. "Thank you for holding. How may I help you?" With a grimace, she waved Raylie out the door. Obedient but curious, Ray took one large step backward into the hall. "Oh, Ms. Johanssen, I'm sorry, Officer McPherson just left the office. Yes, no, I understand."

As Leann fielded the call, Raylie silently shook as if sobbing, then made a noose from Cheddar's leash and pretended to hang herself in the hallway.

Leann almost smiled. "Ms. Johanssen, Ms. Johanssen, remember all those low-cost spay/neuter vouchers we sent you last year? Mm-hmm. Mm-hmm. I know. It must be so difficult to feed so many. Ms. Johanssen, that's why we tried to get them all fixed. Remember? No, Ms. Johanssen, you weren't away. Who would've fed your cats? It says here we spoke on April twelfth. Yes, it's right here. Mm-hmm. Mm-hmm. Can you hold for one teensy tiny second?" She nodded into the phone and pushed the button. Squaring up with Raylie, Leann said, "I can tell you right now you're wasting your time, thinking Ashton's your suspect. I'll bet my paycheck on it."

An unladylike snort preceded Raylie's smile. "Right. You'll bet me your horse he's good in bed and only your paycheck that he's innocent? Property owners with dead animals are *never* innocent. You know that." An expansive wave indicated the menagerie filling the office as proof of what they dealt with on a daily basis. "Why? Who turned him in?"

Solemnly, Leann pushed the receiver to her chest, as if holding it there would cushion her words. Or, she realized, that what she was about to say was oh-so-endearing. "He reported the deaths himself, Ray." She turned and went back to her call.

Rattled by that, Raylie took the keys for car number two and left. Although she knew few people could handle Ms. Johanssen's ramblings better than Leann—those two had practically become buds over the years of confiscations—Leann's endorsement of the man she planned to arrest for neglect and starvation made Raylie frown.

One glass door separated her from the tropical oven, and one last sip fortified her. Cheddar raced up and down the hallway with Bingo, the Border Collie, also rescued, keeping time. Snort the enforcer raged in stiff-legged fashion at the youngsters whenever they had too much fun. Tossing her cup of joe into the trash, Raylie headed out.

It was going be another scorcher. Gray haze filled the skies as only a Kentucky July could accomplish. For the past week, every morning looked like a thunderstorm threatened, and every day that promise left, laughing and unfulfilled. So different from upstate New York. In Syracuse, those gray clouds meant business.

Starstruck was first up on the menu. Eight fifteen a.m. Morning warm-ups would be done, so there'd be no reason why Mr. Ashton couldn't talk to her. She turned the key in the ignition of her green and white work van and aimed for New Spoke Road, telling herself it was only the humidity that was prickling her scalp and had absolutely nothing to do with her dreams.

But as she left flower-filled suburbia and passed mile after mile of whitewashed fencing, she could feel the tension narrowing within her, until it gathered into a tiny knot somewhere around her solar plexus.

She swore the place smelled like money.

A wrought-iron gate complete with video camera blocked the doublewide driveway. She got out and pushed the intercom, straightening her uniform and angling her badge toward the lens.

"May I help you?" The voice crackled with static.

"Officer McPherson. I'm here about the two dead horses."

The woman's voice on the intercom seemed tentative. "Are you…with the police? They said they wouldn't come."

"No, ma'am. I'm with Pause for Paws Humane Society, Cruelty Division."

The intercom clicked off as she apparently consulted with another. Then the door buzzed and swung open, and Raylie got back into her car to drive through.

It was like entering another world, one where gold lined the streets and flags were made of twenties. Livery hands guided massive bays to and from the paddocks, some wearing mesh fly guards around their eyes like equine Zorros. Motorized flatbeds puttered up and down the dirt driveways bearing bales of alfalfa and straw, and young men hopped down to deliver rations to the never-ending rows of brown heads poking out of stalls.

A deliberate cruise down each row revealed healthy animals with glossy eyes and coats. Brushed manes, some braided, decorated the eager friendly faces. She got out, despite her racing heart and the cold sweat trickling down her back, and forced herself to peek over a few occupied stall doors.

Clean, fluffy straw. Fresh water in scrubbed buckets. Leftover grain, as if the horses knew it would still be there when they got back.

Not the typical place one would expect starvation.

Swallowing her fear, Raylie wiped off the pasty sweat from her lips and returned to her vehicle.

She guided the car in front of the massive barn, and got out to watch a trainer in one half working a young colt on a lunge line, while the other side had a young lady riding English, guiding her gray Paso Fino mare around tiny orange cones in a series of complicated steps.

Again the memory surged, replayed over and over until Derrick's death permeated her very pores. Raylie's hands fisted at her sides. Every muscle in her body tensed as her eyes darted around. She wanted to run. She wanted to cry.

"Can I help you, ma'am?"

She turned to the weathered old man at her right, wearing—she couldn't believe it—denim overalls. Her voice felt choked when she asked, "Who do I talk to about the dead horses?"

"Yes, ma'am, that would be the owner. He's right down that hallway, there."

Another bay, tacked with a blue-striped saddle pad and ready for a ride, was led by a little girl from that very hallway. Blue striped. *Blue striped.*

Her headache raged. Her throat clenched shut. She was about to step into hell.

Chapter 2

Not one, but two of his favorites.

He yanked off his Stetson and wiped his forearm over his brow. Plunked it back in place. Picked up his cell and redialed. "Doc Schneible? Yeah, Ashton again. I know. I know." His voice dripped with despair. Doc had a foal caught mid-birth. Scared Thoroughbred took off. Bad situation. Bottom line, his dead steeds weren't going anywhere. "You think maybe poison? Maybe I should call the cops again, anyway?" He listened to Doc ramble on, not hearing his words. "Will an hour screw up blood tests or anything?" He knelt beside Monarch and hid the tiny white spot on his forehead with his thumb. Money's Bull's-eye, he always called it.

But Money hadn't been shot. At least, not with anything as obvious as a bullet.

And Raphael beside him, a darker bay, no white. His head was cranked into the corner, turned up, nostrils flared. But Ralphie wasn't breathing either.

He flipped his phone closed, not even knowing if he said goodbye, and felt his throat swell. Burning stung his eyes as he looked at his two favorites. Ralph was old—that is, twenty—a two-year-old gift from his suddenly rich Aunt Karen on his eighteenth birthday. His first purebred, his first stud. Ralph had a lot of love to spread in Louisville, and the sulky-races showed it. His offspring were slicing seconds off the records every time they set their hooves to dirt.

Monarch, though, he was a brat. *Had* been, he corrected. More often than not Ashton himself threatened to aim for that small white target. But Monarch's head was probably plated in steel. Bulletproof.

He wouldn't pace. Hated the sulkies. Fought constantly with the other horses—stallions *and* mares—even after being gelded. Broke through fences. Jumped the rest.

But his saving grace was therapy. One look at a disabled child and Monarch turned to mush. He'd stand still, let them comb him, brush him, and Ashton finally begrudgingly let one handicapped child ride him.

That was all it took. Monarch was the best damned therapeutic riding horse around. He started a new class for disabled children, bought a few Quarter Horse crosses and a couple Welshes, but Monarch was the one they lined up for.

The two horses that had forever changed his life lay dead before him, and he didn't even have the courage to close their eyes.

He heard a voice behind him and wiped his cheeks.

"Mr. Ashton?"

"It's Lyre," he answered. "Ashton Lyre."

The woman said, "L-I-A-R?" He heard the scratching of a pen.

A common misconception. "L-Y-R-E."

She paused. In a formal voice she said, "I need to ask you a few questions."

Oh, God, it couldn't be good. Whatever vestige of strength he had melted into a puddle of despair at that simple statement.

He turned around and saw a cop, with her hand resting on the hilt of her gun, looking petrified of his gentle steeds. She was average height, with short, cropped brown hair that almost seemed spiky. Burgundy highlights streaked throughout it. It flattered both her color and her high cheekbones. She looked haunted—a little pale—though he wasn't sure how he even noticed that in his grief. But he did, which surprised him. After all, he hadn't even glanced at a woman since Brittany pulled her stunt a year and a half ago. The shadows in the officer's eyes told him she knew exactly what he was going through; it gave him a little courage. He said, "I was told the police wouldn't come here, ma'am."

"No," she leaned back, "sir, they wouldn't." She looked almost shocked that he called the cops, even a little pasty as she glanced around. "Animals are out of their jurisdiction." The way she blanched reminded him of a troll doll left out too long in the sun. "I...I'm a Peace Officer, with Pause for Paws Humane Society."

He straightened. "I didn't think you would really come."

Her eyes widened as he stood up, and her mouth opened a bit. A touch of color brushed those pale cheeks, and he knew he put it there. Then she shook herself, swallowed and cleared her throat. "It's our job to respond to all complaints. I'm Officer McPherson. I've had an anonymous report of two downed horses." That haunted gaze swept behind him, and he saw true pain lingering there. She rubbed her eyes hard, took a deep breath. "Want to tell me what happened?"

He swallowed as well, trying to forget Brittany's backstabbing and focus on the cute pixie standing before him. He removed his hat and held it before him, and she nodded at his courtesy. "Not anonymous, ma'am. I called." He wiped his brow. "I wish I knew what happened. They were dead when the stable hands got here at six."

She groaned. "People at work that early?"

"Yes, ma'am. It's the biz."

The woman picked her way into the stall, examining his gelding with a critical eye he frankly envied. "Freshly shod?" She pointed at the new silver shoes on his horse.

"Last week, ma'am. They all were."

"All of them?" She looked around.

"Every eight weeks, yes, ma'am."

Still continuing her inspection, she squatted down and checked underneath. "No cuts or lacerations that I can see." She stood back up, massaged her forehead. "Looks like he was a good eater. Nice confirmation."

Choked up, he could only nod.

"His stall always this clean?"

Ashton shrugged. "The job of the night shift is to go through and scoop any dirty spots, top up water. I don't know his particular voiding cycle."

She nodded, stood up and scribbled on a sheet of paper. "No manure on his coat. He probably died during his down time."

Down time. The four hours per night when a horse actually lays down. Impressed, he gave her a probing look, wondering how long she'd been a rider.

But she cut him off. "What happened yesterday, to this guy?" She indicated Monarch.

He angled toward her. "It was a normal day, ma'am. Money had a bran mash for breakfast, out to pasture until noon. I showed him his saddle so he wouldn't run away. Classes at one, three and five. Flakes of hay after scrub-down and stalled."

She jotted it all down. "Money?"

He faced her fully. "Monarch, ma'am. But he cost me a bundle in repairs. Dang horse breaks everything."

A shadow of pain flashed across her eyes, and he didn't feel quite so alone with his grief. "That his saddle?" she asked, looking at a bright red one.

"Yes, ma'am. For therapy."

Sharp, light brown eyes studied him. "Destructo is a therapy horse?"

"Yeah. Was. Eight years. Only way to keep him calm."

Surprise crossed her face.

He fiddled with his hat brim. People never understood Money, but he was used to it. "I had to keep him happy, ma'am."

A faint smile crossed her lips. He wanted to see it again.

"And big boy here?"

"Raphael. Ralphie." The words were hard to say. Out loud, it seemed so…final. "Champion sire. Turned out to pasture two years ago."

"And yesterday?" She'd make a good drill sergeant. Fleetingly, he wondered what orders she'd bark out to him.

"No, ma'am. I took him to a show. Left at five a.m., got to Tennessee around seven-thirty. There all day with him. Got home around nine last night."

"Fine last night?"

"Great. A little diarrhea, not uncommon with all the apples. He loves the attention at the shows."

"Got hay at nine?"

He frowned. "You think a poisonous plant? I buy my hay only from Oakbend. Guaranteed free of toxins. Besides, all the horses get the same feed, unless they're sick or pregnant, which these two weren't." He rubbed his neck; he hated all the questions regarding his horses. Sooner or later, he feared, someone would ask the ultimate question, and his whole life would be turned upside down. "But yes, ma'am, two or three flakes."

She pursed her lips and kept writing. Not a smile, but certainly intriguing. "I'd like to get some samples of their grain and hay. Maybe even their water."

She looked up at him, and he saw the catch in her eyes, that momentary hiccup in time when a woman notices a man she finds attractive. He'd seen it countless times giving lessons and trail rides. It was just—well—this was the first time he felt himself responding since Brittany left him for his stable master. "Of course, ma'am."

He waved at a stable hand. "Give this officer a flake of hay in a clean bag, and a big scoop of grain, maybe in a bucket or something. And a gallon of water from whatever source they both drank from yesterday." He looked down into her slightly surprised eyes. "Is that enough? For analysis?"

She settled, jutting out one hip. "Yes, actually. There's a college up north that I'm going to send it to for analysis. It's called Cornell."

He'd heard of it. "In New York."

"Yeah, I'm from there. They'll do a thorough chemical analysis."

"Really? Where in New York?"

She blinked. "Syracuse."

He smiled down at her, wanting to tell her he bought a car from there, but it was too random a comment. He noticed she had nice eyes. "Go Orange," he said, referring to the home team, then immediately felt foolish.

Faint color touched her cheeks again, and she looked down and read from her clipboard. "Is there a pond on the property?"

She looked really attractive when she blushed. He glanced at her hand for a ring. "No. All water's by trough or bucket."

"And the insurance agency? Have you called them about the deaths? They'll want a necropsy."

"Shit." He looked up. "I mean, shoot, ma'am. No. Didn't even think of it. But I already called Doc."

She seemed to consider him in that moment. "How many horses you got here?"

"Eighty-two."

She whistled low. "Lot of flesh."

He caressed Ralph with his eyes, fighting the urge to curl up on his barrel chest and sob. "True, but I've always loved horses. They're my life."

Her eyes softened for a moment at his words, but then she got back to business. "How much were these two worth?"

His throat closed again. Feeling a tentative connection to her, he admitted, "To me, more than anything."

"Insurance cover accidental death? Poison? Acts of God?"

He frowned at her, and his chest swelled in indignation when he saw where she was leading. "You think I killed my own horses? No way. Never. These two horses changed my life." The tycoon mask snapped into place. "Without them, my success wouldn't be a quarter of what it is now."

"The one looks like a leaner. Not much revenue left in him."

"He was my friend." Each word was a sentence.

"And a gelding? No money in him. How much you get now that they're dead?"

Ashton's fists clenched. His stomach clenched. Hell, his teeth clenched. "I would never hurt them. Any of them."

"How much, Mr. *Lyre*?" She deliberately mispronounced his name, then tapped her paper with her pen and looked expectantly up at him.

She wouldn't leave without an answer, and he knew she would come after him if he perjured. "Ninety on Money."

"Thousand," she filled in. "Correct?"

He crushed the brim of his hat. "Yes, ma'am."

"And this guy?"

His hat was probably ruined now. "Three point nine."

"*Million*? For a geriatric horse?"

Ashton dashed his hat to the ground, seeing just another woman trying to determine his net worth. "He was a champion sire, ma'am. Breeders Cup, stud fees, lifetime earnings put him at exactly that. You check his history; you'll see that is his precise value."

"Mm." She ripped off her sheet of paper and handed it to him. "I'll expect the post-mortem report on my desk by Wednesday. You *have* called your vet, yes?" At his stiff nod, she said, "I'll follow up soon." Hand on her pistol, glancing at each horse as if it were fanged, she walked out of the barn.

And suddenly, he didn't think she was that pretty anymore.

Chapter 3

Trying to focus on her job took a whole lot more effort than Raylie anticipated. A score of deep breaths finally calmed her racing heart, but whether from the encounter with the equine persuasion or the cowboy one left her utterly confused.

Double-checking the address, she idled down the street until she found the correct house. She got out, looked at the tidy home with manicured hedges and flowers lining the sidewalk. A chain link fence joined the house corner, and as she walked down the driveway she saw a woman of about fifty lounging in the backyard, clad in a housecoat and curlers and sipping an iced tea with her morning paper.

"Hello, ma'am, how are you today?"

The woman frowned at seeing an armed cop in her driveway, gathered her robe close and eased near. "Can I help you?" She peeked over Raylie's shoulder at the colorful green and white van in the driveway and read the logo on it, frowning.

Raylie smiled and joined her at the fence. The chocolate Lab in question barked once, then jumped up, head resting on the crossbar. "Hi, boy," she crooned, scrubbing him behind the ears until he moaned. "Who's this?"

"Mudslide."

"Hi, Muddy Man." He wasn't. She grinned at the owner, hoping to quell her fears. "I'm Officer McPherson, with Pause for Paws Humane Society, Cruelty Division. Is this your only pet?"

The woman still frowned, tucked a drying tendril behind her ear as she nodded. "Yes, ma'am. Why? Is something wrong?"

She looked around the yard, with the fresh mowed grass, random dog toys and children's balls and hula hoops, obligatory tire swing, then laughed as Mudslide brought her a giant yellow squeaky rubber chicken and dropped it over the fence at her feet. She hurled it into the middle of the yard and watched him bound through the plastic wading pool after it.

Laughing, Raylie said, "I received an anonymous report of a dog left outside with no shelter." She pointed to the doghouse pressed against the back porch, raised her brows. "Would you mind?"

"No, not at all." The woman opened the gate, and Raylie went to check out the cedar structure. Mudslide bounded alongside, raced in and came out with a chew bone, which he promptly dropped at her feet.

Nice bed, lots of toys, smelled doggy, so he obviously used it. Shingled roof. A bucket of fresh water hung on a hook from the deck, right next to the faucet.

The woman said, "We spend a lot of time outside, so we set him up out here. He's inside with us at night."

Raylie scooped up the tennis ball Mudslide had been eyeing and tossed it for him. She wiped off her hands and smiled. "He looks great. Nice set-up. Lucky dog you got there."

The woman pursed her lips and frowned. "You know, two doors down, my neighbor's little girl brought over an original Cabbage Patch doll last week. Remember them? I told her to keep it away from Mud. He likes to gut stuffed toys, and he did. I bet it was her mama who reported me. The doll was sentimental, I guess, since I offered to buy her a new one and she just got mad."

Raylie shrugged. "All calls are anonymous. By the time it gets to me, I'm lucky if I even have an address. But don't worry. He looks great. Keep up the good work." She smiled again, walked back to the gate and practiced one more rubber chicken toss before slipping out and saying goodbye. On her clipboard, under Outcome, she wrote, "Unfounded."

Taking a deep breath, she said, "Good." No teary-eyed cowboys professing their innocence here. Just a healthy Lab lounging around in suburbia.

She packed it in and flipped to the dead cat case on her clipboard, double-checking directions on her laptop.

The poor cat was still laying out in the backyard, in plain view of at least three neighbors. But this case also yielded an emaciated Shepherd-something-something tied up to a rusted-out Buick. Ray dished up a can of dog food for him, and two gulps later, it was gone.

Mr. Belligerent insisted the dog was some rare bony breed and wouldn't sign him over to the humane society.

She used slightly more force than necessary to cuff him.

It had nothing to do with trying to get Ashton's sandy brown hair and gray-blue eyes out of her mind. That, and how his red-rimmed eyes, so filled with angst and pain, mirrored her own. So like hers, even a year and a half later.

No, absolutely nothing to do with him at all.

The dog—named Max, of course, she would change it later—came along more willingly. The dead cat was gathered up for evidence. Mr. Belligerent insisted he didn't own the black shorthair, yet he knew she was six years old and named Pepper.

Hmm.

The poor six-year-old weighed in at a mere three pounds.

The Blue Crew at Louisville Slammer would just love this guy.

She dumped off the perp downtown for processing and drove back to work, talking to Max the whole time. "You a good boy, Max? Yeah?" In the rearview, she could see his nose sticking out through the cage bars. "Don't you worry, pal. You're going to go into a foster home, get your shots, de-wormed, get nice and plump for your neutering, but we won't talk about that right now, huh?"

The Louisville animal shelter looked deceptively small from the outside. Long, low, red brick; from the tiny front, no one would guess they processed more than ten thousand animals here each year. She parked up front and led Max to the admissions door with the necessary paperwork, appreciating the internal view this time. Once a visitor opened these doors, a jungle mural greeted them—complete with wide-eyed monkeys—arching over the well-stocked gift shop.

Raylie had painted the monkeys. Jen, the large tree fronds. Chris, the 'croc, of course, the more teeth the better. Others, the vines and flowers and birds and lizards. Volunteers bought fake palm trees to scatter around.

Beyond that were the puppy pens, blessedly empty. She liked to take credit for that, since she had petitioned the state her first week here for low-cost spay/neuter vouchers and weekend "fix-it clinics," citing one-fourth of their intakes as under eight weeks old. Beyond that were two long rows of indoor-only, ventilated, air-conditioned "suites" for the dogs, where upwards of seventy-five volunteers rotated their time to walk, play with and train the constant slew of refugees.

Cats had the right wall. All eight dozen occupied cages were ensconced in a glass, employee-only holding room, all the better to prevent the spread of the "deadly snot," as she liked to call it, from affectionate visitors touching cat to cat to cat. Technically, it was called Upper Respiratory Infection. Technically, it was also not deadly, unless the five "sick" cages in back were filled, and seven other healthy animals were vying for one chance in the adoptable spotlight.

Raylie tucked Max into a nice quiet kennel—replete with water, bed and food—before heading back for her office. Cheddar's nose peeked into the hallway; the rest of him flopped along the wall and her desk. He raised his head, wagged, then crashed back down.

"Jen brought a tennis ball," Leann explained.

"Ah." She plunked down into her chair.

Those dark eyes sparkled. "One arrest?"

"And one confiscation." She grabbed her paperwork, ignoring Leann the best she could.

"So?" She scooted her chair closer.

Ray knew where this was going. The woman vibrated like a freshly plucked guitar string, leaning forward until the back chair legs were off the ground.

Hands full of paperwork, Ray loudly squared them up on the desk, studiously avoiding those eyes. She felt her heart race, and blast it if her cheeks didn't warm with the memory of Ashton's handsome face. He was a looker, all right. But Raylie wasn't looking. "No, I didn't get to Johanssen's, if that's what you're asking. Did she say how many there are? And when's Matt getting here? I'll need his help."

"Fifteen minutes. I'm not. And at least forty. Now tell me, you like him?"

Spiders crawled all over her neck that moment, making her skin pucker. She blamed the A/C. "He's…cute," she finally admitted. But really, he was *hot*.

"He's hot. If I weren't married…mm, mm, good."

Her cheeks warmed in the office, despite the A/C. Truth was, when he first stood up, hat in hand, eyes rimmed with tears, she finally understood why all the girls prattled on about cowboys. But still, she'd be willing to bet he'd wipe out at a mere fifteen minutes, if not ten. More than willing to prove it, too. Damn, she needed a good romp, and now that she felt an eminent change on the horizon, it was high time she stopped living in her tiny, pink-walled "Cape Cod" and started living a bit.

The fact that Ashton was in need of her particular services didn't hurt her case, either. She'd be visiting him again. Soon.

Derrick, a very handsome Mountie, had liked to pretend he was a cowboy, simply because he rode a horse for a living. But the mentality had never pervaded his psyche, only his ego. He had gotten hired as a patrolman just days after they moved down here to tend to his ailing mama. And although the extremely handsome Kentucky Boys in Blue officially hated his fast-talking New York accent, he had a way of talking circles around the suspects. By questioning everything they said, eventually he'd catch them in a lie.

His arrest record had been exemplary in only five months.

"You know my take on hot men," she finally said.

But that wasn't about to deter Leann. "Just as well. After the headlines, you don't need to get all tangl—"

"Whoa, whoa." She dropped her stack. "What headlines?"

"The—*oh*." The back two legs touched down. "That's right. You were…" her voice dropped, "…grieving Angela."

Without conscious thought, Raylie grabbed her ring finger, remembering her late future-mother-in-law's funeral last November. "What happened?"

Leann drew in a fortifying breath. "Big story. Kid stole a stallion, tried making off with him at night. Sudden storm, washed-out road, something like that. Kid went head-on into a tree and died. Horse survived."

Palm up, Raylie leaned forward, unable to forget the storm raging during Angie's burial. "And? There's got to be more."

"Oh, yeah. Turned out the kid was an illegal, family claimed he was hired to work there. Ashton had no employee paperwork and—check this out—he went on record as saying even if this kid had tenure, he wouldn't pay his family one black dime for raising a horse thief."

"'Em's fightin' words," she said in her best Texas accent as she fell back into her chair. "On record?"

One slow nod. "On record."

"Can you dig this up?"

"Google." Leann scooted back to her desk. "I'm on it."

But one word struck her in that whole tirade, one word that made it…personal. She begrudgingly credited Derrick for teaching her to look for this kind of thing. "Ashton?"

"What about him?" Leann asked as she glanced away from her search.

"First name basis, are we?"

Honest eyes held hers. "Yeah. He was my trainer. Turns out I'm a really bad hunter/jumper. Or, at least, Mole is. But Ashton," she fanned her face, blew out her cheeks. "He could butter my biscuit any day."

"If you weren't married," Ray pressed.

A warm smile crossed Leann's face, and she held up her left hand. The diamond set there glowed. "A very crucial if." She winked. "But honey, a girl like you, and a man like him? Who-ee. I'm all weak-kneed just considering it."

The dreamy bliss she saw in Leann's eyes made her smile. "Yeah, I can see it now." Hands splayed, reading an imaginary neon sign, she boomed, "'Breaking story. Cop Beds Criminal. News at eleven.'"

Those gentle eyes turned sharp. "Already in bed with him, huh, Ray? Can't blame you one bit. Not one bit." She winked and whispered, "Bet you *that* boy can sustain." She clicked on a link and announced, "Here it is. I'm printing it."

Eager to change the subject, she asked, "What horse was it?"

Frowning, Leann scrolled down. "High Eminence."

"Hmm." Ray leaned back, consulted her notes. "Would make sense if it was one of the two that just died, you know, finish the job. But he said they were named Monarch and Raphael."

But Leann tapped the screen and nodded. "Yeah. Son of. Right here. High Eminence was the one-year-old colt of Raphael's Wings, that's Ralphie, the Champion sire, out of Flight-N-Fancy, by High Tide." She whistled low. "Power lineage, for sure."

"But the theft doesn't make sense." She studied the orange spots on Cheddar, the true source of her inspiration. "No one would be able to prove Ralphie was the sire without papers, and no one in their right mind could stud him, show him or race him without being caught."

"That's why your boyfriend took such a beating. The press was all over him."

Ignoring the barb, Ray began skimming the printout handed to her. "If the horse disappeared, he'd get three hundred K."

"Yup. He must have lost at least that on the trial; what with the court fees, the ruined trailer, and the lost income, I bet it all added up fast."

"This man paying his taxes?"

Their eyes met.

She jumped up. "Lee, I want everything you got on this guy. Court transcripts, bank accounts, purchases, sales…hell, I want to know when his horses fart. And you can make ol' Judge Tyler's life a living nightmare. Send him my love."

"With pleasure." She opened a cabinet and began leafing through.

Matt walked in, all bright-eyed and eager to work his afternoon shift. His young fresh face had a smattering of freckles, and his orange hair still hung damp from his shower. "Isn't it a great day?"

Rather than answer, Raylie handed him a pair of high rubber boots.

His face paled to vanilla ice cream with round red sprinkles. "Johanssen's?"

Ray smirked. "Saddle up."

Chapter 4

"I love my job, I love my job," Raylie kept repeating as she opened the back door to her little pink heavily draped Cape Cod, kicking off her urine-drenched uniform and tossing it down the cellar stairs. At least her sneakers were spared; wearing knee-high waders was the only way to survive Johanssen's house.

She heard Cheddar moan as he dropped into his bed, even though she had water running in the pink sink. A handful of scratches; only two grazing bite wounds. All from cats. Either she was getting faster or Ms. Johanssen was beginning to enjoy their company. She scoured the wounds, and then hopped into the pink tub to shower.

This time her thoughts were not on her dreams but the reality behind them. Mr. Lyre—Ashton—had seemed so genuine, so truthful. Anguish had defined him. And he had already reported the deaths to the cops. One call had confirmed that. Of course, if he were poisoning his own stock for the money, he would've had to file a police report. Which would mean samples, evidence, attorneys, yadda yadda. Which would mean whatever drug Mr. Lyre used to kill them would disappear without a trace. Which would mean premeditated insurance fraud.

She washed again, this time with a scented soap, since she was still not convinced she was clean. Then she wrapped up in a towel and headed for the smaller bedroom just beyond.

The double bed filled the room, a white elephant reminding her of how life had been with Derrick, even while tending to his mama. Angela had had the big room up front, and though empty, Ray could hardly even crack open the door without seeing Derrick's mom suffering through those final stages.

The oxygen tank was gone. The medicines were gone. Every personal item of Angie's was gone.

But not the memories.

Never the memories.

She had willed the house to her only son and his fiancée, and when Derrick died, Ray had taken over hospice. She gave too much at work. Too much at home. Everything inside her had been sucked out until only the most fragile of shells encased her.

And when Angie slipped away, Humpty Dumpty fell.

Somehow she had managed the three days of the funeral and friends and family and general sympathizers.

But for six days afterward, she never even got out of bed. Only Cheddar's unwavering internal clock roused her three times a day. And when he came to her bedside and placed his paw on her limp hand, his eyes so filled with the pain she saw reflected there, she realized she couldn't sentence him to her agony any longer.

Their pack was smaller now, but she was still here for him.

Cheddar's cold nose butted into her hand, snapping her from her hallway reverie. The door was still closed. Had been since November. She reached down and tugged on his orange spotted ear, holding back a sniffle. "You're the only thing that pulled me through, pal."

He nudged her hand again.

The phone rang, and she stepped into her room. "Hello?"

A pause. "Officer McPherson?"

"Who's calling, please?"

"It's Ashton Lyre, from Star—"

"How did you get this number?" *Was he a stalker? Dangerous?*

He seemed tentative, confused. "I…you gave it…the write-up. Report. Whatever you want to call it. It says 'Me' at this number, right at the top."

Bowling. Her free hand slowly cradled her forehead. The towel fell.

"I...I thought...maybe...you know...you had heard of the last fiasco. Wanted to find out more. Especially since the case was dropped only two weeks ago."

Her body responded to the uncertainty in his voice, the vulnerability that made her originally choose this profession. His rich timbre vibrated through the phone, making her nipples pebble and a shiver tickle along her spine.

She was probably just cold. "What? It was?"

"Well...yeah. No evidence. I told them I never hired the kid. I thought maybe you had some suspects in mind."

Ray snatched up her towel and gripped it to her wayward breasts. "Mr. Lyre, in my profession, the suspects are *always* the ones who own the pets."

"Damn it, McPherson," she heard a thud through the phone line. A palm along a table? "Doc Schneible was here not two hours after you left. I've known this man for fifteen years. He was my character witness at the trial, for God's sake. He thinks my boys were poisoned. Now, I want to know, do you have any suspects?"

Not many men stood up to a woman with a gun. And he referred to his horses as his "boys." She liked that. Like they were kin and not commodity. Something she understood better than most.

Still...in a composed voice she said, "I think you need to call the Louisville Police Department for that, Mr. Lyre. If you're talking suspects, it's really hard for us to put lie detectors on horses. Hell, even our stool pigeons don't sing."

He grew quiet. She started shivering again. "I thought," he started slowly, "that being an animal cop meant you wanted to help those in jeopardy. Give voices to those who can't speak. See that justice was served." He took a deep breath. "Guess I was wrong about you." He hung up the phone.

"No, you weren't," she whispered before replacing the receiver. Moisture had gathered in a long neglected place, moisture far removed from her shower. For the first time, a man had unwittingly validated her job, her beliefs, her *purpose*, and dang it, it felt good. Her breasts tightened as her nipples strained out of her skin. His face danced in the mirror of her mind, and she imagined those callused hands sliding around her waist, drawing her close.

Humpty Dumpty may be dead, but suddenly Raylie no longer felt like *she* was. "He's my suspect," she growled at herself.

But still…

This was going to be a great case.

She was completely turned on.

Chapter 5

Hermosa cuddled her baby closer to her breast as her own mother, Vicenta, stormed over the threadbare rug. She had been in a rage all day, with an odd light glinting in her eyes, so Hermosa dragged her blanket closer to the pocked wall, where she could sit and nurse and not block the angry path. Noe made a soft cry at the noises, so Hermosa draped him over her shoulder to burp. He felt so good, so solid. Healthy, even.

It still surprised her.

"I told you that boy was no good," her *Mamá* said in Spanish.

The baby belched, and Hermosa agreed with her son's retort. Eshan had proposed well before they made love, not when he discovered her to be pregnant, as her mother insisted.

Her protracted silence must have seemed an admission of guilt to her *Mamá*, for she marched from one end of the studio apartment to the other, taking one random item at a time with her and slamming it down in odd places. "You cannot sleep on the floor forever." A plate plunked down on the chair. "And your baby will need a bed." A crumpled napkin got dropped on the cot. Vicenta then pointed to the blanket-lined drawer in the corner. "He will outgrow that by twelve weeks." She took his only rattle and hung it by the keys.

It was no life for an infant; Hermosa knew this. She stroked the tiny cheek, the soft black hair, the tiny eyes now closed as he resumed nursing. She wondered if, somehow, Eshan knew he was a father. Noe looked just like him. "I know, *Mamá*."

"This is why I told you to stay away from boys. *That* boy. Now you will see how hard it is to raise a baby alone. Now you will see why I said marry first, baby second. No man, no money."

Her son began a hiccupping wail. With nervous instinct, Hermosa began to bounce him along her chest. "Chht, niño, chht." She felt a feeble shaft of rebellion rise within her. "I told you, *Mamá*, we were going to get married last December." But they had eloped instead—an event her mother would never forgive her for, should she learn of it. Hermosa remained mute on the subject.

"It does not matter." She opened up a cupboard, pulled out and shook an empty cereal box. And another. She settled for the last spoonful of jam and slammed down the jar, tossing Hermosa a mutinous look. "He is gone now, and my only child must raise the man's hungry bastard."

"*Mamá*," Hermosa clutched her baby. "It is not Noe's fault."

"No." She whirled on her daughter, that spoon seeming as mighty as any weapon. "Eshan's fault for riding you. Your fault for spreading your legs."

Never had her *Mamá* talked to her like this, and it made nausea roil in Hermosa's stomach. Lucky for her, she hadn't eaten since yesterday. But Noe's appetite was making her thin.

Vicenta loomed overhead; the spoon seemed full capable of peeling scalp from bone. "It does not matter to my family whose fault it is. All that matters is that Hermosa Santiago is no better than her *Mamá*."

Tears stung her eyes. She was better than her *Mamá*. Had kept her legs closed until just after their wedding. Her first and only time with a man had resulted in Noe.

Vicenta grabbed a handful of change. "I go to work now. One of us has to feed this family."

Once the door slammed shut, Hermosa joined her son in a helpless cry.

Chapter 6

Aw, crap. What was he thinking, trying to create an ally in the officer with the sad, sad eyes? When had self-destruction become part of his persona? Still, he stared at the phone in disbelief that he actually hung up on a woman. He was upset, he told himself. But then a smaller voice said, *you need to protect what is yours*. And a guilty voice added, *you were supposed to be a gentleman*.

"Damn it." He paced before the phone, vacillating over an apology call, but somehow he knew that would merely light a fire under her tail.

It was a nice tail, he recalled, then remembered she flat-out called him her suspect. Why the hell would he kill off his two best horses?

Doc said he'd have the blood work results by five.

He looked at his watch. Six-fifteen.

When the phone rang, he snatched up the receiver, choking off the bell before the ring disturbed the air. "Hello?"

The gravelly voice of Doc Schneible came over the phone. "Ashton, it's Doc."

He decided to forego the "what's up, doc?" routine today. Fighting the tenseness in his gut, he asked, "What did you find?"

"Not good, son, not good. The blood work shows elevated potassium levels. Now, you didn't go and change vets on me, did you? Get Raphael started on cardiac meds?"

"No, sir. You're the only vet they've ever seen." He felt cold all over. "What does the sodium level mean?"

"Potassium, son." The vet took a deep breath. "Now, the organ samples I drove to a toxicologist so I won't have results for a few days, even a week. But son," he inhaled again. "Looks like they were poisoned."

A tense silence stretched across the receivers, vibrating with a life of its own. "The case was dropped two weeks ago."

"I know."

"You think…?"

"Could be."

Ashton crushed his free hand into a fist. "You'd think they'd take a hit out on *me,* if they were that mad, not on a couple innocent horses." Tears filled his eyes. He never cried about anything, but here, alone, talking with his friend, the bubble of agony squeezed out of him.

"God." He swatted air. "Ralphie was the most gentle, the best goddamned horse I had." The lump in his throat choked his voice. "He was my favorite."

Doc was silent. "Who knew that?"

"Everyone knew that."

"Everyone?"

With understanding dawning, Ashton's eyes came up. On a deep breath, he said, "Oh no."

"Everyone knew about Trouble, too?"

Destructo, McPherson had called him. "You think it's an employee. But they've all worked for me for years."

"Have your manager go through their case files."

Ashton nodded, feeling worse despite a game plan. "Ed's due back this week. Vacation." Place seemed to fall apart whenever his stable master left, but nothing like this.

"You might want to run criminal background checks."

Ashton shook his head, paced with the phone. "Did that before each hire. Clean, all of them. No one has any relation to the deceased, anyway."

"Someone's got something against you, son. Best find out soon."

"Yeah." He ground his heel into the carpet. There was one possibility that Doc didn't examine, and that was only because no one knew. It was possible—though unlikely—that a Vegas casino owner found out about Aunt Karen and was coming after him.

But Aunt Karen was dead.

Just like Ralphie, the horse she bought with the stolen money. "I'll beef up security. Wouldn't hurt to have a few more men on hand."

"That local security company's got extra men now that their biggest client went chapter twelve."

"Okay, I'll call them first thing tomorrow." He dug his fingers into his brows to crush the pain. Years had passed, years in which Ashton had invested tons into his new enterprise—before he received a lockbox from Aunt Karen's lawyer on the ten-year anniversary of her death. It contained a pile of chips and a newspaper clipping about a poker table scam involving the dealer. It was only then that he learned how she had come into all her wealth.

He heard Doc take another deep breath. "And, son?"

His entire reputation had been built on a lie. "Yeah, Doc?" His face felt hot, as it did every time he thought on it.

A long pause. "Be careful. If this turns out to be a deliberate poisoning…"

I might be next. Ashton almost filled in the words but didn't. "I know, Doc. Animals first, humans second." And those possessing stolen property go straight to jail.

"I'll call you as soon as the tissue sample reports come back 'round."

"Okay. Thanks."

"Bye."

"Bye." The receiver felt cold as Ashton eased it back into the cradle. He stared at it for a long time. *Deliberate poisoning.* Those two words bounced back and forth off the walls of his brain, the conjunction "if" getting lost in the ricochets.

McPherson's phone number still rested beside the phone. He picked it up, tempted to call her, but decided Doc's findings might point her back at her original suspect—him. He scoffed, feeling heat suffuse his cold hands. If she had questions, he would simply give her his lawyers' numbers and have the little barracuda attack his sharks. As far as he was concerned, he had nothing further to say to her. She had made it abundantly clear that he was not only her suspect but also an unwanted caller.

He crumpled up the report, angry she'd called his honor into question when the state of Kentucky had found his character faultless. It would be best if he lost all contact with that nasty, entrancing little viper.

That viper with soft, wavy, burgundy spiked hair and sad, sad eyes.

Eyes that were terrified of the very creatures he so loved.

He flipped open his cell phone, un-crumpled the report and added her to his contact list.

Just in case she ever needed riding lessons on his second-best therapy horse, he told himself.

Just in case.

Chapter 7

She didn't know why the horses were bedded down in money, and why it smelled like alfalfa, but Raylie didn't care. She simply floated stall to stall, seeing two dead horses with Ashton Lyre sobbing over them. Then lots of men surrounded him as other horses walked backward up and down the morning aisles, and wheelbarrows of dung pushed men in reverse from stall to stall.

The two dead horses thrashed and screamed soundlessly in their blackened stable, then came to their feet and munched oats. The sun backed up into the sky and the day continued to rewind. Children ran backward down the aisles and dogs bounded in reverse over the hay bales.

Stable hands gathered scoops full of oats from buckets and flakes of hay flew back into their arms, only to be stacked neatly on a flatbed hand truck. Clouds of dust shrank down toward a broom, leaving a layer of straw on the rubber floor.

And as the morning sun hid under the eastern horizon, soft equine lips collected an apple from an outstretched hand.

Raylie bolted upright in bed and grabbed her temple. "Ow."

A soft whine greeted her, a comforting noise in the cocoon of darkness. "C'mon, Ched." Her forty-five pound linebacker jumped up and stretched out beside her with an explosive moan.

Her head simply throbbed. She turned over and cuddled Cheddar, having a vague sense of horses. Ashton's horses, though she couldn't remember why.

Five forty-five a.m. The post-mortem was due to hit her desk today. Mr. Lyre would maintain his innocence, of course, which would make her job all the more challenging. She needed this arrest. One good case like this would land her that promotion, and she'd be damned if she'd let him get off.

She switched on the navy-blue table lamp, an eyesore in the pink-walled room. She then cuddled around Cheddar's warm back and willed herself to go exercise. Her fingers traced the large orange spots that only decorated the left half of his body, earning him his misnomer, "Melted Cheddar" or "Cheddar Melt." His eyes were almost orange, but probably still technically called brown. And his nose was perfectly pink. The rest of him was a brilliant white, his fur so soft it almost seemed like his puppy fur never left him.

His enthusiasm certainly hadn't.

Within two minutes, she had started her sit-ups, then push-ups, and even a few squat thrusts before Cheddar's whine turned urgent. She got up and went to the back door for his trolley. "One of these days I'm going to teach you about indoor plumbing." Once leashed, he raced outside.

She scrambled three eggs with broccoli and doled one into her dog's dish, along with some dry food. "Men and stomachs," she said as she let Cheddar back inside. As they dined, Raylie couldn't help but think how loud this table had been two years ago when Angie had her incredible moments of vigor. Now all she heard was the scrape of metal on linoleum as Cheddar nosed his dish across the kitchen.

She missed her furniture, scattered to the four winds to help pay for the hospice nurse. She liked clean lines, durable fabrics, sensible materials. Certainly not this claw-foot monstrosity with the thousand-piece glass chandelier overhead. At least the pink walls here were almost white, like a single raspberry dropped into a blender filled with milk. Only at sunset did the walls explode in full raspberry glory.

That was usually her cue to watch TV.

In the dark.

A thunder of paws overhead made Raylie almost spill her coffee. "Oops, almost forgot. C'mon, Ched. We got ourselves a tree full of new friends yesterday."

Expectation filled his eyes as he raced to the foot of the stairs, looking back at her. "Yup. Go get the kitties." He yipped and raced upstairs to the right-hand storage room.

Too small for habitation, Raylie had cajoled Derrick and Angie to let her use it for fostering. So all the stored items now teetered neck-high in the other half of the attic.

As long as she never opened that room again, no one would get hurt.

Cheddar whined and snuffed the door, and squeezed through as she opened it. The four five-week-old wild-caught kittens disappeared like Grandma's rolls at Christmas—not uncommon the first week or so. Three carriers filled with comfy pillows were on the left, the litter boxes were against the back wall, near the A/C, food and water remained on the right, and the jungle gym and toys dominated the floor.

She reached in and collected a white longhair. He hissed, but she stroked his back and he stopped. "Hey, pal." The wee thing gazed wide-eyed at the floor and clutched to her skin. "It's okay. You're safe," she soothed. She sat down and Cheddar immediately began cleaning him. "Oh, Ched," she swatted him away. "He's drenched." She lifted the kitten and touched her nose to his. "I'm going to call you Mr. Skooshie Pants."

He seemed less than thrilled with the honorific. She grinned and released him, then collected the empty paper plates, opened a fresh can of kitten food and doled out their breakfast. The poor things were too scared to eat. So she scooped their litter, patted their frightened heads and whistled Cheddar out the door.

The phone rang. "What the…?" Raylie dashed downstairs. She yanked up the receiver on the fourth ring and glanced at the clock. Six thirty-nine a.m. "Hello?"

"Ray, it's Leann. Did I wake you?"

Alarm bells sounded in her head. "No, not by a long shot. What's—"

"Good. Turn on the news, Channel Seven."

Blood started pulsing in her ear as she walked into the living room. "Oh, God, why?" She clicked it on—she lived on this channel—and saw a sweeping view of Starstruck Stables.

She read the yellow banner across the screen the same time Leann said, "Another two horses found dead."

Chapter 8

It shouldn't hurt this much to breathe, Ashton kept telling himself, but no amount of repetition was going to ease his ache. He stood in the aisle, looking down on the mound of horseflesh that was becoming a common morbid sight. Winnie—sweet, gentle Winnie—was due to foal in three weeks. Although she wasn't a top moneymaker like Ralphie, or even Money, she had been the last gift he got from his Aunt Karen before she died of cancer. Hers was a sentimental role, but an important one nonetheless.

And one more body of evidence that someone out there *knew*.

Young, virile cops littered the place, and the sight made his skin cold in the sticky morning air. Innocent of the crime, but guilty of taking blood money was still guilty in his book.

And yet no amount would make him part with his beloved pastime.

A large van dominated the driveway crossroads, its lights spinning around and around. For a hefty "donation" to the force, Ashton had finagled a mobile fingerprinting unit brought to the scene. All stable hands, livery, trainers and coachers were to be recorded by the week's end. He ambled near the van, aimless in his agony, and saw a line of worried employees waiting their turn.

Doc trudged up and squeezed his shoulder to draw him away. "You think this is necessary, son?"

He shook his head. "I don't know what else to do."

"Anyone complaining?"

"It was their idea." He looked back at the stables. "A bunch of my stable hands are kids. They've bonded with some of these horses and don't want to walk in and…" He looked away, pursed his lips.

"I know. I know." Doc clapped him on the back and gave his neck a fatherly squeeze. "Look, Ashton, without blood work I can't be sure, but this looks like another poisoning." He took off his ball cap and wiped off his dome. He then mashed it back into place and said, "I pulled the foal the rest of the way out. Mucus membranes were all blue. Looks like Windstorm died fast, and her baby smothered."

Hands up, eyes clenched, Ashton said, "I don't want to know this."

Silence stretched between them until Ashton un-tensed and looked up.

Apologetic brown eyes held his. "It's my job, son."

He looked away, toward the flatbed backing up to the barn. Winnie's last ride.

Men behind him started groaning and grumbling. He turned and saw a white and green van chugging up the drive. He and Doc walked back toward the police.

"Miss Fearsome's here," one announced.

"Fearsome?"

Another officer, good-looking and mid-forties, said, "McPherson, Miss Fearsome…she earned her name."

Curious, Ashton tipped his head. "You know her?"

"Yeah, we used to—"

But the first officer swatted him. "Bad luck, man."

Gazes darted back and forth as Ashton tried to determine what happened.

"Cross paths," the second finally said.

She pulled up, got out, walked over. "Boys," she said, her tone a chill breeze in the sticky morning air.

They tipped their hats.

"Mr. Lyre, may I speak with you?"

He frowned at the well-muscled cops, who gave him the barest of warning glances. Then he said, "Of course, ma'am."

She motioned him toward the middle of the driveway crossroads. As he followed, he looked back at the other cops making giant biting gestures with their curled fingers. He tried not to smile as he looked ahead and admired the moving shape of the only other type of flesh he enjoyed riding.

He couldn't handle any more bad news.

Chapter 9

Market day. *Mamá* would take the bus to market and hopefully come back home with some nice fruits and vegetables. Hermosa's stomach growled and she rested a hand there. The only part of her with any flesh any more was where Noe spent his time. Everything in her body went to her son.

Hot, sticky shadows crawled into the apartment, the time of day when *Mamá* made the best deals with vendors unwilling to pack up every ear and bunch and peck.

Perhaps *Mamá* could haggle a sweetbread. One vendor, Jack, always had one on display to lure the bees away from his customers. Jack—if he was there—always gave it to *Mamá* at dusk.

Her stomach growled at the very thought.

Dusk stretched to nightfall when she heard heavy footsteps and loud crinkling of plastic bags. She turned on the lights then and waited at the door.

"Hermosa?"

She undid the chain and lock and bolt and unburdened her *Mamá's* arms. Sweet scents of fresh fruit teased her nose and made her mouth water. She shoved a pear into her mouth as she hefted the bags to the kitchenette.

As if the excitement of food awakened him, Noe cried.

Her milk dropped in response. "Soon, niño."

Energy lit her *Mamá's* eyes. "Only eleven dollars."

"For all this?" At least six bags—filled to overflowing—crowded the counter. She must have begged—or perhaps stolen. It was best not to ask. "Jack?"

"He was not there." Vicenta sorted through the vegetables and took a pear for herself. "The apples are mine. *No tocalo.*"

The pear gone, Hermosa looked up. "Not even one?"

Vicenta held her eyes. "They are for a recipe. I need all six."

"*Sí, Mamá.*" A tomato was her next victim. She took the knife from the drawer and began prepping two peppers for dinner. As her mother stocked the icebox, Hermosa cut slower. "*Mamá?* I was thinking about…maybe…getting a night job in a grocery store."

"A bar would pay better, but no. No job for you."

She let the pepper roll around the counter. "No job? I thought you would want me to support my baby."

Odd fire glinted in Vicenta's eyes. "*Niña,* if all goes as planned, you will never have to work a day in your life." She held up an apple and turned it under the incandescent bulb.

Hermosa heard the knife as it clattered to the floor.

Chapter 10

She hated this part of her job. It always made her feel like a bully, and having the Blue Crew in the midst of this didn't improve her disposition one bit. "Mr. Lyre, as per the Notice of Compliance I gave you, I haven't received the post-mortem report your vet—"

But he cut her off, an aggressive trait she'd had to countenance every day, not only as law enforcement but as *female*. "Wait, officer, this is my vet right here." He walked over, arm extended toward an old man she couldn't believe was even in practice, let alone writing up PMRs. "This is Doc Schneible."

"Oh." Luckily, Doc had an easily distinguishable voice. If Mr. Lyre was pulling a fast one… She held out her hand. "Dr. Schneible, it's nice to finally meet you."

That familiar voice was as rough as his hands. Both of them enfolded hers. "Call me Doc. You must be the McPherson girl. Great job on the Hedder case."

Instead of smiling, she looked down. "Thank you, Doc." She let go and fiddled with the snap on her holster. "Look, the reason I'm here—"

"The report, I know." Doc slid the ball cap off his dome and wiped it with a handkerchief. "I just haven't had time to write it. But he's not guilty, officer. I promise you."

Raylie looked toward the flatbed truck being loaded with the newest victim and her foal and drew in a long breath. "I'm not the judge, Doc. You and I both know how this works. I collect the evidence that you provide me, and the jury sorts it from there."

"Wait, wait." Ashton stepped up. "Is this going to trial? Am I going to be tied up for another year with this nonsense?"

She felt her shoulders stiffen as she met his eyes. He acted so innocent that her gut reaction was to believe him. Damn, she wanted him to be guilty. She wanted him to be the big case that clinched her promotion this fall. And right now, when he gave her that wide-eyed innocent look, she just plain wanted him. So she stood taller. "I guess it depends on how cooperative you are, Mr. Lyre, and the body of evidence we collect."

"Evidence," he mumbled as he paced. "Miss McPherson, I—"

"It's Officer McPherson." He would not hold the upper hand here. He just had to be guilty. For a ten-thousand-dollar-per-year raise, she'd learn the truth.

Mr. Lyre drew in a breath long enough to mimic hers as he watched her—lips? Was he studying her mouth? She felt her body respond with a warm flush that made her acknowledge him as a very virile man. "Officer, I swear," he took off his Stetson, revealing a tumbled mass of damp sandy hair, "you will find me the most accommodating suspect you ever met."

Raylie took an inadvertent step backward. Was he flirting with her? "Really."

"Ma'am," he stepped closer. "I know you think I'm doing this for the insurance, but I can assure you no amount of money would prompt me to harm an animal."

"I agree," Doc chimed in. "The man's off his rocker over these horses."

Both their eyes were so honest. Raylie cleared her throat, although she took another step backward. "Isn't it true that the dispute over your deceased employee—"

"Not my employee," Mr. Lyre said as he bridged the gap.

Another step back. "Ran you about three hundred K in legal fees?"

"Which I paid for, in cash." He pursued her. "In case you didn't do *all* your research, ma'am, I'm quite wealthy. I don't need to kill off my beautiful steeds to pay for anything."

He *had* to be guilty. He was too damned good-looking. "Alimony?"

"She's dead."

Doc glanced sharply over at that. Warning bells clanged in her head.

"Just kidding. I never married." He gave a little grin.

Doc smiled and shook his head as he walked away, but Raylie wasn't about to let it go. "How did your girlfriend die, Mr. Lyre?"

A flash of pain flickered in his eyes. "My *ex*-girlfriend is fine and well and living with the man she left me for."

Ouch. "Someone wealthier?"

"No." His jaw hardened, and he looked off to her right. "My former stable master." She watched his heel grind into the dirt. "I offered her free lessons and an easy life. Apparently it wasn't enough."

She couldn't keep enough space between them. "I'm sorry."

He noticed, for he stepped closer. "What about you? Do you still ride?"

How the hell had he learned that? Her pulse thrummed, and a headache squeezed her nape. She grabbed the area and applied pressure. "We aren't here to talk about me."

Warmth lit his eyes, though. "One free trail ride, with me as your guide. Bring a friend, if you'd like. I'll tell you everything I know about the case. Whatever it takes to prove my innocence."

She leaned back and folded her arms. "Did you try to schmooze the DA, too, Mr. Lyre?"

"It's Ashton. And no."

"Then why me?"

A tiny grin crossed that handsome face. "You're way prettier, ma'am."

He smiled then, but Raylie bit hers away. She would *not* get involved with a suspect. "I don't ride."

"You used to, though."

Frightened that the truth was so obvious, she looked up. "What makes you say that?"

He inched nearer. "Your balance. I can tell. When you've been dealing with horse people as long as I have, you can just see the big ol' invisible 'I ride' stamp on their forehead."

Everything went cold. Her tongue dried, and her mouth dropped open. She met his eyes and said, "I don't ride."

"That's too bad." He stepped closer, and Raylie was running out of room. She backed into a stall door and braced. Seduction laced his hooded eyes and his gaze again lowered to her mouth. One hand landed on the jamb near her head. "Because I'd really like to see you straddle a nice stallion."

A soft *whoof* blew the hair at her ear, and a low whicker told her of the horse just inches away.

"I want that report today," she said as she sidled away, fighting every urge to run. Or cry.

She looked around. Her van. She could sprint to it in six seconds. "Mr. Lyre?"

Sexuality just oozed from him, and she wasn't sure what prompted it. Why her? Why now? "Yeah?" he drawled.

Stiffening her spine, she shot out, "Ain't no such thing as a free ride."

Chapter 11

Shoot, there was just something about that woman that burrowed into his skin and knocked around inside his heart. The way her eyes were so haunted, the way her lips parted whenever he stepped near—he shifted. He was drawn to her in a powerful way. Dust still lingered from her van skidding around and racing for the front gate, and the sight made him smile.

He had gotten to her.

Same way she got to him.

Ashton needed her as an ally, but he wanted her as a man wanted a woman. And he was a fool for even considering either option. A woman like her would ferret into everything and reveal the false foundation of his life, thus ruining him.

Emotionally, he hadn't gotten her face out of his mind for two days. Even when she accused him of such heinousness, the spark in her eyes captured him.

Logistically, he figured four horses dying per week would have him out of business by October, but the bane of the industry by August. He'd already lost one boarder to transfer and heard another three were considering as well, although so far only his horses had been victimized.

He couldn't blame his clients for wanting to board elsewhere.

Doc said something to him, but Ashton didn't hear it. He mumbled some placation and waved him off, his eyes riveted to the wisps of dust curling in the morning air and the last place he had seen that white and green van before disappearing.

McPherson didn't like him—scratch that, she liked him all right. She didn't *trust* him, and actually Ashton admired that about her. He had a suspicion that her trust—once given—was irrevocable. Not unlike a Bureau of Land Management mustang he had purchased at auction. A few weeks of gentling had settled the piebald right down.

He had given her to a neighbor child for a first horse.

Equine lips nuzzled his shoulder, and Ashton reached a hand back to tickle the velvety mouth.

Doc walked back up. "So, you going to do it?"

A nudge from Lilac almost knocked off his hat. He grabbed it and said, "Do what?"

"Take Officer Thompson up on his offer."

Frowning, he looked over. The cops were all standing there, grinning and elbowing each other. "What offer?"

In his 'I'm-repeating-myself' tone, Doc said, "Twenty bucks to get a date with the pretty cop."

Ashton grinned and walked over to the men. Get paid for something he wanted to do anyway? "You're on."

"There's a catch," Thompson said as he walked up and shook hands. A devilish glint shone in his eyes. "You have to be alive to collect it."

Chapter 12

Once she was a mile away, Raylie pulled over and stopped the van. Images of that awful day replayed over and over and her hands shook so badly she had to clutch the wheel. The fighting. The yelling. Curling wisps of air no longer coming from his mouth as his police horse stood calmly off to the side. Snow smelling crisp in the still air. Everyone just standing and watching as she sat there, helpless, radioing in for help.

To this day, the words "Cop down" made her pulse stop.

Her arms quivered. And her knees. Nausea bubbled in her gut just as the tears made their appearance. "Oh, Derrick," she whispered as she pressed her forehead to the wheel and cried.

All because he hated her short haircut. Really hated it.

Agony twisted inside her, squeezed her lungs until her breath came in drowning gasps and every cell in her body screamed in pain. She began heaving and opened the door to vomit.

Nothing happened. The humid air clung to her chilled skin. Fresh goose bumps crawled up her arms. The heavy air calmed her lungs, filled them, or perhaps her misery was running its course.

She hung her head, defeated. "I'm sorry, Derrick. I can't do this anymore. I can't."

She reached for a water bottle in the back cooler and washed her face with some Kleenex. Luckily, she wore no makeup.

Ashton and his horses were going to be in her future for quite a while.

Raylie knew it was time for her to seek professional help.

*

The report was on her desk by four p.m., along with a beautiful arrangement of cut flowers. Leann took one look at the assortment of buds and said, "Wow, I didn't know the bowling alley gave flowers for Gutter Girl."

She almost smiled. "Told you I hated bowling."

With a huff Leann asked, "Did you even try to keep the ball on the runway?"

"Yup." The card read, *The offer stands*, and she knew Ashton wanted her to join him on a trail ride.

She must have smiled, for Leann inched near. "Ashton?"

"Yup." Although the thought of being alone with him—without a uniform and gun—made the color of his flowers seem to glow, her hands began shaking. She could not even imagine getting on a horse again. Not since Derrick. She tossed both card and carnations in the trash.

"Playing hard to get?"

"Sure."

Leann settled into her chair, glanced back and smiled. "He will pursue you, Raylie. Trust me on this." She fanned her face and suggestively wiggled her perfectly arched brows.

Ray busied herself with paperwork and left at exactly five. She couldn't handle being…pursued. Not by a suspect, not by any man. Certainly not by Ashton. A shiver raced through her nonetheless. She placed the sole pink carnation she rescued from the trash on her dashboard, hoping the heat would dry it by tomorrow.

Cheddar bounded in the house ahead of her, and Raylie hovered by the phone. After a few minutes, she pulled out the directory and chose one in the vicinity. Each button pressed harder than the one before. Five-thirty—she'd just leave a message.

"Boughton County Counseling."

Raylie froze at the live human voice. "I…um…I was… wondering if you're accepting new clients?"

"Yes, ma'am. May I ask what sort of counseling you are looking for?"

Unprepared for the question, Raylie felt her mouth move wordlessly. "I…um…I have this association…of horses, with death."

"Oh. Well, dear, you've come to the right place. I specialize in desensitization, and I happen to treat a lot of people with equine-related phobias."

"I'm not phobic. I rode for years."

"Even better. I've just had a cancellation. How about seven?"

Her hands froze. "To…tonight?"

"Yes'm. If you'd like."

She looked around her kitchen—Angie's kitchen—and the blended-raspberry walls threatened to swallow her. Oblivious to the phone call, Cheddar scratched his back by rolling on the floor, curling into spotted C-shapes and moaning happily. Would she ever be so carefree again?

"In for a penny," she whispered. "Seven is fine."

"Are you familiar with our location?"

"I pass it every day."

"All right."

After imparting the obligatory name and phone number, she quickly attended to her pets and herself in order to make her appointment. She arrived about fifteen minutes early and tried to remember the joke about psychiatrists and arriving on time. The waiting room was done in autumn gold and red, with harvest paintings on the walls and the last two years' worth of National Geographic on a bookshelf. Random other magazines covered end tables, and three remained on one chair.

Marta Snood looked like the kind of aunt that everyone wished they had. Plump, smiling, with short curly brown hair and neon blue eye shadow, she had a gentle way and affable manner.

Surprisingly, no fresh cookies were in sight; perhaps they were in her room.

"So you said you're an officer, Raylie?" Marta asked, as she swept her into the room, beckoning her to sit.

An innocent question, yet she still tugged on her lip. "Yes, a, um, Peace Officer. With Pause for Paws Cruelty."

Raylie chose a chair in the corner and pressed her limbs close to her body. Marta dropped into an angled chair facing her. "My two kitties are from there. Dickens and Poe."

Her breath caught. She couldn't believe it. "Two black kittens? Brother and sister?"

"Yes." Joy lit that round face. "You remember them?"

Completely content now with her choice in counselors, Raylie leaned back, felt her arms fall away from her sides. "I fostered them. I named them after my favorite authors."

"They're mine, too." Shared interests made Marta's face glow. "I figured it was a sign, so I adopted them together."

She could just relax in the warmth of that glow. "I'm glad. They were inseparable."

"Still are." With a small grunt, Marta bobbled out of her chair and poured them both some bottled water. "They are delightful cats. The best I've ever owned." Like a hen to her nest, Marta settled back into her chair. "But we aren't here to talk about my beloved cats. You are here because…?"

Snatching the water to sip, Raylie said, "I'm not dealing well with the way my fiancé died." Or any of their life together, actually. She outlined their engagement, the move to Kentucky, Angela's hospice care.

"Your mother, sweetie? Where is she?"

"Never met her."

"Your father?"

It still hurt, but she'd had time to heal from this one. "Lost a long battle five years ago."

"And Angela? Was she like a mother to you?"

"Oh, yeah. We took to each other right away." She smiled and twirled her cup in her hand. It was much easier talking about Angie than the reason she came here. "Derrick frequently accused me of staying with him because I loved his mother." She looked down and picked at the edge of her paper cup. "It's true. The day I was going to break up with him, he told me his mama was diagnosed with liver cancer."

Between him knowing her intentions to end their relationship, and the secret she had recently shared with him, Derrick had decided from that moment on to make her life with him insufferable. She leaned forward. "For Christmas, she gave me her grandmother's china for eight."

Impressed, Marta's lips turned down and she nodded. "Quite a gift." Then she took a breath. "Can you tell me, briefly, what happened that day? The day Derrick died?"

Her throat puffed up on her, and she unrolled the lip of her cup. Even though her voice dropped, and she knew it was a memory, she fell right back into that day. "We'd had a fight that morning. I'd cut my hair." She pointed to her head, not looking up. "He hated it." Forcing herself to say the words, she said, "He claimed people would get the wrong idea about me, female officer with short hair." Barely glancing up, she asked, "You know?"

"Wouldn't happen, darling," Marta whispered.

With a small lip twitch, Raylie continued, feeling braver. "We were both working the Christmas Festival. Derrick was a mounted patrolman doing crowd control and I was at the work booth. We decided to call a truce and go horseback riding for lunch. It was really wet and snowy and cold that day."

Marta nodded. "The horses were warm, though."

"Yes." As if she still held them, Raylie gripped imaginary reins.

Perhaps Marta sensed where this was going, for she said, "You two started fighting again."

His harsh and unfair words of "cop killer" echoed in her ears, and the lump kept growing and growing. When Raylie reached for the tissues, she bumped over her water. The cup clattered on the thin rug, and a dark spot encircled it. She sobbed, unable to hold it in, and grabbed a handful to blot up the spill. "I mean, it was just hair."

Soft hands stilled hers as Marta guided her back to her chair. "It's all right, lovey. Now, we'll go back deeper into that later. Right now I want you to focus on the here and now, okay?"

Mute, silenced by a giant lump in her throat, Raylie nodded.

"Now, how many chairs are in here?"

She looked around. "Five."

"Good," she nodded. "What color is the rug?"

"Brown. Well, tan."

"Is that it?"

She focused. "With one big black wet spot."

"Uh huh. And the walls?"

Raylie took a deep breath. "Light blue. Pretty."

"What day is it?"

"Wednesday."

"Who's your closest coworker?"

"Leann, hands down."

A calming grin crossed Marta's face. "How old are you?"

At that, Raylie shifted. "Twenty-nine. Again."

Marta smiled. "How long were you two engaged?"

One more deep breath seemed to wash away most of the hurt. "Two years. Happily for the first three months of it."

Marta shared a knowing smirk at that. "Now," she leaned forward, hands on her knees, "how do you feel after some routine questions?"

The tears had stopped, but she dabbed her lashes anyway. "Calmer. Not so...torn."

"Good." Marta leaned back. "You are grounded again. The past may define you, but it must not rule you. This is a memory, and a bad one, I grant you that, but it's over. It's not happening now." She paused, assessing. "I want you, whenever you're feeling overwhelmed with your experience, to look around yourself and focus. Doing this will keep you in the present and your memories safely tucked away in the past."

"Wow." Raylie did an emotional inventory and felt okay. "That's a good trick."

"It is a trick." Marta got up and poured her a fresh cup of water. "You see, the brain, in its infinite unfathomable glory, cannot differentiate between real and perceived stress." She waved an arm. "A man coming at you waving a gun garners the same response as this memory. The amigula sends out that all-over-the-news stress hormone called cortisol, which tumbles up your emotions and confuses you, sending you straight back to your trauma." She sat back down and leaned forward. "The hippocampus, though, is our ally here. This part of the brain is the center of thought and problem solving. So we are going to teach you to use the hippocampus to win over this battle."

Marta smiled, not yet done. "Back when bears prowled at our cave doors, this cortisol was a good hormone to have. It prepared us for flight or fight—neither of which is useful against memories. So when you relive this trauma, cortisol floods your body and makes you ready for confrontation, which simply cannot happen when your enemy is grief. So we trick our brain into suppressing that hormone by feeding it logic."

Fiddling with her fresh cup of water, Raylie said, "Again, wow." A genuine smile escaped her, and relief—real relief—eased into her stiff and tired shoulders. She sipped and focused on her words. "The reason I'm here is because…since his death…" Tears threatened, but Raylie looked around and counted chairs. Then the four paintings. Then she studied the wet spot on the rug, looking like a growing puddle of blood that had never materialized. "I can't ride anymore. I associate…"

"Not uncommon. I can help you with that, too, dearie."

Lovey, dearie. Definitely an aunt thing. "I have a big case I'm working on. Lots of horses. And I need to get past this. I don't want something like this ruining my chance for a promotion."

"I understand. Would you like to meet a week from today?"

"Yeah, I would."

Marta proceeded to take notes on her family history, asking probing questions to help fill in holes of her life, which she explained would be helpful in providing a plan of healing. They talked and chatted and Raylie found herself feeling lighter and more unburdened as the sun slipped a notch in the sky.

She looked at her watch. An hour well spent. Raylie wrote out a check and handed it to her.

"Thank you, doll. Would—" Marta looked up and smiled. "Would this be that horse breeder case? The sulky racer?"

"Yes'm. It is."

A knowing smile eased across Marta's face. "I agree. That is one fish you certainly don't want to let get away."

Chapter 13

Three days, and no more horses had been murdered. A huge sigh of relief filled Ashton as he entered the stables and watched the typical Saturday workday play out. Steeds came and went down the wide aisles, and a trio of high school students on work-study mucked a stall under the watch of two armed guards. More paraded the grounds—at least a dozen—their navy uniforms both comforting and chilling in the suffocating heat.

Slightly after six a.m., and already it was ninety-one degrees outside. Sweat started to scratch his chest, but it wouldn't stop him. For two days, he'd waited for McPherson to call, and for two days he held out. But now, sheer need made him pluck a bridle off a peg on the wall of tack—Silver Spoon's. He marched down the aisle, turned left at the intersection and stopped at the first stall on the left.

Henry stopped before him, lead rope in hand, staring at the bridle. "Which one are you taking, Mr. Lyre?"

He smiled. "I'm taking Silly." On cue, the mare spun around to face him and shoved her nose toward his pocket. "Sorry, Silly Girl. Your treat is out those doors." As he slipped the leather behind her ears, he frowned. "Henry, what's that?" He pointed at something orange inside the stall.

As Ashton led the brown mare out of her box stall, Henry ducked inside and retrieved the item, frowning when he stood. "It's a soap dispenser, sir."

"Huh." He swung onto Silly's bare back and looked down at the straw-haired boy. "There's not even a sink nearby."

Chapter 14

An odd sense of calm invaded Raylie's soul as she greeted Saturday morning, odd in that she couldn't place it and even felt it unwarranted after having a stranger dissect her life. Meeting Marta had eased her soul in ways she couldn't explain, massaged sore feelings and wiped unshed tears from a shell she no longer felt was quite so hollow.

Oh, she still was, she knew. Gutted, gored, scooped out, left as empty as a Faberge egg before any jewels were encrusted on her.

Only…it would be years before any precious stone landed on her flesh again. She licked her lips, squeezed her barren ring finger.

Barren.

Another word Derrick had used in his onslaught against her.

On the heels of the disquiet came an old itch, one she hadn't even deigned scratch in almost three years. With her feet barely on the floor and Cheddar moaning as he dropped back into his inner-tube sized blue bed, Raylie tugged on her fingers and left her room. She stood in her pajamas and gazed up the stairs, wondering if the magic had truly left her.

She knew exactly where she had last seen them.

Like the wisps of faerie magic beckoning her forth, Raylie slogged up the steps and lingered at the attic door. Her fist closed before grabbing the knob and turning it. Dust motes danced in the still air, making her sneeze twice as she squeezed in and groped for the red suitcase. The clunky handle felt worn and welcoming despite the years of dirt and neglect. She slid her art supplies close and pulled the door shut before gravity awakened in the slumbering room.

Down in the kitchen, the familiar scent of cracked leather and dust and parchment teased her nostrils with memories so thick her eyes softened with nostalgia. She clicked the latch, half expecting it to be rusted, and pulled out the drawing pad. The sharp knife inside she used to whittle a new point on the charcoal stick, and Raylie turned to the first empty page, not needing to visit with each of her sketched memories anymore.

Some things could never be forgotten.

She warmed up with a large circle, squaring up the bottom, then added eyes and ears. The aquiline nose. Brush-cut black hair, short and incredibly soft, like peach fuzz—her fingers skimmed the paper as if she could yet feel him. The eyes—so dark, so militant. Heavy brows. Derrick.

For a moment Raylie wasn't sure she still breathed. With her finger she smeared the brows, drew them in thicker, darker. But that wasn't yet right. With her charcoal she circled over and over his irises, dulling the point, until she realized it was not his pupils that had seemed so dark, but his soul. The crease of his lids grew thicker, blacker, the set of his lips more unforgiving. His jaw grew wider, harder, stronger, until the harsh words that ended his life seemed to accost her from the very page.

A life that ended at her hands.

Ever since she told him of the article she found in her dad's Bible, he had been a bastard to her. It wasn't her fault—she wasn't even two, for God's sake. But apparently her mother had been driving drunk when she ran over the cop at the check-point, flipping her car on the embankment and killing both of them on impact.

Thus her father learned to fly solo.

Derrick—her former best friend—went from loving and gentle to accusatory and hateful the day she told him, with a constant barrage of "cop killer" falling from his lips lest she forget.

Heaven forbid they break up. No, he would rather keep and torment her, punish her for an act over which she had absolutely no control.

And he lorded his mother over her head. Knew she wanted to leave him and keep Angie in her life and he threatened to get a restraining order if she walked out that door.

Tears rained down on the parchment as Raylie yanked it from the book. "God damn you, Derrick!" she screamed as she wadded it up and tossed it to the floor. The lump in her throat swelled, her chest squeezed shut as more tears leaked from her eyes. She gripped her hair in both hands and leaned on the table to cry.

A cold nose shoved her elbow, and a heavy jaw landed in her lap.

Sniffling, Raylie palmed her cheeks, certain she marked herself like a linebacker in the process. A half-hearted smile was all she could muster as she stroked Cheddar's head.

He whined and bopped her thigh with his chin again—a Pit Bull trait he often employed. "I'm okay, pal."

An orange dotted paw landed on her lap.

She smiled again. "Don't worry. I will be okay."

For a long minute, she lost herself in the velvet of his ears. Derrick was dead. His harsh words were no more than echoes across time. She counted chairs. Listed everything out on her counter. Outlined Cheddar's spots with her pinky finger. Then she studied her dried carnation where it sat in its tiny crystal vase on the windowsill. *Ashton.*

Finally she took up the charcoal and honed a new tip. One long shaky breath filled her lungs. A fresh page beckoned; she hesitated, charcoal in hand. This time she drew two circles.

The one on the right was higher, slightly bigger. With a light hand, she drew engaging eyes under the friendly arch of masculine brows. Sandy brown, as she recalled. A square jaw brushed with stubble materialized, and soon the lazy curve of a Stetson traversed his head. Nice ears with dewdrop earlobes peeked beneath the rim, and tufts of wild hair tempted her to learn their true texture.

Long moments passed as she stared at the face of the man

who was now becoming part of her existence. Smudged fingers trembled over the page, as if touching his picture would render her able to touch him. *Fool. He's your suspect.* She clenched the charcoal tight, her nails digging half-moons into her palm, then gradually moved to the other circle on the page.

With agonizing sweeps of her arm, Raylie slowly added eyes and ears, then tapered the oblong to match her own face. Short, spiky hair completed her self-portrait.

She leaned back and studied the two faces before her. One held life, power, joy and agony, all captured with the touch of charcoal to paper. The set of his lips could either curl in a sensual smile or moue with unshed tears when the next tragedy ripped through his stable.

The other had no life. Flat emotionless eyes stared up at her, as one-dimensional as the media on which they sat.

Disgusted, Raylie swiped a hand down the left side of the page, smearing her drawn face in the process.

And then she got it.

With a fingernail she dulled her nib, drawing long strokes from her crown to her shoulders. Waves curved around her cheekbones, brushed up under her jaw. Peek-a-boo hair made her smile, and she lightly snaked the tendrils over one eye, making the other one seem lively. But not lively enough. So she drew in lashes fortified with mascara, and the tiniest dab added a sparkle to her eye. One careful smear made her eyebrow more defined…refined. And kohl to her lids gave her a seductive look.

Damn, they looked good together.

Good and impossible.

A long, resigned breath filled her lungs. Twisting her lips, Raylie drew a five-pointed star under her picture with the words "field chief" in the middle. Under his, she drew a long box with a random eight-digit inmate number. *Guilty.*

Disgusted, Raylie slammed the book closed.

Chapter 15

He cussed the whole way back. Sweat ran rivers down his torso, and he had already peeled off his shirt and left it at the site.

Silly had keeled over dead beneath him.

He cussed he hadn't carried his cell. Cussed the wretch who was ruining his life and livelihood. Cussed out McPherson for not taking him up on his offer of the trail ride, where he could have shared the details of the case, offered his thoughts, and possibly avoided this latest casualty.

Curse them all.

A stable hand finally saw him crest a hill, yelling and waving his hands for help. The youth disappeared, then two young men on horseback came racing toward him.

Barebacked. Good kids.

"Silly's dead. About two miles from here."

Both of their faces paled.

"Let me up." Ashton was done walking.

One leaned right, offered a left hand. Ashton grabbed hold and hauled himself up. Together they raced for the stables. He dismounted before his horse even stopped, and began barking orders to the assembled masses. "You, call Doc. Tell him I need him ASAP. And find out who those samples were sent to. You, get a guard. And you, I want all the horses inside. Now." Rage filled him. "Where's Henry?"

"I'm here, sir." The boy looked as if he were next on the menu.

"Where's that soap pump from Silly's stall?"

The boy went even whiter. "I... I'll get it."

"Put it in a plastic bag. Try not to get any more prints on it."

"Yes, sir." Relieved, the lad flew out of sight.

"Where's Ed?"

"He took the van, went to pick up that new stallion you wanted."

Stable master gone again. "Call the pound. And somebody get the cops. Don't take no for an answer." He kicked a clod of straw near his feet. "The amount of money I 'donated' to their department, they can damn well get their asses down here."

"Yes, sir." About twenty hired hands scattered.

He went into the deserted stable office and snatched up his cell. With only a few clicks, he got McPherson's answering machine. All anger left him once he heard her voice. He waited patiently for the beep, then took a deep breath. "Raylie? Miss McPherson? It's Ashton. Ashton Lyre. Look, I know you're mad at me, probably don't want to associate with me, but another horse died today. Please, I need to go over the case with you. I can't lose any more. This is my life, my livelihood. I'm on the verge of being ruined. Please. Dinner. Tonight. My treat." He realized he knew nothing of her eating habits. "Your choice. Please call me." He left three numbers where she could reach him. His voice wavered. "Raylie, I…I need your help."

Chapter 16

Billiard balls smashed off the green velvet, rocketing into two different holes as Mack waited for the cue ball to come to a halt. Dabbing blue chalk on his customized pool stick, he ambled around the table in the smoky bar, sizing up his next shot.

Zeke was into him for forty bucks, and Mack was going to push him to one hundred. The kid was sure confident for one so young. Too bad. Money talked and bullshit walked.

This kid was crap in boots.

No music played here, which was why Mack liked this bar above others. Fewer distractions. If a bar fight broke out, he was usually tossing the first punch. Most of the locals avoided him, unless they wished to gamble away some cash. Then he'd put on his friendly cap and buy them a beer.

It was the least he could do, since they'd soon leave a lot poorer.

He was down to the three, plus the eight ball. Kid had four stripes on the table yet. He dabbed another bit of chalk and slid the wooden cue over his knuckles, his personalized *I Got Balls* insignia lined up evenly between his two hands. "Three ball side pocket." He didn't have to call out each shot, but he did. Made the competition sweat more.

One even swipe sent the red straight in, not even knocking around the bumper.

Twenty more bucks would soon be his. The cue rolled back around, just about to where he wanted it. "Eight ball, right corner pocket." He took his time, employing a slow, smooth stroke to ensure even coverage across the length of the table.

The sound of black marble dropping into the leather pouch sounded like a cash drawer being opened. Zeke moaned and handed over his third Jackson. It was almost pitiful the way he dumped out the pockets and prepared to rack the balls again.

Almost.

A soft hand landed on Mack's shoulder, and he turned to smile at the woman smiling up at him. Damn, she was still a hot piece of meat. Brittany plucked the olive out of her martini and held it between her teeth to remove the toothpick. He grabbed her, pressing his fingers hard into her ass so all and sundry knew he'd be riding her hard tonight. Not one to pass up the brass ring, he rammed his tongue into her mouth, claiming the treat she offered and giving her a taste of his power.

She spread her legs as she inched onto the billiard table, and he moved right in, cupping her ass tight.

"You making more money for us, baby?" she asked.

"You know I am."

She smiled at him, licked along the length of the toothpick before taking a sip of her drink. He felt himself harden, knew he could take her right here on this table and no one would bat an eye. Not for Mack.

He practically ran this two-bit piece-of-shit Oklahoma town.

"Got a call, baby."

He looked up at the clock. Only six. Would be seven their time. Too early for her to call. "From who?"

Brittany smiled again, eased her hips against him just enough to let him know what they'd be doing when they got home. Hell, he might even take her in the bathroom. "Another one gone."

"That was fast."

"Mmmm." Brittany wiggled against him. "She's waiting for your next order."

That was five, then. Fabulous. "I'll call her." He looked up to find Zeke had already racked the balls and was trying not to pay any attention to the lovers half-sprawled on the table. He grabbed her hand and pulled her to her feet.

The bathroom was open. As Mack led her there, he said, "Just as soon as I'm done with you."

Chapter 17

She was sweating by the time she got home, but the morning jog felt good, even in this sweltering heat. Cheddar whined and nosed her hand, his sad amber eyes telling her he wanted to run, too.

"Sorry, pal, you'd drop dead out there." She kicked off her shoes, peeled off her sweaty T-shirt and tossed it down the cellar steps. Half clothed, she stumbled into the kitchen for a glass of water. The light flashed on her answering machine. She pressed PLAY and started chugging down her cold drink.

Ashton's rich voice made her choke, and through her panting, she stopped to listen. Cold chills swept her arms—from the central air, she told herself—but when she stopped and replayed the message, it happened again. *I need your help,* he said. "From Humpty Dumpty to Obi Wan," she mumbled, then pressed PLAY for the third time.

Damn, he sounded troubled. And part of her really wanted him to be guilty. Needed him to be guilty. But how could a man ruining his own life sound so desperate?

He sounded desperate because he was. As much as she resisted it, she was going to have to consider the possibility that Ashton Lyre was not a suspect.

The option should have elated her, but as she hit PLAY for the fourth time, and chills raced along her arms, she knew Ashton was a dangerous man to be near, regardless of a lack of criminal history.

Barely stopping replay number five, Raylie made her way to the shower, running blessedly cool water. She stripped and stepped inside, her thoughts muddied.

The man was insufferable. He leaned over her at the stable, thrilling and terrifying her with his mention of riding a stallion—

like he really meant *a horse*. And then the flowers. What with her renewed interest in drawing lovers, and Ashton making it into her drawing pad, the last thing she needed was hearing his rich, deep, troubled voice on her machine.

Her nipples tightened painfully with the thought.

Would he be a gentle lover? Or reckless and wild, the way cowboys were always portrayed? Would he bring a woman to her climax again and again, or would he cover her like a stallion and be off to the next round rump?

Her woman's core flooded with moisture independent of the shower, and she suddenly felt more alive than she had in two years. Perhaps three. With the water sluicing over her, it was easy to imagine Ashton's hands following the trail, from her erect nipples to her hip to the thatch of hair desiring a man's penetration. She wanted him, and considered having him.

What was that motto again? Jump 'em, pump 'em…

Her hand lingered at her nape. He'd be damned hard to dump.

She stood there, feeling the water rush hot over her skin. She missed intimacy. She missed sex. Normal sex. And he was a hottie.

And, if she admitted a teensy truth to herself, she liked him. She didn't want to, because arresting him would be so much better for her career, but there it was.

She liked him.

A lot.

She lowered the temperature and found herself whistling. Cooled and cleaned, Raylie stepped from the shower, tucked herself in towels and headed for her room. She rummaged through T-shirts, tops, polos, discounting all as old or faded. So she dug deeper into her closet and found a flirty top she hadn't worn in years. Burgundy. Sleeveless. Low cut. Feeling a bit foolish, she slipped it on. Braless.

Feeling braver with her decision, she rifled through drawers for shorts, forgoing underwear altogether and finding a short pair with a high slit in the sides. She had nice legs, and though the style was old, she doubted Mr. Lyre would have too many complaints.

The very thought of his eyes on her made her cheeks feel warm. How wrong would it be, really, to flirt? To feel feminine again? Ashton was all male, and Raylie felt every inch the female as she recalled his voice on her phone.

Now dressed and feeling naughty, with crickets bouncing around her hollow core, Raylie replayed the message one more time. Her breasts ached painfully as she wrote down all three phone numbers, and taking a guess, dialed his cell. Her mind raced, not knowing what she was going to say to him. That odd pounding of her heart took up a steady drumbeat in one ear.

He answered on the first ring. "McPherson?"

She almost said *Raylie,* but the old her snapped into place. "Officer McPherson, yes."

He apparently didn't listen. Relief and anguish filled his voice. "Raylie, she died while I was riding her. Silver Spoon died. Just before we got into the woods."

The old training reared its head. "You rode her in this heat?"

"Bareback, at a walk. Slow and easy. And she tossed her head back and screamed, like colic or something, but then she just died." She heard the tears in his voice. "She was only four years old, Raylie."

His grief was genuine. She would bet her job on it. Damn. Before she regretted it, she asked, "Can you meet me now?"

"Where? Lunch? Anywhere, you name it."

Braless and in split shorts? She did some quick thinking. "That café on Corral Drive."

"The outdoor one by the ice cream shop?"

"Yeah." Her body quivered in anticipation, and she clenched her stomach in anger. This was supposed to be business…

So why was she going braless?

"Fifteen minutes?"

"Make it thirty. I just got out of the shower." Now why did she tell him that?

She sensed his pause. "Don't know why you're tempting me with that image, ma'am, but I promise you I can fill in the details on my own."

Her cheeks scorched, and her female parts clenched tight, making the crickets leap with newfound vigor. Any harder and they were going to crack Humpty's shell. "I meant, I need to finish getting…ready." She caught herself from saying "dressed."

"Whatever you're wearing already is fine by me. In fact, in this brutal heat, the less, the better."

Damn. And here she thought she would surprise him.

Chapter 18

Sweet Lord o' mercy, the woman's nipples stared him straight in the eyes. A nudge in his shorts told Ashton he was far more vulnerable to this woman's charms than he should be. A twinge of fear rimmed her eyes, and he saw she felt as unnerved with the meeting as he was. Feeling braver, he stood and smiled, holding his Stetson a little lower than usual—just in case she noticed his physical response.

Her short hair seemed a little damp, which only made him harder as he imagined her naked in the tub. His tub. Some makeup softened her features, and he was certain she hadn't worn any before today.

And those nipples…it took Herculean effort to stop staring at them as they stared up at him.

A tremulous smile crossed her face, and Ashton knew his own came out warm. Maybe too warm. "I like you in civvies." He nodded at her clothes.

The smile disappeared. "Um. T-thanks."

With his hat, he indicated the chair opposite him, then jumped to push in her chair. "Thank you, Miss McPherson, for agreeing to meet me."

He settled into his seat, grateful her eyes stayed on his and not the bulge in his shorts. "Miss McPherson now, is it?"

He smiled at his gaff and shifted his hips. "I took the liberty of ordering you a glass of ice water and a lemonade."

He took delight in her moment of surprise. "Thank you. That was kind."

"They have the best pink lemonade here." Nervous, he took a sip, set the glass down back into its ring of condensation.

She mirrored him. "Truth to tell, I've never eaten here. Only passed it a bunch of times."

"You won't regret it." He met her eyes, holding his breath. Damn, now that he said it, he meant it in so many more ways than lunch. Would she understand?

Red crept up her throat, and she batted her lashes and looked down to draw on the sweat-covered glass. "What do you recommend?"

Food, he guessed. Not what he really had in mind. *Yet*. "You like meat? They have a Great Griller hamburger that's amazing. Their chicken caliente is pretty spicy, really juicy. Or if you're vegetarian, they make this fruit pizza that's out of this world."

"Covered all the bases, I see." She spoke quietly now, turned her glass around and around in place.

He swallowed, watching her. Where had all the fire gone? Suddenly he felt like a big clumsy oaf. "Raylie?"

She looked up, her mouth drawn, sadness in her eyes.

The look she gave him nigh killed him. Deflated, he said, "I need whatever help or insight you can give me." He indicated her legal pad. "Should I start from the top?"

She nodded, quiet, and he wondered what he had done to take the spark out of her. He thought he knew. "You like wearing the uniform? Being a Peace Officer?"

Those tempting lips curved into a small smile. "Yeah, I do. I've always wanted to be an animal cop. As far as the uniform," she grinned, "it keeps the urine off my real clothes."

Clothes that let his imagination know far too many details about that beautiful shape God gave her.

They were still pointed straight at his eyes. Suddenly the straw in his drink wasn't what he wanted to suck on. He sucked on it anyway, almost choking when he saw them pebble up even harder under that cottony veil.

He dared a glance to her face, but she was lost in spinning her glass on the table. So he took his leisurely fill of those nice round breasts.

"You really like them?"

Caught. Feeling guilty, he snapped his eyes to hers. "Beg pardon?"

"You really like me in civvies?"

And out of them. "Yes, ma'am. I'm not half so intimidated by a woman in short shorts."

The compliment warmed her eyes. "I haven't worn these in years."

He sucked long and hard, swallowed and said, "You got the perfect shape for 'em. Ma'am."

Color brushed her cheeks again, and he was enough of a fool to know he enjoyed putting it there. A teenage girl bobbed at his elbow. "Hi. My name's Kristin and I'll be your server. Would you like to place your order now?"

He realized they hadn't even glanced at their menus. "Raylie?"

She smiled and pushed the menu toward the girl. "I'll take the Great Griller, salad on the side. You got beer?"

Kristin nodded. "Bottle or tap?"

"Ooh, tap."

Beer? He was flat-out in love. "I'll take the hamwich, side of fries. Tap as well." He handed over his menu and the girl flounced off for their food.

One deep breath seemed to focus Raylie, for she grabbed her legal pad and unclipped a pen from it and settled into her chair. "From the top?"

He leaned back and grinned. "I was born at a young age, in the usual way. To a woman, nonetheless."

Her shoulders dropped, and she indulged him with a grin.

He chuckled, crossed his feet. "Ma'am, it started on a cold, dark and stormy night last November. A young man reputed to be twenty-one stole into my stables and made off with High

Eminence, a now two-year-old colt, born of Ralphie and out of Flight-N-Fancy. One of his very last offspring, if not his very last. I'd have to check. The last ones were all born within days of each other."

She seemed to be jotting down notes, so he continued.

"Highway patrol said the road was washed out, causing the kid to barrel into a tree headfirst. He died on impact; Eminence was banged up a bit, but okay, at least physically. A week later I get a call from a Mr. Lucatelli telling me his son died while in my employment and demanding restitution."

He leaned over, watching her write out the name. He spelled it out for her. "What did you tell the man?"

"Same thing I said in court, Raylie. I never hired the kid, didn't need to hire any more help, so I certainly wouldn't have taken on an illegal immigrant, and there was no way on God's green earth I was paying one dime to reward a horse thief's family. If I'd have caught him, I would've hanged him myself."

A teasing grin played along those lips. "Rebel justice, Mr. Lyre?"

"God's honest truth, ma'am."

"You said the horse was 'physically' okay; what did you mean by that?"

"Oh," he leaned back…more like collapsed. "Can't trailer him ever since. Fears the van, can't get him anywhere near it. And he's the fastest racer I got."

"That's too bad."

"You're telling me."

She took a deep breath and got back to her notes. "Where did this Lucatelli live?"

"The father, in Italy; the kid, forty-five minutes away."

"He dating anyone on your staff?"

"None that I knew of. Good looking kid, actually. Kind of a shame he was on the wrong path." The picture from the coroner's office, the kid's face all banged up and restful, still haunted his dreams at times. The senselessness of his death prompted Ashton to donate a thousand to the local center for troubled youths. Perhaps the extra money would help prevent just one needless death.

"What was his name?"

"Diego Lucatelli. *E.* Lucatelli. Must be a common name."

"What's the E. stand for?" She kept writing.

He frowned. "Don't know."

She looked up and held his eyes, and he felt himself falling forward. Something changed in her eyes, subtle and seductive, and he battled his inner demon to lean over and kiss her right there. A slow smile spread, exposing white teeth, and she whispered, "Got any enemies, Mr. Lyre?"

He chuckled, banishing his fiend. "Hell, yeah. I think I'm number four on PETA's hit list."

She frowned, so he explained, "No, I'm not cruel. They just hate the racing industry." He leaned back, gazing off to think. Any casino owner would be after Karen, not him, although the choice of killed horses was pretty damning. He vacillated on telling her. "None come to mind."

"No disgruntled employees? Jaded merchants? Spurned vendors?"

He shrugged, spread wide his arms. "People love me."

But Raylie gave him a "don't-mess-with-me" look and leaned forward. "Ex-girlfriends, dead or otherwise?"

Nothing like a woman to kick a man in his glory. "Brittany didn't hate me. She's just power-hungry."

The pen began tapping on her pad. "This the girl that left you for the stable hand?"

"Master, yes."

Doubt in her brows, Raylie asked, "Okay, forgive my ignorance, but how is a stable master more powerful than, well, you?"

Somehow the interrogation was teetering on personal,

threatening to dive into that murky realm of past relationships that all prospective lovers wish to know. He took and released a deep breath, then a long draw on his lemonade. "Brittany was sexually abused as a child. A lot. Sex is a tool for her and harsh displays turn her on." He took another sip. "I was getting some complaints from class members and staff that Malone was too harsh on the horses, and when I watched and caught him I dismissed him. Even taught the next three weeks of classes until I could get another trainer in here."

Scribbling away, she said, "Malone hate you after that?"

"He got the girl and the Lexus I just bought her."

"You're kidding."

"I wish." He shook his head. "Don't know what more he could want."

Pensive, Raylie looked at him. "Revenge, Mr. Lyre?"

He scoffed, leaned back. "Why won't you call me Ashton?"

Their food came, and he waited until the girl left. When she made no reply, he started over. "It was just a job to him, Raylie. Trainers are mobile people. I don't know any who even stay in business more than a few years, let alone devote their life to one stable. They're the handymen of the horse world, do a job and move on."

She bit into her hamburger and moaned. "This is good." She chewed, swallowed, and said, "You stayed."

He smiled, tore into his bun. "I'm the king. They'll have to mutiny to get me to leave."

At that, Raylie leaned forward. "Perhaps, Ashton, they already are."

Chapter 19

After an hour of notes, Raylie was no closer to solving the case than she had been on Monday. One thing was abundantly clear, though: Ashton was not her suspect.

This troubling realization put him in a whole new classification of dangerous.

"What about you, Raylie?"

She looked up, not knowing which direction the conversation was taking now. "Beg your pardon?"

"I told you all about my sexually abused ex-girlfriend who left me for another man. What's your story?"

Fear punched her square in the chest. "I-I don't have a story."

That comment made him crack a grin. "Everyone has a story. You dated a cop, right? You knew those policemen at my stable."

Thump, thump, thump. The pulse thrummed loudly in one ear. She didn't want to lie to him, but didn't know how much she could handle telling him. She opened her mouth, and after a minute said, "I was engaged to one."

Ashton leaned forward, crowding the table. With a crooked smile and an exaggerated accent, he said, "Want me to drag him out to the back forty and learn him a lesson?"

Cold swept her. Her heart beat louder. She started counting items on their table. "He's dead."

That cocky grin dropped hard. "Oh, Raylie, I-I didn't—"

"It's okay." But it wasn't, really. Nothing was okay anymore, least of all her head. Two ice cubes rattled in her glass, and she stuck her fork down there to retrieve one. As she tried to scoop it, she mumbled, "Turned out he wasn't that nice a man."

One strong tanned hand rested gently over her fingers at that. "Are you okay?"

Burning behind her eyes told of oncoming tears, so she blinked rapidly, gulped down the sudden lump in her throat. She stopped fumbling with the glass, relishing the human contact and fighting her defensive urge to yank away. "I…will be."

He stayed that way, his hand on hers, just watching her. When she felt she could, she looked up into the most understanding eyes she had ever seen. He stood, pulled her up with him. "Come on." He reached into his wallet and dropped a fifty on the table.

For lunch at a café? "Ashton, that's too much."

But he winked and claimed her elbow. "You're worth double that, Raylie. Cheer up. I'll buy you an ice cream cone."

Just like that, she was his toy. "I don't eat ice cream."

His fingers wrapped a little more snugly around her elbow. "Everyone eats ice cream." With an impish grin he said, "You're getting a cone, just so I can watch you lick it."

She gasped, feeling heat suffuse her cheeks, knowing he was bent on embarrassing her and helpless to go to battle.

So he chuckled. "You're not going to tell me you're lactose-intolerant, right?"

"No," she groaned, "just trying to watch my weight."

Smoldering eyes appraised her every curve. "Baby, there ain't nothing about you that's in the wrong place."

Again her nipples tightened, and this time she knew for a fact he noticed. A lazy satisfied smile crossed his lips, and—blast him—he moved closer to smile down into her face. "Nothing at all."

She held his gaze, wondering if he was going to kiss her right there on the sidewalk, but he slid his arm around her back and guided her into the ice cream line.

When was the last time she had indulged herself with an ice cream? Thirty-one flavors tempted her, and she read the options, trying to decide.

"Double-chocolate chunk?"

She looked at him. "Me? No."

"Raspberry swirl?"

She grimaced and shook her head, abhorring pink in all its flavors. "For you I'm thinking Mocha Loco."

He laughed. "Mint chocolate chip."

"Maple walnut for me."

He ordered for them, and Raylie never felt so self-conscious licking an ice cream as she did with Ashton. He watched her, his eyes betraying without doubt where he wanted her tongue.

The way he kept looking at her, she was tempted. The look in Ashton's eyes made her feel desired, not dirty. A completely different beast than Derrick's.

But Derrick had taught her the frailty of trust; any secrets she might harbor could not be shared—only her body, which he wheedled her to do without mercy.

The promise in Ashton's eyes held deep appeal, and—she admitted to herself—a mighty dose of curiosity.

"Any kids?"

"No, you?" This had definitely become a date. When, exactly, she wasn't sure, and right now she didn't feel like complaining.

He shook his head. "Someday, though. I have a legacy to pass on."

"Legacy." She rolled her eyes. "Are we back in the Middle Ages?"

He stepped close again, with just enough room for their cones in-between. "Come on, Raylie, you wouldn't want Starstruck's horses to be scattered across the country, would you?"

The crickets jumped like popcorn at his nearness. "I've got nothing invested in it." *Take that*, she thought.

But then his eyes softened, and he said, "Not yet." And he leaned over and stopped a half-inch from her lips. Her heart raced, and her nipples thrust up with her labored breathing. People brushed past, but even that was not enough to keep Raylie from stretching up the last tiny measure to join their softness. He kissed her, slow and gentle, and her head tipped back with the blessed chill mixed with his warm lips slanting against hers. Maple oozed along her knuckles in the heat, and another rivulet bumped down along her fingernails.

He pulled back, his expression gentle and filled with awe. "You're dripping," he whispered, and she wondered how he knew. But then he grabbed her hand and proceeded to lick the ice cream rivulets off her knuckles.

His tongue, both hot and cold, thrilled her. Abashed at his wanton behavior in public, Raylie backed up. "Ashton…"

He stopped and looked up, her knuckles in his mouth like an ardent medieval courtier. "Better in private?"

Half the crickets leaped for joy. The rest sang. And a wet painful clenching began in a long-neglected place as she witnessed the promise in his eyes. *Yes.* "I…"

"I'll get a wet towel." He dropped her hand and marched inside, leaving her bereft.

Her phone rang, the ring tone ominous. Shaking off the stickiness on her hand, Raylie rummaged into her pocket. Work. Never good.

"Yeah?"

"Raylie, it's Leann." She heard a sigh.

"Yeah, could tell by the ring tone. What's up?"

She heard the hesitation, and Leann said, "It's Starstruck again."

Raylie looked up to see Ashton pushing open the glass door, a wet brown paper towel as his prize. Her voice dropped low, not wanting him to hear. "Another death?"

"Worse." Leann sounded torn. "Raylie, there's a fire."

Chapter 20

The look in Raylie's eyes was one he had grown far too accustomed to over the past six days. He saw the cell in her hand and almost stopped dead in his tracks. He heard her say, "We'll be right there," and just knew.

"Another death?" He braced, waiting for the inevitable.

Raylie tossed her cone into the nearest trash. "Worse. Fire. Let's go."

He cussed with vigor as he dumped his ice cream and rummaged for his keys. "My place?"

"Yeah." She turned and said, "I'll meet you there," but Ashton would have none of it. His Mustang sat fifteen feet away, and Raylie had parked the next block over. He grabbed her arm, hit the button on his keychain, and heard the *bloop bloop* of his baby.

"Get in," he said as he raced around to the driver's side.

Almost as if she were fearful, Ashton watched with impatience as she pulled open the door of his convertible. "Come on," he urged, turning the key and revving Chastity up.

She dropped down and locked the door.

Glancing into his side views, Ashton tore out into the street, did a u-turn, and gunned it for home.

Fear made him lead-footed, whipping all two hundred twenty-five horses to full speed. He raced through a yellow light, swerved around a senior citizen doing the speed limit, and opened her up on the straightaway.

To her credit, Raylie made no retort. Guilt over his recklessness made him glance over. She hadn't moved, hadn't paled, merely sat there with frown on her face. He took a deep breath, noticed her touch a small cigarette burn on the dash—the only flaw with the car. "I'm sorry, Raylie, I hope I'm not scaring you. I just got to make sure."

"Don't worry." She turned to meet his eyes. "I'm not scared. At least, not about your driving. A sixty-six Mustang can handle anything you throw at it."

Impressed that she knew about cars, he looked over, opened his mouth to say something.

"Curve," Raylie pointed up ahead.

He touched the brake, then gunned her up again at his first chance.

"Do you think it's intentional, Ashton?"

"Hell, I hope not." He leaned into the wind, floored the petal. The needle climbed to ninety. "I had my staff put all the horses inside this morning, after Silly—" he couldn't finish. The lump in his throat dared him to speak. God, if all his horses went up in flames…

Ninety-six, ninety-seven…

Sirens crept up behind him, and Ashton edged up one more mile. Black curls of smoke danced ahead in the thick air, the banner defying him to hope all was well. He slowed, hit the automatic door opener for the gate before fishtailing into his driveway. The officer's siren followed behind him, the noise annoying in the smoky air.

A few horses stood around outside, held still by some youths. Firemen sprayed water on one corner of the stable, with other firemen already flattening down the hoses. From other stalls in opposite buildings, curious equine heads watched the activity, none overly concerned.

Ashton skidded Chastity to a halt and got out, only remembering at the last minute to close Raylie's door for her. His hands felt slick as he grabbed her palm, knowing it was for his comfort and not hers. Still, feeling her nervous squeeze reassured him that she, too, knew the stakes.

He approached who he assumed was the chief. "No damage?"

The man appraised him. "Who are you?"

"Ashton Lyre, the owner."

"Oh, Mr. Lyre." The men shook hands. "We got it under control. Once the smoke clears, we'll go in and see what's what."

He nodded, feeling mute as the enormity of what he almost lost kicked him over and over in the gut. Raylie's hand stayed firmly in his, and he thumbed her knuckles over and over as he watched the wisps dissipate in the murky air.

"Jesus Christ, Ashton." He turned and saw the cop—Thompson?—coming near, shaking his head and frowning. "You had me up to ninety-five, you bastard."

He swallowed, but no moisture filled his mouth. "When it's your home, see how fast you drive."

"But damn, boy, you nearly broke every—" He stopped and frowned deeper as his eyes shifted left. "McPherson?"

Ashton admitted Raylie looked a lot different wearing makeup and flirty clothes, but she had no reason to step back. He felt her tense and clutched her hand tighter.

"Hello, Chuck."

"Damn, boy, you did it. Never thought I'd see the day."

Mortification made him close his eyes. He sensed Raylie staring at him, defying him to respond, but the chief called him over just then, granting him a brief stay of execution.

If it weren't illegal, he would cut Thompson down right now.

"Yeah, boss?"

"Got the report." The chief led him into the barn, and Ashton made sure to keep Raylie's hand tight in his own. The last thing he wanted her to do was yank away angry, in front of Thompson. Water dripped from the ceiling beams, and straw-filled sludge made the aisles slick. The sweet smell of burning wood and shattered dreams hung thick in the cloying air.

The chief pointed to a melted blob in the middle of a pile of ashes. "Near as we can tell, a pair of electric clippers caught on fire."

Confused, not seeing how it could be arson, Ashton stared at the smoldering black pile of pudding. "Um…how?"

"Frayed cord." He held up what could have been the cord. "Looks like it was chewed."

"Chewed." Try as he might, he couldn't wrap his head around what the chief was saying.

Raylie glanced between them. "You got dogs here, Ashton?"

Dogs? He studied her. "Yeah, a few. Why?"

"Dogs chew things. Any puppies? They chew on cords all the time. There's probably one that's acting a little weird right now, spacey with the electric shock, depending on its size and the volt it took."

"Dogs."

She almost laughed. "The furry things that bark."

"I know what dogs are."

She grinned a bit. "Just checking."

Still in shock, he looked at the chief. "So, this was not arson."

"Arson?" The chief looked at him as if he were nuts. "Accident to me."

"Leash your dogs, Ashton. Crate the puppy."

Relief swelled his chest until he thought his shirt would split with it. Gratitude filled him—sweet, blessed gratitude—as he looked at Raylie for affirmation.

She looked pissed.

Thompson came up. "You two dating now? An honest-to-God date? Wow, Fearsome, I thought you swore off men."

"No, Chuck, just assholes," she said, and the look in her eyes should have bored holes through his bulletproof skull.

The man just grinned, reached for his wallet. "Well, Ashton, you're just going to have to give this back to the state when I ticket you for speeding, but you actually got a date with Fearsome. Lucky dog." He pulled out a bill.

The goddamned fool. Ashton swatted away the money. "Go away. Write me the damned ticket and leave us alone."

Raylie leaned back and glared at Chuck. "You're ticketing him when his stables were on fire?"

Chuck just grinned. "He didn't know that. All I saw was a Mustang doing ninety-six."

So Raylie flipped open her cell. "He did know. I just got the call."

But Chuck shrugged it off. "Can't prove it." He bent over his pad to write out the ticket.

She scoffed. "Three years later, and you're still an asshole." When he glared at her, she said, "And it was ninety-nine, for the official record. Faster than your piece of shit Crown Vic can go."

With a scowl, Chuck tore off the ticket to hand to them, and Raylie wordlessly snatched it. She spun away, but surprisingly didn't yank out of his grip. Instead she turned her back on the officer and faced the fire chief again. "So, it was an accident, no major damage?"

"Yes, ma'am. A few beams might need to be replaced, some grain or hay…and the clippers."

"Good." She faced him then, all serious. "Then can you drive me back, Ashton?"

From magic to manure in ten minutes flat. "Of course."

She allowed him to lead her to the car, saying, "Stay out of potholes, Chuck," as they walked past the cop. His face darkened, and Ashton knew she got in the last word.

He hoped he was not her next victim.

Chapter 21

Clinging to Ashton's hand like a lifeline actually kept Raylie from tearing Chuck's pig-like eyes from his skull. Weasel eyes. Rabid-hedgehogs-with-quills-up-their-asses eyes.

Now that the imminent danger had passed, Ashton guided her to her door—her door—and settled her into the car. She touched the cigarette burn, disbelief stunning her to silence. What a day.

He got in, revved up her old car Charlie until the whole herd rumbled under the hood. Careful and diligent again, he backed up, turned around and drove back down the drive. Hesitant now, no longer the charging knight—in a white Mustang, nonetheless—he looked over at her. "Want to tell me what that was all about?"

She met his eyes. "How long you have this car?"

Perhaps he sensed this conversation would be a volley, for he studied the road for a long moment. "I don't know. Twelve, thirteen years? Why?"

"Where did you get it?"

He almost smiled. "Guy in New York. Just outside of Syracuse, why?"

"Remember his name?"

"How could I forget? John Smith."

"John C. Smith."

That caught him off-guard. Mouth open, he just kept looking at her. "Spill it."

Of all the things to come full circle. She never once thought she'd sit in her old car again. "This burn was from my high-school friend Kaitlin. It was the first and only time I let her in my car. She thought she was so cool, smoking in a sixty-six 'stang, wanting her upper-crust friends to see her as I drove to class."

"This was your car." He didn't even have the capacity to ask.

"She snubbed it out just as we pulled into school, and I flipped out. My dad had begged this car off his best friend—a car enthusiast—and I spent a lot of my childhood in it as we went on trips and whatnot. To have Kaitlin scar it the first week…" Even now, eighteen years later, she wanted to wring the girl's neck. She traced it with a finger. "I tried putty, plastic, wood filler, anything I could think of. The dealership had no recommendations other than replacing the whole dash."

He shook his head. "It was your car." Something changed in his eyes, but Raylie didn't know him well enough to read his expressions. "I was told the same thing. About the burn." He paused. "Why'd you sell it?"

She shrugged. "College. It killed me to, but I needed the money. Dad couldn't work full-time anymore and I really wanted higher education."

His voice softened. "Your dad still around?"

Her shoulders dropped. "No."

"Mine either. I was orphaned young. My Aunt Karen raised me from about ten. Left her husband, in fact, to raise me."

Confused with that, Raylie looked over. "That's strange."

"He was a rough man, she said. Didn't want to subject me to a bullying step-uncle and a conniving cousin, so she moved out into a small apartment and took me in."

She nodded. "Your needs superseded her own." They were quiet a moment, so Raylie patted the dashboard. "I'm glad Charlie here is with someone who truly appreciates him."

He chuckled. "Charlie? Girl, this is Chastity."

"Oh, no," she moaned. "That's a hooker's name."

He smirked, "Wanted to make sure she kept herself for me."

Groaning, Raylie dropped back into the seat. "Chastity. You not only changed his name and gender, you added a *bloop bloop* to him, too."

"I protect what's mine," he said seriously, then laughed and looked over at her again. "What about that officer?"

Just like that, Raylie leaned back, crossed her arms and legs. "What about him?"

"Are you ever going to trust me?" He offered her his hand, fingers spread. "Come on, talk to me."

That hand stood there, asking her to bare so much—things she wasn't even ready to tell her newfound therapist. But he jiggled his fingers, and Raylie found her own intermeshing with his. Satisfied, he placed their hands on her lap.

His warm strength filled her, grounded her. And memories of a daring teenager barreling Charlie uphill to the tune of eighty-seven mph gave her courage. "Derrick worked with them. He was a mounted patrolman." Her thumb circled around his nail, played with a rough spot on his pad. "Chuck was…well, still is…a pervert. He was always making bets. On anything." She met his eyes, willing him to realize that a ménage à trois was his biggest goal in life. With her.

That warm hand squeezed hers. "Raylie, I want you to know I had every intention of asking you out before he even dared me. Look at your phone; I asked you to meet me the first time we met. I hope you know that."

Still fiddling with his callus, she avoided his eyes. All of Chuck's bets focused on sex. How many other bets did he make? Would Ashton win a C-note on getting some ass tonight? Aware of her silence, she said, "I do now."

"Is he always that big of an ass?"

Grinning, she said, "He hates me for turning him down. Made my life as miserable as possible at every opportunity, and he had many chances, being Derrick's closest friend."

Ashton slowed down, and Raylie saw they were nearing the ice cream stand. She didn't know if she should tell more or shut up while she was still dry-eyed.

"For the record, he wanted to see if you would chew me up and spit me out if I asked you to dinner, which, again, I was going to do anyway."

A cautious expression turned to him. "That's all he bet on?"

He turned on his directional and waited for a car to leave its spot. He held her eyes. "That was it. Nothing perverted. Had I known you two had history, I would have told him to go screw."

She liked the truth she saw there in his eyes. It made her smile when she realized how easy he was for her to read.

"And the pothole comment?"

She chuckled, loving this tale. "After turning him down for like the fifth time, he got on his cycle and popped a wheelie down the road. He hit a pothole, flipped the bike, bent the frame, it was great."

Ashton laughed out loud as he pulled into an empty space. Afternoon heat crawled along the street, making sweltering lines waver above the cars. "And Derrick? Where was he in all this?"

She let go, but Ashton still held tight. "He knew." Shame writhed in Humpty's shell, filling it with serpentine coils. "He…" she dared a glance at him. "Wanted to watch. Us. Started pressuring me all the time about it. I think he just wanted to make me squirm."

"That's just wrong."

The serpent vanished. "That's what I said."

"What man wants to watch his girl get it on with his best friend?"

"And his wife," she added, looking down.

Ashton turned off the engine and faced her. "You're kidding."

"I wish."

Taking both her hands in his, Ashton met her eyes. "Some men are just twisted, honey. I hope you know that not all of us are like that. I'm certainly not."

Honey. The endearment sent the snake packing and had the crickets leaping all over inside. Angry at her physical response when she vowed to keep to her motto, she whispered, "I know." She nodded good-bye and got out, but Ashton ran around.

Just like a formal courtier, he led her to her car, where she stopped to face him. His hand rested on her hip, and the crickets all jumped on her veins now, making her blood race. "I'd like to have you over for dinner tomorrow night. Six o'clock?"

Sex o'clock, more like it. "Should I bring my handcuffs?" After she said it, she realized it could mean either for protection…or pleasure.

He smiled and leaned close. This time, his kiss held heat and promise, and as her buttocks pressed against the car door, Raylie found her fingers trailing along the curve of his elbows. Strong, rugged fingers dug into her hips, making her own splay along his strong chest. His hips rolled along hers, and she found all her female skills intact enough to note his package rubbing up along her abdomen. Her body activated with a heady sense of yearning.

He had no dinner plans based on this kiss. Only sex, and Raylie found herself in a generous mood, willing to accommodate him. Countdown to climax initiated.

He pulled back, eyes wide and wondering, and smiled down at her. "No handcuffs. Just a swimsuit." He grinned and walked away.

Chapter 22

A house like Ashton's probably had a private swimming pool, Raylie kept telling herself; so private that no one could see in.

Still, she couldn't quite make that leap to deliberately not pack a swimsuit. She elected to wear her yellow and pink string bikini set in lieu of underwear.

A constant ache pervaded her system, sending tingles along her skin as she tried to fill her day with monotony. She glanced at the clock again. Three-twenty-nine. Still. Two and a half hours to go.

God, she needed a good lay.

If all went right, he'd wine and dine and sixty-nine her, and Raylie would get a great release. Man, she needed one. She bought and packed fresh condoms in her purse, and even tucked some into her pocket as well. Hopefully, he'd last at least ten minutes.

Everything ached. Part of her couldn't believe she'd be rushing into a physical encounter like this, but the other part couldn't wait.

Jump 'em, pump 'em…

Tending to Cheddar and playing with her foster kittens took a good hour, and a long bath filled the rest. She wanted to smell lovely when she de-robed tonight.

By five, she had tried on half her wardrobe, deciding on a yellow button-down to match her bikini top and left it half-open. She vacillated tying it at the waist but held off. She could always do that later, like if he needed a little encouragement or something.

She donned a pair of flattering butter yellow capris over the pink bikini bottom, added some sandals and headed for her SUV, wondering if he wanted a good romp as much as she did and if she would chicken out at the last minute.

The drive went slowly, even though Raylie hit the petal hard. But Broncos and Mustangs were simply not the same animal. She hovered at the gate at five-fifty, waited while it swung open, and stepped out of her vehicle to be inspected by three armed guards. They got her driver's license and plate numbers, her thumbprint, and looked through her car. Looked like Ashton wasn't taking any more chances. Satisfied, they let her take the paved drive to his grand white house.

Or, more precisely, mansion.

He greeted her outside the door, standing tall and proud in a sky-blue polo shirt, long black shorts and his Stetson, with one hand behind his back. She smiled and got out, and Ashton produced a bunch of long-stemmed red roses. "For you," he said, planting a kiss on her knuckles.

But Raylie wanted more than a chaste kiss. She stared at the flowers, and then smiled up at him. Didn't red mean love? "And here I was hoping for a real kiss."

Gentle eyes skimmed her face. "You'll get one. Or many."

Her body thrilled in response. She accepted the flowers and placed them on the passenger seat of her car.

"From a Mustang to a Bronco, and you claim you don't ride?"

"Cowboys ride horses. I ride cowboys." She slammed the car door and leaned against it, giving him a suggestive look and hoping she wasn't blushing as furiously as it felt.

With a matching smile and a chuckle, Ashton's hand claimed her waist as he guided her to the door.

Money practically slapped her as she stepped inside, timid on the black marble floor. A long hallway stretched to the left, but immediately next to her was a sitting area with one white leather couch, two sleek black overstuffed chairs and a black coffee table with a milk-white vase and red flowers. Green throw pillows and a red-and-white zebra rug were the only colors to offset the monochromatic scheme. A large Ansel Adams print dominated the only wall. Formal; perhaps a waiting area?

Straight ahead another hallway beckoned, and she saw a glimpse of a stainless steel kitchen. White French doors stood to the right, leading to what she assumed to be the dining room.

All glamour aside, Raylie loved this house. The simple lines, the monochromatic color scheme, the modern art, all spoke to her, appealed to her. *This* was the style of furniture, the colors, the layout, she craved.

She practically creamed herself on the spot. At this rate, Ashton might just outlast her.

"Let me give you the tour," he whispered, and Raylie hoped it ended in his boudoir.

"Okay."

"Guest parlor," he said, pointing to the black and white cozy nook, then drew her along. The next door on the left revealed a library, with two floor-to-ceiling windows channeling the late afternoon sun across the art nouveau rug. "Gentleman's parlor, for smoking," he said at the next room, filled with burgundy chairs and tables, and when she frowned at him, he laughed. "I don't smoke. But a lot of my guests are cigar aficionados."

She nodded.

"The next room is a game room." Ashton's hand never left her hip. He opened the door, and a pool table dominated the green and white room, along with a dartboard on one side, pinball machines on the other, and a myriad of shelves containing board games. He released her hip and strode to the center of the room. Plucking a cue stick from the rack on the wall, he smiled. "You play?"

Hmm, the pool table would do nicely. She shut the door and turned the lock, leaning against it suggestively. "Badly." She wished she wore a skirt. Bending over the table, wearing a thong…she felt her pulse race as she sashayed into the room.

A wolfish grin crossed his face, and Raylie knew they were on the same page. He handed her a shorter stick, racked up the balls, then gave her the chalk square. "Need help breaking?"

Oh yeah. "Probably." Aroused and awkward with the cue, Raylie leaned over the table. She fumbled with the stick in earnest, and nearly scratched the felt. That was when Ashton's arms encircled her, his face hovering near her ear. Strong fingers wrapped around hers.

"Focus on your quarry," he said, his voice rough. Then he slid the cue through her fingers, over and over as if to teach her the rhythm, his forward thrusts forceful, putting her in mind of the other thrusts she wished to experience. She closed her eyes, and the stick blasted into the cue ball.

She gasped, stood up, finding her bikini bottom offered no protection against Ashton's nearness.

"Nice shot. You sunk one. I'm solid."

Yeah he was. The ball was not what she really wanted sunk, but it would do. For now. He analyzed the table, and when he leaned forward to shoot, Raylie grazed her hand down his back, glancing at her watch. Six-o-four.

His shoulders dropped, his eyes closed. "Raylie, you're going to drive me to distraction."

She grinned. "Go ahead. Sink a ball." She winked, fiddled with her top button. "Or two." Who was this flirtatious woman wearing her clothes? She wanted him with an ache she couldn't refuse, and the words that tumbled out of her mouth frankly startled her. But then her sex would clench with need, and Ashton's eyes would meet hers, and she knew she would have him this night, case be damned.

He groaned, looked up at her with wolfish humor. "You want to play?"

Her brows waggled. She undid the top button. "With balls? Sure."

He dropped the stick, stood before her. His hand wrapped around hers, peeling the cue from her fingers. It clattered to the thin carpet, and Raylie backed up onto the pool table, spreading her knees a bit.

He stood there, taut and hard like a mountain lion sizing up its prey. "Raylie, I'm not a man who easily changes his mind. If you want me to start this, I'm not going to stop until we're both completely satisfied. Do you understand?"

"Wow." She held her breath, held his gaze. The thought of him promising not to stop aroused her like nothing in her imagination ever could. "Do you promise?"

Not one to apparently pass up an invite, Ashton inhaled a deep breath and stepped near. The hardness dissipated from his eyes, but not the tautness as he eased between her legs. Her body vibrated with readiness, ached so deeply she could barely stand it. "Raylie," he whispered as his hand brushed along her jaw and throat. "I didn't invite you here for this, just so you know. But I'm not going to lie about my attraction."

Hands skimming up his shoulders, her sex clenching with need, Raylie knocked off his hat. He groaned, grabbed her hips, and it was all Raylie could do not to shed her clothes. She whispered, "Is it possible to skinny dip on a pool table?"

She felt him harden, and her legs wrapped around his hips to draw him closer.

He touched her jaw with his fingertips. "You are the most enchanting woman I've ever seen."

She opened her mouth to him, and he smiled at her, dipping his lips to hers once, twice, three times before making contact.

It drove her wild.

His fingers trailed over her jaw, her throat, stroked the short hairs at her nape as his tongue tickled hers.

She moaned—or whimpered, she wasn't sure—and locked her ankles around his waist.

He pulled back, wonderment on his face, and studied her before drawing her into his tight embrace. His kiss possessed her, weakened her. She sensed his controlled passion like an anchored ship with the sails billowing against the wind, a kite snared in a tree against a hurricane gale...

A stallion behind a teaser wall, chomping at the bit.

And Ashton himself held those reins in check.

She couldn't get any wetter.

She yanked his shirt from his shorts and tore it over his head. The look she gave him decried her need.

He leaned close to her lips and whispered, "Raylie, are you sure?"

Despite his claims that he wouldn't stop, she knew one "whoa" from her lips would forestall him. She drew a telltale foil square from her pocket and handed it to him.

Ashton needed no further encouragement. He stepped away from her and marched to the back wall, held her gaze as he reached behind the bookshelf and flipped a switch. "Don't want the boys in Security getting an eyeful, do we?" He sauntered back to her, reclaiming his position between her legs.

"You watching out for me?"

"Would hate it if you wound up on YouTube." He touched her chin. "I've said it before and I'll say it again: I protect what's mine."

"And you think I'm yours?"

"Not yet." He gave her a wolfish grin. "I have to thoroughly explore the territory before I can stake a claim."

"And I'm territory?"

He felt his face soften as he studied her, this amazing woman of burgundy fire. "There's so much to explore. There are mountains and peaks and valleys, and if I'm really lucky, I'll find me a gushing well."

"Something's gushing. You best get started."

Driven to touch all of her, Ashton's hands flew to her buttons, undoing one after another before the creamy white swells displayed what he had originally suspected—she wore her swimsuit. What there was of it. He delighted in the strings at the shoulders holding it together, for one tug freed those lovely handfuls to his ministrations.

"I found mountains." He nuzzled her throat, licked along her sternum as he continued to attend the line of buttons, unpeeling her and exposing the delectable fruit underneath.

Just like before, those nipples stared him straight in the eyes, and he took great delight in finally savoring their flavor. "And some very rocky peaks." Raylie tossed back her head, whimpering, and he saw her yank her shirt hem from her pants.

He pushed her back on the bumper, swept the pool balls to the edges as he laid her down. Her flat stomach quivered under his spread palm. "Ooh, earthquake." He stuck his tongue in her naval as he untied the strings on her pants. The zipper folded open to reveal a barely there pink bikini, and he swelled so hard he wanted to plow into her on the spot. "Hidden treasure," he heard himself whisper.

God, she was beautiful. He had hoped to woo her, wine and dine her, sway her to his cause. Perhaps being in her old car made her see some cosmic sign that women always prattle on about where men and dating are concerned, or perhaps she felt equally as drawn to him as he was her, but right now all he wanted was for her to hiss out his name.

The cottony pants came out from underneath her with a tug. He followed each inch of new flesh with a slow kiss, and when he dropped the material to the floor, he rubbed her foot, massaging pressure points that he knew would make her writhe in pleasure.

Her hips came off the bumper, right on cue.

He grazed his teeth over her tiny toes, and she gasped, breathing out his name.

He covered her, spreading her shirt around her ribs, exposing her stiff rosy nipples to the room. Images of them poking out from that burgundy shirt yesterday made him suckle her as he had the lemonade straw, this flavor divinely more satisfying.

Her fingers raked through his hair, her hips rocked, and Ashton hooked a finger under her thong and traced it to the source of his desire. Slick, hot liquid guided him to her core, and he drew circles around her nub, around her opening, rewarding his efforts with a fresh burst of liquid.

Geyser jackpot.

"Ashton, I want you."

How hard could a man get without snapping? Every word she uttered made him thicker, stronger, but still, he would bring her to her glory first. His lips trailed down, his tongue leaving a wet pathway that made her hips buck every time he blew across her dampened skin.

Her legs spread wide, and he nudged the flimsy material aside and dipped his tongue into her wet core.

Hard fingers dug into his scalp, and Ashton thrust his tongue inside her over and over again. He grabbed the material at her hip and tugged both strings of her thong to untie it. Yanking it off, he continued his thorough ministrations, hoping she didn't miss his hands as he unbuckled and lowered his shorts.

He found the foil packet, fell to his knees to nuzzle and kiss her calves as he slid it on.

Another earthquake quivered her skin.

God, he'd never been harder.

He stood, pushed two fingers into her to stretch her out, then grabbed her thighs and drew her bottom off the bumper.

One long slow thrust brought him home.

"Oh, Ashton."

He closed his eyes, lost in the feeling, the ecstasy of Raylie's tight channel and soft whimpering cries. He studied her, her pert breasts, her stomach, her shapely thighs wrapped around his waist, and knew she was the most perfect woman he had ever met. Their coupling felt so right, so spontaneous and intense, and he knew he wouldn't want another woman in his life after this.

Hell, after this, he'd just want to take her again.

He swelled, even under the raincoat she wanted him to wear, and Raylie arched up into his thrusts. He pushed harder and harder, leaning over to suckle her, his fingers toying with her breasts as he panted against the sweet curve of her throat.

He loosely rolled her bikini top into a long tube and rested it against her breasts, holding the ends.

"What are you doing?"

"This." He plowed her, and her breasts bounced up and down under the stretched material he held, and he watched her nipples peak higher and higher with the added stimulation. He grinned with male satisfaction as her eyes opened and darkened with pleasure.

He managed to wiggle his thumb between them, rubbing along her sensitive nub, and was rewarded with the cry of Raylie's violent release. She arched, quivered, twitched and clenched, and he restrained her hips, holding her, controlling her, riding that bucking mare until she milked him of his own moaning climax. Panting, lowering his forehead to rest on her shoulder, he nibbled her earlobe and waited for his own breathing to slow as well.

Damn, he wanted her again. Right now.

He gathered her limp body in his arms and slid her to the floor. A handful of foil packets littered the carpet; he exchanged his used raincoat for a new one.

Raylie raised a weary eyebrow as she watched him slide it on. "I didn't tire you out?"

He grinned and covered her, sliding back into her damp depths. "I could never tire of you, Raylie."

She grinned against his lips, but his pumping interrupted the kiss he planned. He was still so damned *hard*. He rolled to his back, wanting to see her breasts bounce as she rode him.

"Alley oop, McPherson."

She grinned and straddled him, and the arch in her back felt like she would snap him in half. He felt himself grimace as she rode him hard toward the finish line.

He made sure he came in second place.

Raylie collapsed atop him, sweating and heaving and quivering with her release. He cradled her in his arms and lowered her to the floor beside him, tucking her head to his shoulder. He kissed her damp brow, brushed her wet hair from her forehead. Her lips seemed pouty; he cradled her head and kissed her until their softness seemed made for his lips alone. When she sighed with satisfaction, he eased back. "Are you okay? I didn't hurt you at all, did I?"

"Exquisitely," she purred.

He chuckled and drew her close. He whispered, "We make a good team, McPherson."

Someone jiggled the door. When it didn't open, a sharp knock disturbed the atmosphere. "Sir? Dinner is served."

He closed his eyes, reveling in Raylie's warm body tucked to his side. Trying to find his voice, he took a few deep breaths. "We'll be right there," he called out.

She moaned and lolled her head back and forth on his shoulder as she slowly came back down to earth. "You aren't going to tell him we're *coming?*"

He chuckled, knowing with certainty he wanted this woman as his. From now on. He claimed her whole breast in his mouth for one long lingering moment before pulling her limp body to a sitting position. Thumbing her pert nipple, he whispered, "Do you think I missed any crucial geographical areas?" He nuzzled her neck, nipped the curve of her ear.

She gave a throaty laugh. "No."

Raylie's spent eyes trailed around the room, then finally up to his. She took a deep breath and wiped her damp hair from her forehead. She glanced at her watch, paled, then jumped to her feet and announced, "I have to go."

Chapter 23

He couldn't believe how fast she got dressed. He looked at his own watch, disbelief practically stoning him from all angles. Six-fifty-nine. "Raylie? What's wrong? Are you mad that dinner's late?"

She shook her head, yanked on her pants, found her sandals as he unpeeled his raincoat and looked around for a trash can.

Grasping at straws, he said, "The seafood truck was a little late. I had to wait for the shrimp… "

"It's not about dinner, Ashton." She talked into the shirt she buttoned.

He yanked on his shorts and faced her. "Then what is it?"

Angry, she whirled on him. "I didn't come here for food, all right?"

Now *that* confused him. He frowned, trying to replay all he had said to her over the past week. "You didn't?" He gasped. "Did you only want to conduct another investigation? Have I trespassed, Raylie? Please tell me you wanted this as much as I did. Do." God Almighty, he'd wring his own neck if he overstepped her boundaries or caused her anguish.

She looked at her watch again. "Fifty-five," he heard her mutter as she shook her head. "No, Ashton." She assumed a resigned pose. "Look, this isn't about dinner, okay? It's about sex. That's it. We both had an itch to scratch, nothing more."

He'd never met a woman like her before. All he could manage was a blank stare.

She huffed, tucked in her flimsy shirt. "I'll call you when I have any more details on the case, okay?"

Some detached part of his brain recognized that their roles had somehow reversed—that she now played the wanderlust male, and he the bereft woman.

The knowledge offered him little consolation. He didn't want casual sex with Raylie—he wanted Raylie. Gravity pulled him toward her, and he felt helpless against the McPherson orbital draw. "May I call you tomorrow?"

A rueful smirk crossed her lips. "Let's not make this into something it's not, okay?"

No words crossed his tongue. He fell mute to her callousness. Last item of apparel in place, Raylie nodded and practically flew out the door. Seconds later he heard her car engine roar to life.

Something he did had made Cinderella fly the coop.

Ashton leaned down, picked up her pink bikini thong and tucked it into his pocket.

Prince Charming only had to make a shoe fit.

He never once had to make amends.

Chapter 24

It took every last vestige of strength for Raylie to keep from barreling through the security gates and running down the guards that hovered there. Wouldn't that be just perfect? Confirming her "cop-killer" status to a dead Derrick as she tried to run from the most passionate man she had ever bedded? Irony tasted sour on her tongue as she waited impatiently for the men to clear her leaving with Ashton. Apparently he told them she would be spending a few hours.

Fifty-five minutes told her more than she was ready to accept.

Ashton could sustain.

And if he could pull that off in a moment of spontaneous passion, what else about him had she mistaken?

His voice, thick with concern, clicked over the guard's walkie-talkie. "Is she okay?"

The man eyed her and stepped away. "Want me to detain her, sir?"

The unit bleeped. "No, no. I don't know why she's upset, but just let her go."

The guard eyed her, suspicion etched across his brow. God, were they all cut of the same cloth? "10-4." He walked to the guard's station and flipped the switch. With Herculean effort, Raylie resisted sticking out her tongue at them as she escaped.

They were not her battle.

She was her own battle.

The roses on the passenger seat mocked her. She vacillated tossing them out the window, but didn't want Ashton to think she rejected him.

She was rejecting herself.

The sooner she solved this case, the quicker Ashton and everything sexy and manly would be out of her life.

Time for some accelerated healing courses. She flipped open her cell phone and left a message with Marta.

Chapter 25

"*Mamá* has been acting loco," Hermosa whispered to little Noe, smiling as he beat his tiny fists in her direction. She leaned over and kissed his knuckles, earning a coo and some bubbles for her effort.

The rattle had disappeared, but Hermosa had found a red feather and batted his tiny nose with it. Something akin to a giggle escaped his ruby lips, and she bent to place a kiss on his soft head.

Keys rattled in the lock, and her *Mamá* burst into the room, arms filled with flowers. "Look, *niña*," she said, holding up a cell phone. "Look what I have."

"*Teléfono*," Hermosa said, feeling joy at the sight of it. Their last phone had been disconnected. "Can you afford it?"

"It is a gift." Her *Mamá* beamed. "It came in the mail, from my boss."

Hermosa stopped tapping Noe's cheek at that. "*Señor* Lyre mailed it to you?"

"No, my other boss. He will mail me minutes to use the phone, too. I must save twenty minutes each month for him to call me, and the rest I may use. Is that not nice?"

"*Sí*. Now you will not have to use the payphone."

The cell rang in her *Mamá*'s hand, and together they determined how to answer it. She pressed the ON button and together they heard, "Vicenta, I have another job for you to do."

Chapter 26

Sweat dripped down him as he danced around the punching bag, giving it a left-right power combination that set the bag to quivering. Ashton had been at this sack for fifteen minutes already, and a burning ripped through his arms and shoulders, but he wouldn't stop until physical exhaustion claimed him.

Anger at his inability to control himself made him punch harder and harder. No gentleman would have invited a lady to his home for dinner instead of taking her out to a fine restaurant. No gentleman would have bent a lady over a pool table. And no gentleman would have taken a woman on the floor of a gaming room.

Damn.

He moved to the smaller teardrop shaped bag hanging over his head, imagining his face on it as he pattered a barrage of blows along its brown surface. No wonder she ran.

And he got the "fifty-five" comment after she left. Minutes. He had been too passionate with her, too hasty. A woman with a former rough boyfriend didn't need passion; she needed tenderness and courting. And here he had gone and focused on bringing her multiple climaxes instead of wooing her and granting her a chance to gradually explore him, to grow slowly comfortable with the idea of another man in her life.

Hasty and stupid.

Double damn.

He would give her a few days to regain her composure. Maybe heal, since he had been a rough bastard with his need of her. He punched the bag so hard it made a *twang* sound.

One of his servants knocked on the gym door.

"Come in," he bellowed.

Timid, his Mexican housemaid eased in, extending him a cordless phone. "*El Doctór.*"

Doc, calling on a Sunday? Panting, Ashton bit the laces and untied one glove, then the other. "Doc?" The hitch in his breath had nothing to do with the vigorous physical exercise. He watched the servant leave and close the door.

"Son, I got those results back. Not good at all."

"Poison?"

He heard the doc take a deep breath. "Deliberate. Based on the levels, it's most likely oleander."

Still breathing hard, he tried to focus. "Isn't that a tree?"

"Flowering decorative shrub. Any around your house?"

"No, sir. I told the landscapers my needs, and they didn't plant anything toxic."

Another pause, then Doc said, "I'm going to fax you some photos, so you can look around the neighborhood for them. They might be blowing over a fence and into your pastures."

Ashton wiped the sweat off his face and lip. "Okay. But Ralphie was in Tennessee all day. How long does the poison take?"

"One to three days, depending on the volume ingested."

"So it would have been the day beforehand, right?"

"At the earliest. Maybe check your staff three days prior?"

"I'm on it." He paced, hating to deal with this, the deaths, and worst of all the callous deliberateness. "You call Raylie yet?"

"No, son, thought maybe I'd leave that to you."

Damn. "Um, okay, all right. I will."

But Doc picked up on it. "You, ah, seeing her?"

He threw a glove at the wall. Hard. "Uh, yeah. I guess. Yeah." He squeezed the other one tight.

Doc paused. "I know it's none of my business, son, but McPherson and I have worked on many cases together. She had kind of a breakdown last November, what with losing her cop fiancé and then his mama within about three months' time."

That caught him off guard. "She did?"

"Yeah. Had that skinny kid filling in for her for a full week. Nice kid but clueless. I had this case—the Hedder case—some guy dragged his dog behind his Chevy about two miles. Dog barely made it, took me hours to patch him up, and the kid there couldn't make the arrest. Raylie comes back, kicks in the door, gun trained on the guy, and handcuffs him. Then she ties a tow rope to his cuffs and goes to her hitch. Tells him if he confesses to aggravated cruelty he won't share the same fate as his dog."

He almost grinned, picturing that spark of passion in her eyes, but the depravity stopped him short. "She could have lost her job."

"He didn't press charges."

Ashton wiped his sweaty jaw on his shoulder. "Why are you telling me this?"

Doc huffed out a long breath. "Because Raylie's going to solve this case for you. She's a go-to girl."

"Or a loose cannon." Breath held, Ashton waited for Doc to refute his comment.

He chuckled. "You're on the right side of the law, son. Don't you worry none about Raylie." He chuckled again. "And, son?"

Exhaling a relieved breath, Ashton said, "Yeah?"

Doc paused. "Don't tick her off." He hung up the phone.

After standing still for so long, sweat made Ashton's shorts cling to him, even though the air conditioning in his gym kicked on at seventy. Exhausted and disheartened, he climbed up the stairs, exited to his sweltering back patio, then punched in the code for his privacy gate around the pool. He closed the gate, stripped off his shorts, and dove in.

Blessedly cool water greeted him, and after a few laps, he felt refreshed, his limbs limp with fatigue. Leaning his nape against the wall, Ashton floated, trying to make his thoughts as light as his body.

This was not the way he wanted to be naked in his pool. He had hoped Raylie would have joined him after dinner, and perhaps he could have taunted her into some physical sport, just so he could have touched and held her.

His penis swelled despite the water temperature. He wanted her. Now. But Ashton had never been the child to have everything handed to him on a silver platter. No, he always had to work for what he wanted.

He got out and headed for his own bedroom, collecting his shorts for the laundry. The patio doors opened easily, and the bathroom had a pile of white towels stacked next to the Jacuzzi.

He dried off. It was time to get to work.

Chapter 27

The cursor on his screen blinked at him over and over until Ashton decided what he had to do. He typed his list.

> 1. *Find a way to make Raylie forgive whatever I did wrong*
> 2. *Find the horse killer*
> 3. *String him up by his intestines and drop him into a pit of fire ants*
> 4. *Make Raylie fall madly in love with me*

He sat back and studied the list. Then he revised number three: *String him up by his intestines and drop him into a pit of fire ants after feeding him oleander all day.*

He nodded, thinking his addition might more closely reflect his vehemence on the matter. He looked at the clock, although truly he didn't care. Nine p.m., still Sunday. Raylie would be going to work tomorrow, and Ashton needed to keep himself first and foremost in her mind. It couldn't have been just for sex. He refused to believe it. What he felt with her could not be relegated to the mashing of two bodies. She connected with him, and he'd be damned if he'd let that slip by.

Besides, he promised her a trail ride, and, by God, he wasn't about to go back on his word.

But Raylie feared his horses. A new fear. He sat back in his chair and studied the monitor. Something to do with Derrick? Perhaps. She said he died, but not how.

He booted up Google and typed in "November Derrick cop killed" and got a few hits. He skimmed through a couple of them and found one that made a whole lot of sense.

Ashton spun out of his seat and left his black and white office. It didn't matter. He loved her—complete with fears—and he'd find a way to complete his list.

Starting with number one.

Chapter 28

The entire hallway smelled like peonies and roses. As Raylie stumbled her way down a dim Monday morning corridor into the office area, everyone she nodded to just stared at her.

In fact, everyone waited outside their doors, just watching her with a strange kind of anticipation. She balked before crossing the wide expanse of linoleum. "What? I'm fifteen minutes late because Jim wanted my input on something." His new truck. Like she was an expert on engines, of all things.

Smiles crossed their faces, and knowing looks exchanged between them. No one spoke.

"Whatever," she mumbled as she mentally rolled herself into the hedgehog position and trudged to her office. Cheddar ignored everyone, so she could, too.

Leann giggled when she opened the door.

"Oh my God." Raylie froze at the tropical jungle that invaded the Cruelty Department. Okay, maybe not tropical. But it definitely explained the floral scent in the hallway. Peonies and roses and baby's breath and irises and flowers she couldn't name all vied for attention as they crowded the desks and floor and file cabinets.

Everyone burst out laughing.

Leann's knowing smile told Raylie she gleaned everything she needed to know about the weekend but would certainly listen to all the details. Every last one.

She shuffled her way between the pots, dashing her hand to prevent the beatific heads from banging into her own. "Get these out of here. I'm allergic, for cripes sake."

A chorus of "aws" trailed into her room, and she skulked at her desk. *Damn.* She'd never been wooed before, especially not by a one-nighter. And the burning humiliation of dragging the entire shelter staff into it really got her goat. "Will someone please take these out of here?"

One by one her coworkers trailed in, claiming a potted plant or vase or basket. Leann placed a protective hand over a white vase containing red roses and kept it on Raylie's desk. When the foliage had all blown away, Leann closed the door. "Tell me everything." She perched on the edge of Raylie's desk, her expression stating no work would commence until she had her fill.

"We had lunch, ice cream and sex. Satisfied?"

"Ooh." Leann shivered with joy. "The question is, honey, were *you*?" She waved a graceful arm about the office. "Because I know he was."

Raylie couldn't meet her eyes. "He was, well, yeah. We had a nice time."

"Nice?" Leann almost fell off the desk. "Four hundred dollars worth of flowers nice?"

She cracked a grin. "Really? You saw the invoice?"

"Don't be silly." She waved off the question. "I worked at a floral shop before here. I know my plants."

Raylie tried to nudge Leann off her clipboard, but she had none of it. "I want all the details. I've heard he's got talent."

Clipboard abandoned, Raylie shoved away to pour some coffee, but none had been brewed. "I don't know what you mean."

Now Leann stood up, following her. "Come on, girl. You always told me about Derrick. I'm old and married. I need to live my sex life vicariously through you."

"You're, like, nine years older than me." The wet filter filled with old ground beans gave a satisfying thump when she hurled it into the trash. "With Derrick, there was nothing to tell."

"O-ho!" She clapped, dropped into her chair. "I'll fill it when you spill it, girl. So Derrick was a dud stud, huh? You never told me that."

Perhaps therapy helped, or perhaps Raylie had no more reason to protect him. Or herself. "He was as big a pervert as his best friend."

"Oh." She leaned back. "Oh. I never knew."

"Yeah." She fiddled with an empty cup. "I never told."

"So why now?" Those dark, luminous eyes met hers.

With a huff, Raylie turned and dropped back into her seat. "Because Ashton's different, I guess."

"Good in bed?"

Cracking a grin, Raylie said, "We didn't actually make it to the bed."

"Couch?"

"Pool table."

"*Pool table?*"

"And then the floor."

Leann squealed in joy, tossed her hands in the air. "Oh, baby, that's hot." She stomped her feet, covered her face to giggle. When she looked up she said, "When are you going to see him again?"

"I don't know." She shrugged. "Whenever I get more info on the case, I guess."

Jumping from her chair, Leann said, "Absolutely not." Like a mother hen, she hovered over Raylie. "There is no way on God's green earth I'm letting you let this man walk away from you. Now, you need to call him and thank him and tell him what a beautiful gift he gave you."

Hands up, Raylie said, "No way. I'm not getting tied down to another man right now. I'm just barely getting over Derrick."

A soft smile crossed Leann's lips. "He doesn't have to tie you up, girlfriend." The phone rang, and she sauntered back to her desk. Tossing her a coy look, she added, "Although, with him, those ropes might just be made of gold."

Chapter 29

"Thanks for meeting with me so soon, Marta. I know this is a big imposition, but—"

"No imposition here," she said, beckoning Raylie to a chair. "I know time is of the essence, and you have a case to solve before more horses are killed."

She nodded, not trusting her tongue to spare Marta the details of her time with Ashton.

"Now, I did some thinking, and I've made a list of horse-related items. On a scale of one to one hundred, I want you to tell me how anxious you get when you think of these, okay?"

"Okay." She settled into her chair, ready for the crash course. Or, at least, the crash.

"Seeing a picture of a horse."

"One."

"Talking about horses."

"One."

"Planning to ride a horse."

To ride? "Eighty."

"Holding tack."

She took a deep breath, imagined the smell of leather and horse sweat. "Sixty."

"Remembering a time as a child when you rode a horse."

She thought of Snowflake, a pony she rode at a carnival, and nothing happened until she envisioned walking up to him again. "It went from five to ninety-five."

"What changed?"

"I saw myself walking up to Snowflake."

"And that became ninety-five?"

She nodded. Marta scribbled it down.

"Playing with toy horses."

"One."

"Being on a horse trail."

She considered that one. "Five?"

"Seeing horses on that trail walking toward you."

"Eighty."

"Walking around Mr. Lyre's stable."

In a flat tone, she said, "One ninety-seven."

She smiled. "Okay." Marta leaned back and set aside her notepad. "I have a good idea of where to go from here. Now, since we're going to have to work quickly, I'm willing to step outside my normal parameters and offer you some latitude regarding how we're going to go about this. Do you," she leaned forward, "have something that makes you completely relaxed, makes you forget all your daily toils?"

Sex with Ashton made her more physically relaxed than she imagined possible, but the ensuing complications knotted up her insides after she left. She had been a fool for thinking she could ride that particular hunk of flesh and emerge unscathed.

Marta sat waiting.

"Oh, playing with my foster kittens. They crack me up. And they've come around socially to the point where they act like lightning lunatics now."

The comment made Marta grin. "Okay, next session I want you to bring them."

"Here? You want me to bring a litter of lunatics to therapy?"

She shrugged. "Why not? I have paper towels if they make a mess."

"You'll need a vacuum cleaner and a kindly God if they make a mess," she mumbled, but the thought thrilled her. They'd get socializing while Raylie healed. "What a great idea."

"Glad you like it. For today, I want you to pretend you're watching your foster kittens play. Can you do that?"

Raylie nodded, loving this exercise. She leaned back in her chair, closed her eyes to do as bade. Marta turned on some music, spoke in low tones, encouraging Raylie to unwind. She even lit some lavender incense and let the aroma fill the room.

As Raylie imagined little kitten tails racing back and forth, Marta said, "Now, when you're ready, open your eyes."

Lavender and soft music worked. When Raylie opened her eyes, a poster, held by Marta, showed a beautiful white Arabian.

"How do you feel seeing this?"

"Fine. It's a beautiful creature."

So Marta read some facts about the breed's history, then looked up. "Any reaction?"

"Nope."

"Good. Now, I want you to close your eyes and pretend you're on that horse path I mentioned. Are you there?"

Raylie closed her eyes, imagined the birds chirping in the trees, the whisper of rustling leaves, the startled squirrel darting up a trunk. "Yes."

"Now, when you open your eyes, I'm going to have five horses here. Ready?"

She gripped the chair arms, grounding herself in Marta's room even as she imagined the scent of flowers on the air. When she opened her eyes, five model horses stood in a trail line on the floor.

"Oh!" She dropped down and picked them up. "I used to collect these. This one is the Indian Pony, and Five Gaiter, oh, he was my very favorite. Where did you get them?" She picked them up, noting the scratches where they were played with and loved, not unlike the ones she finally retired.

"My niece. She has about thirty." Marta wagged a finger at her. "You are supposed to be imagining the trail horses."

"But these are more fun." She took Five Gaiter and plunked back in her chair, making the horse gallop before her.

Contemplative, Marta drew her chair closer and claimed the

horse from Raylie's hands. "I'd like to try something. Close your eyes."

Obedient, Raylie did as she was asked, smiling after her micro play session.

"I want you to think about a horse standing before you, but as you do that I want you to reach out and touch this model instead."

Her heart leaped a bit, but mentally she reminded herself she'd be touching a toy. She pictured the gray mare she first saw at Ashton's, being ridden by a child, forty feet away. She raised a hand, almost fearful that the horse would…what? Give her an aneurism? But as she reached out, she bumped into plastic.

Fingers curled into a fist as she battled her imagination. Then she opened them again and stroked a finger down the plastic nose, pretending to trace a white stripe on the mare. Her finger wedged between the plastic ears, but she envisioned the soft ears of a horse as she continued the exercise. Down the bumpy mane she went, trying to recall the nylon-like feel of a real mane. But as her fingers eased down the swoop of back, lingering over the withers for the saddle, sweat broke out on her upper lip. She snatched away her hand and opened her eyes. "Can't do any more."

Marta set the horse on the carpet. "Were you envisioning a live horse?"

"Yeah," she said as she wiped her brow. "The gray mare at Ashton's." She swallowed. "I was okay until I got to where the saddle would be."

"That's good. You managed to see yourself patting a horse's head and neck. That's very good, Raylie." She folded her hands on her plump abdomen and leaned back. "How is Mr. Racing Horse these days?"

Raylie sucked in a long breath. "He filled my office with flowers today," she admitted.

"Really? Wow. What prompted such a nice gesture?"

Breath caught, Raylie wondered how much to share, but then

remembered that the doctor/patient relationship would remain confidential. Still, she couldn't just blurt out that she slept with him.

"I slept with him."

"Hmm." Head cocked, Marta asked, "Did you want to?"

"That's all I wanted."

"How was it?"

Phenomenal. She tried to shrug. "It was sex."

Marta seemed to consider her. "Do you feel that this intimacy may complicate your case?"

"Nah, I'll just send the kid instead. Matt needs the experience, anyway."

"So it did complicate things."

Her breath caught. "How so?"

Marta shifted. "If you are sending someone in your place, then I'm inclined to ask you, why are you avoiding him?"

That hit home. Raylie lowered her head. It took a while to find her voice, but she said, "My motto."

"What about your motto?"

The deep breath she took didn't make her any braver. "Well, ma'am…he's blown it all to hell."

Chapter 30

For two hours, he waited for Raylie to return, sweating up a storm and alternating between running his A/C and pacing on the strip of grass off to the side of the shelter. He watched a volunteer—identified by the green and white apron—take out one dog after another, walking them and playing with them and even training one puppy to sit. Fourteen dogs she handled as he waited while morning eased into a sultry afternoon.

From here, though, he also watched people file in with animals they relinquished. A box of puppies. A laundry basket teeming with kittens. A guy hitting his Doberman as he dragged it inside.

Ashton's teeth clenched at the cruelty, and he made a step toward the man just as the volunteer raced up and claimed the dog from him. By the look in her eyes, he assumed it to be a sight far too common at this doorway.

A new understanding of Raylie's life filled him. Her duty involved protecting animals from the likes of people like that.

And, until he could prove otherwise, the likes of *him.*

A loud truck or van rounded the bend, and by the pace of it, he assumed it to be a staff member. He peered around the corner and watched as a Pause for Paws cruelty van screeched to a halt. Soon Raylie got out, and he inhaled a deep breath upon seeing her exit the vehicle.

She seemed pissed.

Whipping open the back door, Raylie cocked a knee up on the van and yanked open a crate. Easing out, her arms burdened, he saw a limp dog lolling from her embrace.

She raced to the door, and without thinking, he popped out from behind the corner and pulled it open for her.

"What are you doing here?"

"Waiting for you," he said as he reached ahead and opened the next set of doors. "What happened to the dog?"

"Neglect happened. Turn left."

He did, and she directed him down the hallway and into a hospital area. He watched the dog's mouth open in agony, and felt fear clench his chest. "Is it going to die?"

The clinic staff stood waiting, and she eased the dog onto a blanket-covered exam table. He had heard the shelter now did all their own spays and neuters, and assumed this was the place where it was all done. Five young women and two young men in matching green scrubs stood waiting, and he saw a female doctor in the surgery room, gowned and masked and leaning over an animal covered in a blue drape. He assumed it was one of their daily surgeries. "If she does," Raylie replied, "it goes from a misdemeanor to a criminal charge, and I'm tossing his ass in jail."

Fluid bags hung from mobile stands, and he watched in awe as the staff inserted not one, but three catheters.

"He says he gave the dog food and water yesterday," Raylie said, doubt thick in every word.

"Yeah, right," he heard someone mutter.

Ashton watched as another doctor approached, this one a male in his fifties, and he peeled off his rubber gloves and tugged his mask from his face. He grabbed a stethoscope from the nearby counter and came to the dog's side.

"X-ray's on, Doc," someone else said.

"Temp's one-o-seven," a girl said, pulling out the beeping rectal probe.

"One-o-seven? Get cold towels." The doctor pointed to the sink.

"I'll get the alcohol." Raylie ran to a cupboard and pulled out the clear cosmetic type. She grabbed some gauze and poured the liquid over the dog's feet, and soon the typical hospital aroma filled the air.

"What's that for?"

"To cool her down," she muttered, as if she really didn't want to be answering his questions. Her voice rose. "She's in pain," Raylie said to the doctor, her voice suffering along with the dog. "Cried the whole way here, really increased breathing."

He watched as staff laid soaking wet towels on the whimpering patient to cool her down, layering ice packs in between them. No different from horses, he told himself. But then again, his horses weren't starving and bordering on heatstroke.

"Hmm," the doctor said, putting on his stethoscope and listening to the dog's abdomen. "No gut sounds."

"Bastard," Raylie hissed as she wiped and dried the dog's feet, then poured on more alcohol.

"What's that mean?" Ashton asked, looking around at the impassive faces. But no, they weren't impassive…they were pissed. All of them.

"It means the dog's starving to death," the doctor answered matter-of-factly. "No gut sounds means no food inside."

"Lidocaine in the bag, Doc?" A girl hovered with a hypodermic needle aimed at the bag of IV fluids.

"Yeah, she's painful," he said. "Ten ccs to start. When her temperature's down, mix up a slurry of Gerber baby food and canned a/d, see if she'll take anything. She's weak; be careful not to choke her." He looked down her throat, checked her eyes and ears, then shook his head.

In shock, Ashton stared down at the dog, only about thirty pounds, yellow shaggy coat covered with caked-on mud and burdocks. "What kind is she?"

"Golden Retriever."

"You're kidding." He frowned. "Aren't they big dogs?"

"I smell maggots," a girl in scrubs said, and two others sniffed the dog.

"Yeah, me too. Flip her."

They rolled her, legs under, and gags and sounds of disgust soon rippled through the staff. Someone grabbed clippers, called out for flush and forceps, and Ashton turned away before he lost his breakfast. "And I thought botflies were bad."

The dog being tended to, Raylie faced him, arms folded, hip cocked. "How big, you asked? Double that. The dog should be sixty-five pounds of life." She spat the last word. "Why are you here, Ashton?"

Some curious eyes looked up, and he looked back down at their emergency case. "What are her chances?" Somehow, it seemed very important that this dog make it. More cold towels landed on her body, leaving the infested wound exposed.

"About the same as getting you to answer my question."

Her passion flared, and Ashton tried to tell himself it was because of the dog. Tried. He looked at his watch. One-fifteen. "You eat yet?" Not that his stomach would hold food right now, but in twenty minutes…

"No."

"Come on." He opened the door with one hand, tried scooping her shoulders with the other, stopping only because of the volume of witnesses. Surprisingly, she came along. "How long of a lunch do you get?"

"Half hour."

"Come on," he said softly, knowing a woman in need of emotional support when he saw one. "My treat. Where do you want to go?"

She shook her head. "There's a pizza shop around the corner. I usually just grab a sub."

"How about Chinese?"

Hope lit her eyes. "I didn't call anything in."

He smiled, pulled out his cell. "What do you want?"

She didn't hesitate. "Sweet and sour chicken, an egg roll, and dumplings." She gave him a significant look. "Think I'm going to have to pass on the white rice right now."

Suppressing a gag reflex, Ashton said, "How does a dog get infested like that? With those—" he shivered, trying to erase the image by waving his hands over his face.

"We call it 'fly strike.' Bed sores. Too weak to stand."

"So this has been going on for some time now."

She almost shattered right there on the spot. "Ashton, just call in the food, okay?" She didn't look at him.

Feeling like he disappointed her, he said, "The chicken sounds good." He dialed one of the numerous restaurant numbers he had programmed in that morning and placed their orders. "Hop in. I'll drive."

He left Chastity home today, opting for his BMW with all the bells and whistles. She didn't seem impressed as she got in.

"You trash my car?"

He laughed and started the engine. "No. I wanted A/C today."

"Better not have," she warned as they drove off. Then she took a deep breath and faced him again, seeming weary and broken. "Why are you here, Ashton?"

"Can't a man pick up a beautiful lady and take her out to eat?"

"Sure, but..." she huffed, raked her fingers through her hair, "...it was only supposed to be a one-night stand."

"Not for me it wasn't." His gaze felt hard when he looked at her. Too bad. "We're on this case together, Raylie. Until it's solved, you're going to be seeing a lot of me. I don't want that kid filling in for you, either. You're the one I trust."

She eyed him. "Trust? Why? What are you hiding?"

"I...nothing." He felt his neck grow warm. "I mean, I trust you to solve the case."

"Mm-hmm."

Damn, she was going to start digging. He cleared his throat. "Doc says it was oleander poisoning. You believe that?"

"Yeah, I got the report." She faced him. "And the flowers. They were really nice. What a great way to advertise to everyone that we slept together."

He gasped. "Raylie, I—"

"Forget it. I know the looks people were giving me. They're wondering why I don't just go into a professional escort service."

"Raylie, that's not—"

She hit the dash. "Do you know how much you humiliated me? God, Ashton, I didn't even want to walk into my office today."

"I didn't mean—"

She slumped back into the seat. "It was just like being with Derrick all over again."

He swerved the car to the shoulder and slammed it to a stop to face her. "I'm not Derrick, Raylie. I would never do anything to deliberately hurt or humiliate you."

Tears glistened in her eyes, but she squared her jaw and stared straight ahead. He sighed, unlocked the doors and undid his seat belt. He put the car in park, pulled his keys out of the ignition and walked around to her side.

Wary, she watched him. When he opened her door, she actually recoiled. "What are you doing?"

He bent over her and undid her belt. "Come here." He tugged her out of the car.

She resisted, but not enough. So Ashton drew her up and out and guided her back along the side.

"Ashton…"

He knew a woman in distress, and what Raylie needed right now was some old-fashioned comfort. Despite the heat, he gathered her into his arms, holding her fast against his car.

"Ashton, I…"

"Shhh." He traced a finger along her ear, down her arm. Nudged the nape of her neck and breathed in the scent of her skin.

Her fingers clenched his sleeves, and he felt the strength of her anger sizzling under the surface. Soon she relaxed, tipped back her head, completely placid in his arms. A car raced by. "We're blocking traffic."

His voice deepened. "No we're not."

Her arms trailed up his back, drew him closer. "You sure?"

She felt so good, so right, in his arms. "As sure about this as I've been about anything." He kissed her cheek, her neck, her jaw. "Raylie," he whispered, and thought he heard her sniffle.

Her stomach growled. She leaned away from him, looking down. "Food?" she asked hopefully.

He grinned, stroked her bottom lip with his thumb. He wouldn't kiss her. Not yet. He wanted her to want him before he made any move that could seem aggressive. She already compared him once to that abusive ex and that was once too many.

"Yeah, I'm hungry, too. Let's go."

With renewed hope, he tucked her back into the car.

He couldn't wait to read his fortune.

Chapter 31

Shot, maimed and blown straight to hell. That's what Raylie's motto was right about now. But she sipped her cola and dabbed her dumplings in soy sauce and tried to forget the side of her life that Derrick had never wanted to hear about.

The deaths. The suffering. The abusive bastards. No wonder he didn't want to hear about them—too close to home.

But Ashton…he stayed, watched, asked questions. And blast his soul, he held her. *Held her.* Her eyes watered again, just like they had there on the side of the road. In his arms. Being held.

Something cracked. Humpty? No. It felt warm. Ice? Her heart? Thawing? She looked up into his soft eyes and noticed him smiling at her. Another glacier split, the crevasse racing like lightning across the frozen tundra of her soul.

"I have a lot of respect for what you do. I've never seen anything like that before."

Remembering his reaction, Raylie found herself grinning. "Yeah, first time's the worst. I have to say, you have the Icky Dance down pat." She mimicked his cringe and hand-flapping.

He chuckled, but he shook his head. In his eyes, his entire soul glittered there. "It must break your heart."

Her throat swelled, and burning stung her eyes again. She looked down. "Some more than others," she whispered.

"You think she'll make it?"

One tear raced down her cheek then, and she tried to dash it away before Ashton noticed, but his radar had been trained on her for fifteen straight minutes now and he didn't miss a beat.

"Raylie?" He tucked around the table and slid onto her bench. "Raylie?"

This one wouldn't be contained. "It's my fault if she dies."

"Honey," he took her hand. "It's not—"

She yanked away. "It is." Defiant, she met his eyes. "This guy was banned from owning any animals after he starved his Beagle last year." She shook her head. "I should've checked on him. I knew better."

"Aw, honey." He scooped her close, drawing her head to his shoulder, and Raylie didn't care that other people in the restaurant noticed her moment of weakness. "You are not responsible for the actions of other people. Don't you know that by now?"

"It's my job," she muttered into his shirt.

"And he's responsible for his own dog. Even a five-year-old has enough sense and heart to feed a hungry pet."

She gulped down the lump, took a moment to relish the drum of his heartbeat as it pulsed under her cheek. "Did I tell you I had a Golden growing up?" She managed to raise a hand to wipe off her tears.

Gentle fingers stroked her hair. "No," he whispered.

"She wound up getting cancer at six, and my dad couldn't afford the surgery, so we had to put her down. At only six." She swallowed. "Her name was Brandy. She was my last pet before college."

He kissed her temple and rocked her along his shoulder. "That explains so much."

She looked up at him, confused.

"You couldn't save yours, so you'll try to save all the rest of them." She shrugged and looked down, but he drew her close again, still rocking her. "Is there anything I can do? Does she need twenty-four hour care? I can take her to the emergency clinic."

Abandoning the idea, Raylie waved away his words. "The shelter can't afford critical care. Besides, the only one who will work with us is all the way in Lexington."

"But I can." He pushed her to arm's length. "Does she need it, Raylie?"

Mute with his offer, she could only nod. "Why would you do this?"

A gentle smile played at the corner of his lips. "Is it important to you she make it?"

Tears filled her eyes. She nodded and tried to swallow. "Yeah. It is."

He stroked her chin, smiling down into her drippy eyes. Perhaps he weighed out his words, for a moment of silence stretched between them. Then his mouth descended on hers, but instead of kissing her, he paused and met her eyes. "Then I need no other reason."

Everything in Raylie fell limp. She thought for sure he would kiss her then, but when his phone rang, he had no problem abandoning her to answer it. Just as well, she thought, but felt her face cloud up nonetheless.

"Hey, Ed."

Ed. His stable master.

"Again?" Ashton asked, and he shook his head to Raylie. "Even tranquilized?" He huffed out a breath and told her, "High Eminence still won't trailer, even sedated." Into the phone he muttered, "There goes that win." Frustration poured through him when he said, "My fastest two-year-old, and I can't even get him to a race track."

Raylie held Ashton's eyes, but then he frowned and turned away, keeping the phone out of earshot. Alarm bells rang, but instead of reacting to more bad news, she could tell Ashton hid something from her.

"How far—" he glanced at her. "Tell me more details."

A brief nod punctuated the silence, and she watched the frown deepen across his handsome brow. He glanced at his watch, then looked at her again. "I'm with Raylie now. We can be right there."

Mouth open, she glanced at her watch, too. She shook her head, mouthed *No,* touched her watch.

Work-related, he mouthed back. Then Ashton stood, offered her his hand to stand, and snatched her last piece of chicken and the tab. Still listening to Ed, they checked out and left.

"We're leaving now," he told him. "See you in ten." Ashton hung up.

Seizing her chance, Raylie said, "I have to—"

"It's work-related." He appraised her, and the look made no sense to her. It held—reverence. "You need to be there. Trust me."

With his hand on the small of her back, he led her to his car. There she braked. "If it's work-related, I need my van."

He grinned. "No you don't. And you'll be back within the hour, I promise."

Something hid in his eyes, something mischievous, and Raylie felt his simmering joy as a contagion. Needing a break from the imminent death of the Golden, she conceded. "Okay."

She studied him. "You know, it might help to sedate the horse while he's stalled, or early morning, before he gets too awake."

"Early mornings are for workouts. And he loves to run."

She shrugged. "Adrenalin tends to counteract sedatives."

"This from all your horse experience, Raylie?"

She clammed up, so in relative quiet they rode the familiar path to his estate, an odd smile hinting about on his lips. Through the security gate they went, up and around the hillocks, and on a gravel road between pastures until they stopped at a gate about seventy acres away. "She's out here."

Without pretense, Ashton got out and came around, taking her hand and pressing it under his muscular biceps. Unable to resist his strength, Raylie gave a squeeze. "She? She who?"

A thick rope looped the gate to the post. Ashton opened it, guided her though. "You'll see."

A stable hand nodded at them. "Over the hillock, sir."

"Her name is Missy," Ashton said with a gentle press on her fingers. "Mystic Time."

Her feet stopped. "A horse?"

But Ashton smiled and patted her hand. "A horse in need. Come on."

With phenomenal effort Raylie trudged forth, gripping his biceps with claws extended. When they breasted the hillock, a brown lump faced her, the horse downed.

"Poisoned?" She moved forward one step.

Strong arms grabbed her around the waist and held her still. "No. Shh." Setting her away from him, Ashton stepped closer. "Hey, Missy."

The horse raised her head, made a soft whicker and lay back down. So Ashton came nearer and knelt by her head. When the horse settled, he waved Raylie to him.

All she could see of the horse was the rump and tail. Both brown. Not dying, but in need. Emotions warred in her, seeing Derrick lying prone with his horse standing over him. But that was winter, with snow gathering on cold skin too chilled to melt it.

Sticky heat greeted her now, and lush green grass surrounded her. Still Ashton waved her close. Now, not then. Therapy. Horse in need. Focusing on the tail—one association that didn't trigger anything—Raylie eased near.

The tail rose up, and Ashton said, "Just in time."

And then, in a gush of fluid, a thin sack with two little hooves appeared.

"Quick. You may need to pull."

A baby. Foaling. Horse in need. Feeling awkward and yet relieved, Raylie knelt down by Missy's tail. "What do I do?"

"Pull on the next contraction, but only if the baby doesn't advance."

"Uhhh…okay." *Right*. Wiping her hands on her pants, she grabbed the slimy sack and felt the strong hooves in her hands.

Apparently Ashton found her position amusing. He chuckled and said, "Fourteen years ago, I was right where you are, helping this mare begin her new life." A soft stroke to the horse's jowl accompanied his words.

Somehow she knew he honored her with this, giving her a chance to bond with a horse the way he had.

A threat, and yet a promise. She licked her lips and waited.

Two contractions later, the baby slid to the grass, relatively unassisted. Her heart swelled with the sight of it.

Missy rolled to her feet and turned to sniff the foal. Knowing this much, Raylie tore the sack from around the nose and peeled it back, feeling as if she had just stepped into another world. Missy took care of the rest.

Stunned and awed, Raylie sat there, mesmerized, as the foal stirred and blew out its nostrils and lifted its ungainly head off the ground. It was the cutest thing she had ever seen.

Diligently, Missy cleaned and groomed the foal, and soon the baby did its best Bambi-on-ice impersonation, complete with tousled hair looking like a shag rug after a rainstorm.

One peek underneath told her what she needed to know. "It's a colt." A beautiful, perfect, chocolate-brown colt.

"Either sex is welcome here." Like a proud papa Ashton stood there, hands on hips, unmoving, merely watching events unfold. Then he radioed the stable hand, who walked over the hill bearing iodine and a tiny bridle. Like the lover she knew him to be, Ashton ran those strong, gentle hands over the foal and applied iodine to the umbilicus. While the baby nosed his mother's leg, Ashton slipped a tiny bridle—complete with bit—into the baby's mouth.

"Break 'em young?"

He looked up, eased the headpiece behind the foal's ears. "If their first memories are of a bridle, they accept it far easier next year."

"Really."

"Yup." Then his hands stroked every inch of the baby's hide—checking for conformation and soundness, Raylie assumed—and she would have given anything to have that bridle in her mouth. But then he eased it back off and guided the colt to his mother's milk. "Here you go," she heard him whisper.

Two steps brought him to her side, and that strong, gentle hand pulled her up and drew her close. "He needs a name."

"Yeah," she agreed, watching the perfect little foal guzzle his first meal.

Those fingers stroked up and down her arm, lulling her with their rhythm. "His father is named Fear Me Now."

Up, down, up, down. Ashton's touch did not border on absentmindedness, but rather titillation. His touch told her he stroked her strictly for the pleasure of pleasing her.

Lulled by the song of his fingers, soothed by the music of birth, Raylie forced herself back to the conversation. "Okay." Something forced her to look up at him when all she wanted to do was purr.

"It's customary to use the sire's name, if possible." Pride simmered in his eyes, telling her he knew how his stroke affected her senses. "Raylie," he whispered, angling to cradle both elbows, "I'd like you to be the one to name him."

Chapter 32

The ride back to her van seemed hazy. He wanted her to name a horse. Craziest thing she'd ever heard.

And a fantastic honor.

She looked over at him, admiring his handsome profile. "I'll check on the dog first thing."

Her comment made him glance at his car clock. "It's been almost two hours. Do you think her temperature's dropped?"

"By now, yeah."

He met her eyes. "I meant what I said about critical care. I'll cover her costs, Raylie."

She nodded, relaxing in the fact that Ashton took control. "I'll just need to clear it with the director, especially since I'd have to drive to Lexington. I'd be gone for hours." Not unpleasing a thought, really. "If anything, we can sock the owner with the emergency bills and mileage."

"Even if I pay for them?"

A sniff of derision slipped out. "The price of neglect, I guess." She shrugged.

They pulled in to the shelter, and Raylie led Ashton straight to the clinic. The dog had been moved to a kennel, and one girl sat right there with her, monitoring her vitals. Ashton joined her in the vigil, so Raylie dialed the director and got the all clear to transport. Next she called the emergency hospital and told them they were en route.

They. Another two hours with Ashton. This time, she would be in control. She opened the cage and tossed a chilled blanket over the dog and eased her out by carrying the thick dog bed she was on. "We're going to Lex Crit Care. I'll get copies of everything." The staff watched, solemn, as she and Ashton made their procession out of the building.

Hopefully not a funeral procession, she thought, as Ashton opened the doors and readied the crate in the van. Soon they were packed up and heading out onto the highway.

Apparently the inside of her van intrigued him. "Laptop?"

"For directions."

"No porn sites?"

She smiled. "No, it's a girl's computer."

"Ouch." He pointed to the clipboard on her dash. "What's this?"

"My workload. Top are ones I need to visit, with critical first."

"Really?" He grinned. "Where's mine?" He flipped through.

She let him explore, smiling, letting him wonder. After about twenty sheets, the clipboard lowered. "Where's mine?"

She grinned and pointed to the plastic filing container on the floor. "Special case. Front pocket."

Without a word he popped open the top, flipped through and quickly found his report. "I'm special, or the case is?"

"The case." She tried not to grin.

The top clicked back in place. Ashton's head dropped until he had to look up at her. "Not me? Not even a little?"

She tried to swat him, but he caught her hand. "What are the pink sheets in the back here for?"

The last twenty on her clipboard had caught his attention. "Dangerous cases."

"Pink is dangerous?"

"For me, yeah."

Genuine warmth lit his smile. "Why pink?"

"Because it's too hard to read the report on red paper."

"Oh." He flipped to read one. "Why are they dangerous?"

She reached over and grabbed the clipboard, shoving it hard onto the dash. "Because those are the ones that need constant supervision. Like the Golden." She grabbed it back and dropped it on his lap. "Last page. 'Check monthly,' I wrote. But did I? No. Not last month. It was six weeks since my last scheduled visit. Two weeks late, and this is what happened."

Long tanned fingers flipped to the last page. He read it quietly, and then slid it back onto her dashboard. "Honey, you couldn't have known."

"Don't call me 'honey' anymore, okay?" She swallowed hard and changed her mind. This was a bad idea, trapping herself with Ashton for two hours.

Silence stretched between them. Even the dog drifted off to sleep. Ashton broke it by asking, "Why do the cops call you Fearsome?"

She almost smiled then, glad to be on familiar ground. "I came here from New York. The anti-cruelty laws are far stricter there than they are here. Did you know that Kentucky is one of the few states left where you can still cockfight? Everyone else outlawed it. Anyway, New York City was the first place in America that initiated anti-cruelty laws, so New York tends to be pioneering in the field. Any dog left outside must have insulated shelter. Insulated shelter, not a garage or lean-to. And fresh water, not standing. So, to come here after working north…well, let's just say I'm a bit ambitious."

"A lot of arrests?"

She grinned. "Yeah. Even if they're let go, a few days in the slammer seems to be a great wake-up call. No one wants Fearsome sniffing at their door."

"Baby," he faced her. "You can sniff at my door any day you want."

"Bold words for a suspect."

He didn't smile. Instead he studied her, and something hardened in his eyes. "Why did you assume we were only a one-night stand?"

Her shoulders wouldn't shrug. "I'm not your type."

"What, female?"

A dark look answered that one. "Barbie doll. Rich."

"You think that's my type? Because I was too rough with you?"

Without thinking, Raylie said, "You weren't too rough with me."

He collected her hand again, not letting her pull away. "Fifty-five minutes' worth of too rough?"

Damn, she must have muttered it out loud. Not surprising, the way he had shocked her with his vigor. He acted hurt. Or wounded. "You weren't rough with me, Ashton. Not at all."

"Then why did you leave so fast?"

Trapped. In a moving car. With questions she plain did not want to answer. Would she ever be able to tell him it was the best hour of her life? "I don't want to talk about it right now."

"Okay." He leaned back, her hand ensconced in his. "How did Derrick die?"

"Oh my God." She tried to yank away. "Is this twenty questions?"

Still, he held her. "Did it have something to do with horses?"

Her jaw tightened. "I don't want to talk about it."

"Are you afraid of horses, or just me?"

"My God, Ashton. Can you please worry about the dog in back, instead of my head?"

"Ah-hah." He nodded and sat back. "Your head is messed up."

Now he ticked her off. "What about you? What about this, 'You're the one I trust,' bullshit? What are you hiding, Ashton?"

She scowled at him, catching a glimpse of fear in his eyes. "I told you. Nothing."

She managed to yank away. "What kind of name is Lyre, anyway? What family even names themselves after an instrument? I mean, you never hear about the Oboe family, or the Kazoo family. So why Lyre?"

He blanched, she was sure of it. "It was my aunt's name."

"Mm-hmm." At that point, Raylie knew she'd have to do some serious digging on him. Skeletons rattled loud right then. But how did one go about looking for name changes? She'd check with Leann after dropping Ashton off.

"I didn't mean to upset you, Raylie. You're just so…guarded."

How to respond? Silence eased into the gap, widened it. Finally she said, "I have a lot at stake right now."

"Tell me. Let me help."

God, when had someone last offered to help? "I don't think you can."

Somehow he shifted to face her. "Let me in, Raylie. I will help you. You know I will."

Endless rolling hills stretched to the north and south for several long minutes as she cut across Kentucky toward Lexington. Whitewashed fences swelled up and down on bluegrass waves as far as the eye could see. The breath she inhaled shook her, rattled her chest. Words came slowly, required inordinate effort. "Derrick had an aneurism when we were both riding patrol for the Christmas festival. I…I haven't been able to be near horses since."

Slowly Ashton eased back into his seat, digesting her words. "I'm so sorry, honey. I never would have…I mean, I thought something had happened, but not…I didn't…today you did fine." He hung his head, pinched the bridge of his nose and exhaled.

"I've been getting help. Crash course style, to finish this case."

He eyed her then, cautious. "To be free of me?"

Mixed emotions clamored within her. Normally she would lash out, injure with her words, create distance. Now, she wasn't so sure she wanted to be that person. "Initially, I thought to arrest you, solve a great case and get that field chief spot opening up. Our director likes men behind bars, and a guy from out-of-state and I are both running for it. More arrests would make me look better."

He harrumphed. "Don't you know promotions are just an

excuse to load people down? You'll be buried in paperwork."

"I need the money." *So close to being free of Derrick's oppressive squashing thumb*. Selling off Angie's house would clear her of all her debts and enable her to get a fresh start on a new life. Three more mortgage payments and she could claim ownership to sell.

"I'll support you."

"I need to pay off Angie's house to get—what? What did you say?"

No humor filled his eyes. "I've never had a peace officer on staff. Why not? You get free room and board, free meals during your shifts, and—" he glanced at her clothes, "—well, you'd probably want to wear your own uniform."

Crazy. "You're serious."

"I said I'd help you. If you'll let me." A small grin twitched his lips. "Besides, then I could make sure you were working twenty-four/seven on my case."

So she jerked her thumb to the back. "And let dogs like her die."

"Okay." Hands up, Ashton leaned back. "Twenty-four/seven is a little ambitious. I'll let you work for the shelter on Tuesdays."

Her own laugh caught her off-guard. It felt good. "Only Tuesdays?"

He tipped his head. "I golf then."

Such chuckling eased the burden she felt, and sharing it—really sharing it—made her troubles smaller.

"So who is Angie?"

Good mood gone, Raylie focused hard on the road. "She was Derrick's mom. Really, my mom. Probably the only one I've ever had. She willed Derrick the house, but I hate it. I hate the style, the design, the colors, the layout, the furniture…ugh. And the memories. Both good and bad. With the promotion comes a free house. It's old, but nicely maintained."

Ashton nodded, frowned, then asked, "So when are you going to start arresting people on my case?"

"When I have evidence. Why? You volunteering?"

A wolfish grin stretched his lips. "Are you going to handcuff me, officer?"

She frowned. "Do you really keep all your staff on the premises? *And* feed them?"

"Ninety-plus percent." He nodded. "I also have tennis courts and a pool, and have someone come in twice per week for lessons."

Surprise, surprise. "You're good to your staff, aren't you." It almost came out as a whisper.

"I take care of what's mine. These people have access to everything I value. The best way to protect what I love is to keep them happy."

"Hmm." Another mile sped by as she muddled around with that revelation. But something struck her as odd. "You said ninety-plus percent. Can you give me the names of those who live off-site?"

"Sure. There's only, like, six or eight."

"Okay."

"Why? What are you thinking?"

"I don't know." They neared their exit, so Raylie slowed and got into the right lane. "It would seem that someone living off-site would have the least investment in your enterprise, and therefore, with proper motive, possibly the most to gain."

Chapter 33

With the dog stabilized, kenneled and admitted under G.S. 12—for the twelfth Good Samaritan case—Raylie and Ashton returned to Louisville. About halfway back, she noticed him sulking. Guessing his distress, she touched his forearm. "She'll be fine."

He sighed. "I know."

Attempting levity, Raylie said, "With your credit card on file, that dog'll be tap dancing fit for Broadway when she's discharged."

He only shook his head. "It's not the money. It's my horses. Maybe you're wearing off on me." He stared at her clipboard of cases, eyes fixated on the pink sheets.

"In what way?"

Pain edged his eyes when he looked at her. "Maybe if I can save her, the rest will live."

She squeezed his strong forearm. "A wise man once told me I can't be responsible for the actions of others."

Chuckling, he pressed her fingers into his arm. "More like a wise guy than a wise man."

"Yeah. I agree."

He touched the pink sheets. "Pink for dangerous. Same with red. What does yellow mean?"

"Caution."

"Blue?"

She grinned. "Case resolved."

"Purple?"

That one stumped her. "Don't know."

"Green."

"Mm." She smiled. "Day off in the park."

For a moment, he studied her. "Most of your colors have to do with work." His thumb stroked gently over her hand. "What color do you associate with love?"

Heat suffused her cheeks again, blast him. She thought for a moment, about love, lovers, and only one color came to mind. "Pure white. Like the white of a drawing pad before the charcoal ever touches it."

"Sounds like you're an artist."

"Used to be."

He regarded her for a moment. "What happened?"

She shrugged. "Life, I guess." She remained quiet for a moment. "I used to go to this park near where I lived, in Syracuse. There was this little bridge over a creek, and a bench nearby. Couples used to hold hands on the bridge, or kiss, and I would sit and watch and sketch them."

"Voyeur. And you think men are perverts."

He still stroked her fingers, and the gentleness coaxed a reluctant truth from her lips. "I like love. I like capturing it on paper. I like seeing how the chemistry between two people can be caught with a bit of charcoal." She thought of the picture she had drawn of them and felt her throat tighten. They *had* looked good together.

He raised her fingers to his lips for a lingering kiss. "Have you forgiven me for Sunday night, Raylie?"

Sunday night? "The pool table? I wanted that, Ashton. There's nothing to forgive."

He rubbed her fingers back and forth along his chin, where a bit of stubble tickled her knuckles. "Then, why did you run off?"

With one hand on the wheel and one hand trapped, Raylie stared at the road. "Can you turn up the radio and A/C?"

He only turned the A/C switch. "Did I hurt you?" He nuzzled open her palm and kissed it.

Shivers raced up her arm, straight down her spine to her woman's core. Moisture spilled from her, and when Ashton stuck his tongue between her fingers, she nearly bucked off the seat.

Her van lurched as she inadvertently punched the gas. Ashton smiled a confident grin. "Did I?"

Completely wet and aroused, Raylie tossed him a coy look. "Well, you *are* big."

He grinned like an idiot, then stopped. "Too big?"

"Not too big." Heat flamed her cheeks, all the worse in the cold air blasting on her, and she shook her head at their conversation.

"Just right?"

God, he loved to push her. "You are an arrogant man, Ashton."

He slid her finger into his mouth and sucked on it. A low moan escaped her. "Ashton," she whispered.

He nuzzled her wrist. "Need a refresher course?" His tongue licked a trail to her elbow.

"My memory is perfect." *Jump 'em, pump 'em, dump 'em. Dump 'em!*

His voice turned gravelly. "As is your body."

Somehow, step three of her motto experienced technical difficulties. "Thank you," she managed to whisper.

"And by the way, just so you know, you're completely my type. For as long as I can remember, I've been attracted to girls who look kind of like you. Short, athletic, brown hair." He crooked a smile at her. "Although burgundy is new, I'll admit." He unclipped his seatbelt and squatted down between the bucket seats, one hand resting on her thigh. "How about we start over?" His fingers tucked under her pant leg hem and stroked the skin over her sock. "You, me, dinner at Georgios."

Georgios. Seven-dollar soft drinks. "I…I have appointments every day after work."

"Cancel them." Those fingers eased up to her knee.

"They're with my grief counselor. I'm not canceling them."

"Saturday?"

Shit. "I'm…taking my dog to the park."

"Sunday?"

"For the weekend. Camping."

He let go and eased back. "Raylie." A warning. "You can't

run from me forever." His fingers skimmed down along her arm. "Saturday."

To go from fast and furious to slow seduction melted her reserves. "What time?"

"Nine a.m."

"You're kidding."

"We'll spend the whole weekend together."

Her thighs clenched with promise. "Doing what?"

He leaned in, nuzzled her ear. "Leave the details to me." And he planted a kiss on her head and returned to his seat, ignoring her as if he didn't just flip her horny switch.

Swirling emotions coursed through her. The truth was, she trusted him with the details. Knew he'd plan a wonderful date and she'd have a great time and want him in her bed by noon.

Problematic.

Hot, rich, and problematic.

One deep breath later, she asked, "You go to college?"

"Yeah. U Tech."

"Utah?"

He shrugged. "I wanted to be a computer analyst."

"What stopped you?"

He smiled. "Ralphie. My aunt gave him to me on my eighteenth birthday. Within one semester, I had three stud fees from him and four more lined up. I had to skip a few days of school here and there to breed him, and within a year my GPA went from three point eight to two point four and my savings account went from one hundred fifty-seven dollars to over seventeen thousand." He shrugged. "My passion chose my career for me."

Raylie harrumphed. "I find that hard to believe."

His mouth opened as he stared at her. "It's the truth."

She grinned. "A three point eight? You're not *that* smart."

He laughed, and the sound of his joy warmed her to her core. She liked that she could make him laugh. "Sorry to disappoint.

If it's any consolation, I took online classes a few years ago and graduated with a three point zero. Is that better?"

"Tolerable." She realized Ashton was the holy trinity of guys: hot, rich, smart, and caring to boot. Damn, there had to be a catch.

He reached over and squeezed her knee—a gentle, playful gesture. Another fissure cracked the glacier in her chest. She acknowledged him with, "You really love your horses, don't you."

He claimed her hand. "As a horny teenager, I just liked watching them breed."

When she eyed him, he merely grinned. "Learn anything?"

"Yeah. Don't get kicked."

She laughed, then grinned back at him, but she saw his eyes look deep into the past, so she waited.

"Ralphie was a fantastic stud, and I don't mean in the money-producing way that most breeders mean. He was a gentleman, you know?"

He looked at her for a second, then faced forward again. "The first time I went to breed him, it was to an experienced mare. He got all ramped up and tried to jump on her, and she tore right into him. He immediately had to come up with a new plan of attack. We were about to separate them and put the mare behind a teaser wall, where the stallion can rouse her and not get kicked?"

"I know what they are, yes." Raylie nodded for him to go on.

He nodded in reply. "But Ralphie had other plans. He immediately went up to her face and nuzzled her neck, settled her down, started nipping and grooming her. He worked all down one side of her, to her tail, and the mare stood perfectly still for him, tail flagged and everything. But he wasn't done. He ducked around to her off side and began nuzzling her some more. By the time he was done attending to her, she was more than willing to breed."

A small smile crooked one corner of Ashton's mouth. "I thought I would put his message into use. I went into bars and tried picking up women. I had this one move, where I would place my hand on a woman's shoulder, near her neck, and whisper if she'd like a drink. Or, if she already had one, I'd think of another reason to move in, maybe compliment her perfume, or the scent of her skin. It was a brash move, you see, a little aggressive, a little possessive, and the ladies all fell for it. It was a game to me to win their time.

"But after I started making money, the tables turned. The girls would start buying *me* drinks, trying to get me to take them home. I stopped going to bars about that time."

She scoffed at his tale. "Well, I'm certainly glad that your stallion helped you get laid." Even to her own ears, she sounded bitter, damn it, and jealous.

He chuckled again, and took a deep breath as he stretched out in his seat. "I did some soul-searching about Ralphie's motives about that time. I tried to get into his head, to see why he acted the way he did. Eventually it dawned on me: he knew his job was to make them happy, or at least complacent. He wooed them. He worshipped them. He took great care with his woman." His voice dropped. "He turned a geeky teenager with little experience in the dating world from the arrogant, cocky rogue into to the respectful man you see before you today."

She felt her face heat up with the memory, and felt compelled to softly say, "His student was an apt pupil."

Tears glimmered in Ashton's eyes, and she thought she heard him sniffle a bit. He raised her hand to his lips and pressed a hard kiss to her palm for what seemed an eternity. When the kiss ended, she no longer saw the telltale shine lingering in his orbs, just a calming presence in the aftermath of an emotional memory.

Still, she couldn't just let go of that story. "Playboy millionaire" were the only words that seemed to bounce around Raylie's head right now, and she had to admit she didn't like the sound or flavor of them. "You didn't do that move on me."

"You're no game to me, Raylie." Ashton's fingers had been tracing little lines on her hand while he spoke, his gentleness mimicking the words he spoke. "Ever since you walked through my gate, you have been the most important person in my life." He grinned and squeezed her hand. "And it's only gotten better every day."

A different sensation coursed through her belly at those words, words she had never heard another man utter to her in her life. It didn't feel like butterflies, or crickets, or serpents slipping away. It felt…

Fulfilling.

Like an empty tank taking on fuel.

Ashton was filling her up.

Humpty's shell no longer had cracks, and the heavy feeling of being cared for warmed her up, gave her nourishment. She felt the gooey albumin of Humpty's innards give her substance she hadn't felt in a long time.

She realized some of it was leaking into her panties.

She had to say something to distract her from her growing response to his words. "So, what great deed did you do to earn a prize like Ralphie?"

His humor faded. "My…aunt…came into money. She…didn't want her husband or stepson to come after it, so…she invested it for me."

"They know about it?"

He licked his lips. "No, but…she was…worried her name might…appear in the paper or something… and they would want their share."

Something struck Raylie as falsehood. "Poor memory, Ashton?"

He sat stiff in his seat. "No. Why?"

"Your speech. It's—" she made chopping motions, "—halting."

For a moment, he remained quiet. Then Ashton said, "Angie was to you what Aunt Karen was to me. She did everything for me."

His voice dropped. "Too much, even. It saddens me sometimes."

Mentally, Raylie replayed the conversation. "How did your aunt come into money?"

She swore he blanched. "I don't…I… Raylie, I don't want to talk about this." He wiped off his lip, took off his hat and leaned back in his seat.

She knew right then he tried to cover a lie. Not well, but he tried. At least now she knew where to start.

Her CB radio beeped. She lifted the hand piece. "Yeah?"

"ETA?" Leann asked.

"Oh. I don't know; maybe fifteen minutes?"

"We have another round-up. Johanssen's been hiding cats in a vacant house two streets over. It's bad." The last word dragged out.

On a moan, Raylie said, "Great."

"How's the dog?"

Not that Leann could see, but Raylie shrugged. "Stable, I guess. Time will tell."

"My former trainer with you?"

A frown crossed Ashton's face. He took the unit from her and asked, "Leann? Is that you?"

With a Southern purr, Leann said, "Hi, you handsome hunk of man."

"I thought I recognized that voice." His smile lit up the whole vehicle. "You still sound like sweet maple syrup."

Leann laughed. "Raylie treating you well?"

Running interference, Raylie snatched the hand piece away from him. "What are you up to, Leann?"

"I just wanted to tell Ashton not to take no from you because you're too dad-beamed stubborn to know a—"

"Leann." Her tone felt deceptively mild. "Aren't you late for a manicure or something?"

"Hang on." Leann switched back to business. She clicked off, and Raylie experienced a breath of relief. "Knew that would get her."

But she buzzed back in. "Raylie, you better hurry."

"Now what?"

She heard Leann exhale, felt the pause preceding doom. "Some kid from Starstruck just called, crying. Something about a mass poisoning."

Chapter 34

If it hadn't been so danged dangerous, Ashton would've yanked Raylie from her seat and floored it. Also, he knew the top-heavy vehicle wouldn't survive his lead foot.

Raylie wasted no time. Apparently well-versed in calculated recklessness, she swerved in and out of traffic, yanked the emergency brake to round a corner, and gunned it again toward his farm.

Once inside the gate, his guard waved them over. Raylie rolled down the window, and Ashton barked out, "What happened?"

"Storage barn, sir. Most of the guards are there."

He didn't like that at all. "If everyone's there, who's guarding my horses?" The man paled, and Ashton swore. "What happened to the storage barn?"

Still pasty, the guard stepped back. "You better see for yourself, sir." And he pointed, as if Ashton didn't know the location of his own barn.

Raylie must have sensed his disgust, because she punched it on the dirt road, peppering the guard with gravel. By pointing the way, Ashton guided her there.

Too many guards loitered. Ashton brushed his way through them toward the door. Steeling his voice, he asked, "Anything dead in there?"

"No, sir."

A small measure of relief unwound the coil inside him. He pulled open the wide door, but going from the bright sun to the windowless barn ruined his vision. After a moment, he noticed the flowers draped over all of his hay bales.

Raylie drew near and sniffed one. "Pretty sure this is oleander."

"Shit. That's what Doc said the lab tests showed." Hundreds of them adorned the wall of hay. "Ruined, all of it." He kicked the dirt floor. "Hay's not that expensive, but what a waste of time. Now all the horses are going to be on one-hour rotations for grazing. That's a pain." He looked back at the guards. "Anyone call the cops?"

Few men moved. A couple shook their heads. "No, sir."

Raylie groaned.

"This is a crime scene. Call them. Have them cordon off the area. And get back to guarding my goddamned horses."

Most of the men vanished like dried leaves in a dervish. All but two. Good.

Raylie looked around. "We know who called?"

One of the lingering guards nodded. "She's in the kitchen."

With a nod, Raylie indicated the house. "This is the part I'm good at."

"Interrogating?"

"Sympathizing. Perps share a lot more when you show them you care."

On impulse, he grabbed her hand. "I'm glad you're here, Raylie."

Softness edged her features when she looked at him. "Me, too," she whispered, but then loudly said, "Your operation needs constant supervision."

He grinned, pulled a few bales off the stack. "Look at this. The oleander is actually nestled in between the bales. Someone spent some time in here yesterday." He pulled down a few more, finding an increasing amount of oleander.

"Don't touch it, Ash. It's really toxic."

"Yeah," he groaned, then plucked a pair of work gloves off a hook. Motion in his periphery made him turn around. He was positive someone was hiding. "Who's there? Come out."

Nothing moved, but he noticed Raylie unclip her gun, hand

hovering ready. But the movement he had seen had ducked behind the hay bales, and he would not see Raylie harm herself, armed or not. Not for him.

He waved her closer, in the guise of showing her where he saw something, but once she neared him he eased her to his back.

There. Someone short. A sliver of face peeked out. Vagabond? "I see you. Come out."

Nothing happened. Raylie's gun appeared at his bicep, held steady by a trained hand. Still, she was a woman, in his home, and he would protect her, not the other way around.

Something flashed, and he heard a crack the same time a burning pain ripped through his arm. Another crack—Raylie's gun—as it discharged beside him.

Gunfire.

They were caught in gunfire.

He shoved Raylie behind the bales he just moved and went charging after the person who dared defile his home.

A scream—a woman's scream—as he neared her point of assault. She ran, and he grabbed a handful of cloak as she raced for the back door. Somehow she shed that layer and squeezed through, slamming the door on his arm when he tried to follow.

A string of curses tumbled from his lips as an irate Raylie jogged up. "Done martyring yourself?" She peeked cautiously around the door, and then motioned for him to follow.

"I'm no martyr," he groaned as he covered the wound on his arm.

Wryly, she said, "Dead heroes are either saints or martyrs." Lazy eyes perused him up and down. "And you sure ain't no saint."

He pointed. "House is close. She must've gone inside."

"Woman?"

"Yeah. Short. With long black hair."

Together they crossed the lawn, seeing no signs of people except for a nearby guard running up, gun aloft and ready.

He pointed to the side door. "Cover the exits."

The guard spoke into a walkie-talkie on his shoulder and eased off around the corner.

He whipped open his own door with a bang, and a servant dressed in black with her hair in the appropriate bun tossed her arms in the air, the broom and dustpan clattering to the flagstones.

"Oh, *señor*! You have scared me *muy mucho*." Panting, she placed her hand to her chest and stooped to clean up her mess.

"Anyone come in here?"

"*Si, señor*." Her arm pointed all the way down the hall to the stairwell at the far end. "There."

Lips pursed, he grabbed Raylie's hand and led her deeper into his house. When he reached the staircase, he stopped. "Was she dressed all in black?"

"She?" Raylie studied him. "The servant? Yes. Why?"

"Damn it." He raced back, but she was gone, with only a wide open door to denote her passing. "That was her."

"The shooter?"

"Yeah. Not in uniform." He kicked the floor. Checking outside, he heard the spin of tires on dirt, and looked up to see a nondescript gray sedan with no license plates careening for the gate.

"Call the guard. Block the gate," Raylie ordered.

"Can't. Intercom's at the other end." So they raced over the rolling lawn, arms waving, and Raylie stopped short and riddled three rounds into the bumper.

The car fishtailed onto the driveway, bolted for the gate, and the gatehouse guard waved her off.

When the engine revved and the car showed no signs of slowing, the man withdrew his gun and aimed for the windshield.

Four rounds went off, and still the car sped on. He ducked out of the way as the sedan plowed through the gate, the doors slamming wildly on their damaged hinges.

Two cars swerved off the road as the gray blur swung onto the blacktop, grabbed hold and raced out of sight.

Raylie slowed to a stop at the gate, barely winded, although Ashton found his breath a little short. He'd have to start jogging again soon. A two-year lag already showed its toll.

A strange smile crossed her face when she turned to him. "The Mustang could catch up."

Rubbing his neck brought him no relief. Stress erupted inside him until he thought—like a volcano—he would explode. "Forget it. We'll let the cops take care of it. I don't want to get into a shootout in Chastity." He closed his eyes, trying to dig his fingers into the cord under his skin, when Raylie's hand began massaging the other side of his neck.

"Are you okay?"

"I'm fine."

Her voice dropped. "You're bleeding."

Those gentle fingers traced from his neck to his arm, and pain suddenly flared in all its throbbing glory.

"Wow. I never noticed."

"Adrenalin's a pain killer. You would've noticed it soon enough."

"Bullet wound?"

"Graze, yeah." She clasped his other hand and said, "I have some gauze and stuff in the van. I'm no doctor, but I can clean and wrap it until you can get into your doctor."

He needed no wrapping. Really. It was just a scratch. But the bullet grazed him across his shoulder, and the blood had drenched his sleeve. He'd have to take his shirt off to feel those gentle hands administering to his ails.

Hmm. He smiled. "Then, take me to your healer."

Chapter 35

He looked even better shirtless than her memory could recall. A thin rivulet of blood oozed down his biceps, and Raylie managed to pour chlorhexidine on a white gauze pad and apply it without him noticing her shaky hands. Some triple antibiotic cream, a Telfa pad, and plain brown rolled gauze completed the wrap on her patient who sat and leaned so casually, framed in the open back doorway of her van.

Any lightheadedness she felt must have been from holding her breath as she ran that brown roll over his arm and shoulder and across his muscular chest. Why she had held her breath, though, she couldn't say.

Her fingers burned from brushing against his hot skin.

"You okay?"

She coughed out a laugh. "I should be asking you that."

Warm fingers from his uninjured limb trailed up her forearm. When their eyes met, Ashton wrapped his fingers around her arm and tugged her close.

Stupidly helpless, she watched, almost mesmerized, as her lips came down to his. They were full and soft and dry and pressed against hers in a sweet, gentle kiss. A sense of disappointment filled her, because she knew him to be passion-filled, but when their lips parted, he said, "Next time I'll let you tie me up with this stuff."

Heat suffused her cheeks, and his thumb brushed across her bottom lip. "Thank you," he whispered.

She grinned. "I *should* tie you up. You're worse than a junkyard dog. You could've gotten killed."

He stood and cradled the nape of her neck. "So could have you. And I wasn't about to let that happen."

Another fissure cracked inside, and she felt the glacial waters spraying through. "Why me, Ashton? Why risk your life for me?"

Pain edged his eyes when he tried to move his injured arm, so he drew her close and stroked her cheek and neck. "Because you're the one worth dying for."

"You could have." She felt really guilty about that.

He smiled. Almost. "In duty to my heart."

Duty. She straightened, cleared her throat. "Speaking of…we need to interrogate the caller."

"Great," he moaned, and she followed his gaze up the driveway.

"Great," she snorted as the black-and-white rounded the bend. "Bet it's Chuck."

Ashton's fingers looped with hers. "It is."

"You detain him while I go chat with our caller." But when she walked away, Ashton drew her in, dipping her backward with his kiss.

Yeah, this was what she knew his lips could do. As she felt every bone liquefy and every nerve tingle with electricity, Ashton stood her up and let go.

"There," he whispered. "That'll give Chuck a good ten minutes worth of questions to ask me."

Her legs didn't want to work. "Wow. Um, okay. Yeah. Thanks."

He pinched her chin and winked. "Go," he whispered.

By forcing herself, Raylie pulled out of his gentle grasp and marched toward the house, doing her best not to turn around and smile.

His kisses, she feared, would be her undoing.

Chapter 36

Hiccupping wails broke the strained silence as Hermosa bounced Noe on her shoulder and paced the kitchen under the watchful eyes of one of her *Mamá's* boss' guards.

Two people entered, a uniformed woman with spiky hair and her *Mamá's* boss, *Señor* Lyre—the one who hired her when her *Mamá's* other boss asked him to.

Subdued excitement seeped from the pair, and Hermosa recognized the scent and look of two people in love. Perhaps Noe did too, for his wail turned to a low gurgle.

They made a handsome couple.

"Hi," the woman said as she pulled out a chair and sat down at the table. "I'm Officer McPherson. I heard you made the phone call about the poisoned hay." She motioned to a chair across from her. "I'm curious why you called, since they were only flowers. Did you have any idea they were toxic?"

The sympathetic expression in the officer's eyes convinced Hermosa to sit down, albeit on the edge of the seat. "I…I do not know this word. Toxic?"

"Deadly. Poison. *Muy peligrosa.*"

"Ah, *sí*," she nodded. "*Señora*, I believe the flowers are bad. My *Mamá* would pick them and say to me, *no tocalo*. Do not touch."

The woman smiled wide at Noe, who stared at something over her head in his little baby way. "Why did your mama pick flowers that were bad when you have such a beautiful baby in the house?"

She kissed her son's thick topknot of hair. "*Gracias, Señora.*" Her lips stayed there as heavy tears filled her eyes. She looked up to *Señor* Lyre, who leaned casually against the door. His near shoulder displayed a torn shirt and a dried pool of blood. Her tears slipped out as nausea grabbed her stomach, fearing his cut to be anything but accidental. Sniffling, she pressed Noe to her shoulder. "*Señor* Lyre, you have been very good to my *Mamá*, but I am afraid she has not been good to you."

He stopped leaning and stood straight. "How? In what way?"

This was bad. Those tears fell down her cheeks as she met his eyes. "*Señor*, my *Mamá* is a good person. She only wants the best for my son. But she is acting loco for months now. She yells a lot. She—" her hand waved, "—paces. Over and over. And yesterday she filled the apartment with flowers. 'For my coffin,' she told me." Hermosa wiped her face. "Today she did not go to work. And a strange man picked her up. When I opened the bathroom cabinet, her things were gone. And her closet and drawers."

The woman with the crazy hair leaned forward. "Do you know what kind of car? Or what color?"

"Gray." She shrugged. "I do not know what kind. But," she frowned, "it had no license plates."

"That's our girl," *Señor* Lyre said.

Officer McPherson leaned over the table. "What made you call? And why did you come here and not call from home?"

"No phone at home. And I wanted to see if she came to work. Then, when I was told she hadn't, I looked around for the flowers. I had a bad feeling," she touched her stomach. "I did not like it."

Now *Señor* Lyre stepped forward. "How did you get in? I mean, past security?"

"Oh," she rolled her eyes. "They were terrible, *Señor*! I had to tell them over and over who I was. I had to s'y my *Mamá J*'s birthday. I had to tell two people. Someone walked me all the way inside. Once inside, Maria remembered me and was very nice to me."

Although his nod seemed to hold satisfaction, his eyes felt harsh. Noe started to fuss, so she tapped him on his back, making his cries come out in a staccato rhythm. "Please, *Señor*, do not hurt my *Mamá*. She is not well. In the head."

Her words only made him point to his arm. "I watched her shoot me." Red colored his cheeks as her fear made gurgles churn her stomach. "No amount of mental sickness entitles a person to—"

The officer's hand rose to him, and his words and color faded. Then the officer faced her, sympathy in her eyes. "The best way to help your mama is to let us take her to a hospital."

"Jail," *Señor* Lyre muttered, but then he shook his head and settled back against the jamb.

Officer McPherson ignored him, so Hermosa followed her lead. "When people suddenly 'go loco,' there is usually a medical reason. I see it all the time, even though I deal with pets and not people."

Hermosa chewed her lip as she tucked Noe under her chin.

"Help us help your mama. Please tell us where she went before she winds up killing someone." The officer reached out a hand. "The police aren't going to be nearly as forgiving."

"Especially Chuck," *Señor* Lyre muttered.

"Who is Chuck?" Hermosa asked, looking back and forth between them, feeling nervous and scared now as she hadn't when they first walked in. Even Noe grew fussy as she waited.

"That guy out there," Officer McPherson said, and Hermosa looked out the window to see a policeman talking to another servant and taking lots of notes.

"We have maybe five minutes," Officer McPherson said. "Can you tell me who she went off with? Where they're going? Or why she's been picking deadly flowers?"

Her heart raced, and she began bouncing Noe so nervously that he began to wail. She had to tell them. *Mamá* would never forgive her, but for all it looked like, *Mamá* was not coming back. She swallowed, then swallowed again. "*Señor*, all this started when my husband died the day he tried to deliver your horse."

Chapter 37

"Wait, wait." Ashton abandoned his spot on the wall and leaned over the table, placing his weight on his good arm. "Let's get one thing straight—he wasn't *delivering* my horse, he was stealing it."

Hermosa's rage made her hair fly around her head like a witch's. "Eshan didn't steal anything. He was a good man."

Smacking the table, he yelled, "He was found dead in my truck with the engine in his lap. If that doesn't—"

"Enough," Raylie yelled, hands flung up in between them. "Even I know the details of the case, so let's not rehash them now, okay?" Color sparked along her cheekbones, making her hair complement her hue even more. She looked ravishing. So he quieted and backed away.

A long moment passed, a moment in which the young mother's piquant mood finally waned.

Raylie took the lead, stepping forward to stroke the baby's hair. "You got married young, didn't you?"

The girl nodded.

"Ah, young love. Did you know him long?"

She shrugged and kissed her baby's cheek. "I loved Eshan from the moment we met."

Ashton frowned when he heard the name. "Eshan? That wasn't his name. It was Diego Lucatelli."

But the girl nodded. "Diego Eshan. He went by Eshan." Then her eyes turned hard and unforgiving, and Ashton braced for the next verbal assault. She did not disappoint. "And he was working for you. He gave me the money you paid him. One thousand dollars. I saw the check. Starstruck Stables." The fire in her eyes defied him, dared him to deny it.

"Impossible. I sign each and every paycheck. I never wrote him a check because I never hired him. And I *never* give any of my staff thousand dollar paychecks."

"You did." The girl moved close, her youth and passion showing a rashness he wasn't used to. "We used some of the money to elope. He rented a tuxedo and I rented a bride costume so my *Mamá* would never know."

"Receipts," Raylie whispered to him.

"I can look up the dollar amount in my checkbook, you know," he told the girl, making his tone as menacing as he would grant any impertinent minor. "If you're lying, we'll know."

Despite holding her son, the chit was all flailing arms and spitting words. "You do that. You'll see my Eshan was a good man. Your stable hired him and he did just what he was told to do. And now he's dead and the money went to bury him." Tears filled her eyes, but her war raged on. "I was with him when we cashed it. Boughton Bank. On Center Road and Cliff Run Way. You check with them. They'll show you I'm telling the truth."

"This is ludicrous. I never hired the kid. Eshan," he corrected when he saw the mutinous look in her eyes. "Going on a wild goose chase for this alleged check is just a waste of time. *I never hired him.*" He pounded the table on each word. "My shifts start at six a.m. and three p.m. Not ten at night."

"You're a liar," the girl screamed as she charged him. But Raylie stopped her by restraining both arms and looking at the baby. That simple glance made the girl crumble into a puddle of tears.

She was so adamant about this. Something felt wrong. He had no employee records, no visa, no pay stubs or W-4 forms or anything on Eshan, only a widow and grieving parents who both claimed he had hired him.

Brittany came to mind, but he abandoned the idea. She wasn't smart enough. Or motivated. Perhaps Mack, but what would he gain? It made no sense.

Still the girl cried, and Raylie squatted beside her, looking up to him, waiting for him to say something.

He cleared his throat, eased around the table. "Look, I…I didn't mean to make you cry." He waited, and he could tell she listened. "Do you have a name?"

"Hermosa. Hermosa Lucatelli, but my *Mamá* thinks I'm still a Santiago."

"Hermosa." He took a deep breath. "Look, I'll go through my check register again, okay? Something here doesn't make sense."

Hermosa and her baby both sobbed, but she looked up and held his eyes. Accusation filled them when she said, "I thought you went through them for the trial."

"I did." He knelt down. "But both you and his parents swear I hired him. I swear to you I didn't. I don't run my stable that way. I don't pay my kids thousand-dollar paychecks. I don't transport at night. And the few times I've shipped horses, either I or my stable master drives them. Not a kid. Okay?"

Wariness in her eyes probably reflected his own. Both, it seemed, had been lied to. But by whom?

One small nod moved her. "You sound like you're telling the truth."

"So do you," he said, gripping his knees to stand, "which is why," he felt his mouth dry as he heaved a breath and uttered the dreaded words; "I'm going to reopen this case."

Chapter 38

It took every bit of effort to drag herself into Marta's office that evening. The plastic carrier rocked to and fro with the kittens' antics from within.

"Ah, you remembered." The smile on Marta's face eased the trouble in Raylie's soul. "How was your day?"

Setting the carrier down, Raylie said, "Well, it started with a half-dead dog and ended with tampered hay at Starstruck."

"Oh my."

"Yeah." As soon as she opened the carrier, four fuzz balls tumbled into the room.

"Aw, aren't they cute?" She tried to catch them as they raced by, their tiny tails standing upright as they stretched their legs.

"They're holy terrors. Every morning at two a.m., *kathunk, kathunk, kathunk.*" Her hands imitated the kittens' bounding, making Marta laugh out loud.

With a groan, Marta eased her way to the floor, her eyes on the kittens. "So, are you ready to begin your advanced desensitization?"

The floor seemed like a good idea. Raylie pulled two toy balls from the carrier and rolled the foam one across the carpet. "Yeah, sure."

"Good. I'd like you to play with your charges for a few minutes and get nice and relaxed. Don't worry if they make a mess. I hate to say I'll leave it for the cleaning lady, but she'll be here in an hour." She grinned.

"Okay. They have a small litter pan in the carrier, anyway." She pulled her Cat Dancer out of a compartment on the carrier and unrolled the long wire. By twitching it, all four kittens began stalking the rolled paper at the end. Soon they tumbled pell-mell after it, making it nearly impossible for the women to control their laughter.

Marta pulled a leather leash from behind the trashcan and handed it to Raylie. "Here, use this."

A clip adorned one end, and two six-inch pieces of leather hung from the other. Tassels, perhaps. Raylie whipped it over their heads and beyond, and two of them pounced. So she tugged it along the carpet to reel them in.

"It's a decorative rein from a bridle," Marta said as the kittens wiggled and stalked the leather.

"Yeah." Thinking it and knowing it really did make a difference. "I know." She stared at it for a moment, and her voice dropped. "I never thought to use old reins as kitty teasers." She forced herself to continue playing. Really, they liked it. Probably something about the thick texture. She grinned, feeling the racing fear settle and then calm in her chest. "This was a good idea, Marta."

"I'm glad. Looks like everyone agrees." She indicated the rein. "You ready to put that back where it belongs?" The steady look in her eyes told Raylie this was another step in her process.

"Um." She licked her lips, took a deep breath. "Yeah."

So Marta opened a drawer and pulled out the bridle, holding it at arm's length.

In for a penny, Raylie thought, and forced herself to accept the bridle. She clipped the rein to the bit and studied the contraption. "You know, Ashton bridles his newborns. Just for a minute. Says it makes for easier training."

"He would know." She shrugged. "How is Mr. Lyre?"

Still holding the bridle, stroking it the way Ashton stroked the foal and desperately trying not to remember Derrick's death, she said, "Fine." A deep breath helped. "He took me to lunch, offered to support the dying dog and brought me to Starstruck to help deliver a foal."

"Wow." A kitten raced by, too fast for Marta to catch. "Does he know about Derrick?"

"Yeah, I told him." Still she fingered the bridle. "He had to weasel it out of me, but he knows." The leather smelled old and worn and perfect, the way all horse tack should. One kitten scrambled over her knee and tumbled onto its sibling before tearing off again. "You know, I'm glad he knows." Her hands clenched the bridle hard. "In fact, outside of you, he's the only one who knows how difficult it's been for me. Maybe Leann has her suspicions." She let go. "I hate being weak, you know? Doesn't look good for a woman with a gun."

"You are human first, officer second." Marta indicated the kittens leaping for the bridle, so Raylie dragged the reins across the carpet, luring two to the chase. After a moment, she gave it back to Marta, who put it away.

"Mr. Skooshi Pants, are you sleeping?" Raylie collected a tired fur ball and cradled him. A contented purr soon trailed across the room as she rocked him to and fro. "Ashton lets me be weak around him, and it's weird, but I feel stronger afterward."

Marta's head shake didn't dull her grin. "Human, Raylie, not weak." A beatific smile crossed her face. "It sounds like he lets you be yourself. Does he support you?"

She thought of the restaurant, her head on his shoulder, the wonderful roadside hug, and smiled. "Yeah, he does."

"A fine trait in a man, is it not?" Overly plucked eyebrows waggled as she spoke.

"Way better than Derrick," she muttered. "But, yeah, it's nice. Really nice." The kitten continued to purr as Raylie cradled him.

Marta cleared her throat. "This may be a little awkward, but I'd just like to share some knowledge I've gleaned over the years. Since you have been, ah, intimate with Mr. Lyre, and you are in close contact with him for your job, I just want you to reflect on how he treats you abed. I've always maintained that men show their true colors when they're devoid of clothing. Is he gentle? Courteous? Does he share? Take time for your needs? Talk to you? Enjoy your happiness? And afterward, does he hold you? Talk to you? See to your comfort?" Leaning back in the chair after her soliloquy, Marta added, "All these are great reflections of a man's character."

Raylie looked down. Ashton had been the most perfect lover imaginable. Derrick…not so much. She swallowed and stroked the soft kitten asleep in her arms. "I spent years with the bump-and-run variety. Chose it, actually. I know a good thing when I see it."

"I'm not spying on your sex life, dearie. I just want to help you analyze your life during this difficult transitional phase." Marta got up and moved to her desk drawer.

"No, I, um, thanks." She looked up and smiled. "Really. I never thought of the truth of a naked man."

"Our egos unearthed." Marta rummaged in the drawer and pulled something out. "Here, brush him with this." She tossed it near.

The horse brush fit in one hand. A face brush, really, with the gentlest bristles, designed for the tender noses of horses. But Mr. Skooshi Pants didn't mind as she stroked the corner over his head and exposed belly.

"He wants me to name the foal, Marta."

"He does? That's quite an honor 'round here." She got up and unfolded a blanket from the seat of her chair and spread it out.

Except, it wasn't a blanket.

It was a saddle pad.

Almost identical in pattern to the one Derrick had used that last day.

Marta couldn't have known it; it was probably just an extra one she borrowed from a friend, probably the most popular saddle pad made. Still, her heart raced as she looked at it, seeing Derrick fall over and over, the blue and navy striped pad echoing the blankets they had tossed over their horses' withers that day.

And ultimately, over Derrick's body.

Oblivious to Raylie's paralyzing response, Marta continued, "Have you thought of any names yet?"

Breathing fast and shallow, feeling sweat bead on her lips and tears leak down her cheeks in the icy-cold air of memory, Raylie merely stared at it. Mesmerized with the blaring stripes, unable to look away or stop the rewinding death, it took a few very long moments to ground herself and respond. She had to keep counting chairs, the colors of the carpet, the pictures in the room. Name the kittens. Twice. Look out into the hot July sun. Remember Ashton holding her hand as he told her she was the most important person in his life.

Marta stood silently by and watched her work through her anguish.

Once her heartbeat slowed, she wiped off her damp lip, used her shoulders to brush off her face. Looking up at Marta, feeling drained and weak and pale, she said, "Yeah. I'm naming him Fearsome Time."

Chapter 39

Icy cold fingers tickled Ashton's spine as he cracked open the newly delivered safe where all of Aunt Karen's incriminating evidence sat and looked within. Poker chips, damning news articles and Ralphie's Bill of Sale, dated three days after she mysteriously disappeared from her job. Name change documents. Fake IDs leading to real ones. And the one that turned his stomach the most, his adoption paperwork, turning him from Ashton Bennett to Ashton *Liar*. All delivered as per Aunt Karen's final wishes, ten years after her death.

Some days he could still see his parents, laughing as if they were standing just before him, ready to fly to a destination they would never reach. Aunt Karen's wrongdoing would not be something his parents would ever have suspected. In fact, she had been as much a mother to him as his own mom, even when she was still alive.

But not today.

He closed the heavy black door and spun the dial.

Definitely not today.

He picked up the phone and called his bank. "Yeah, this is Ashton Lyre. I'd like copies of every check written out for one thousand dollars in the past year. Front and back, yes." He waited, then gave out his account number and personal information. When told he'd have copies in ten days, he said, "How much to have them by tomorrow?" He listened, nodded, said, "Well, charge it to my account, then, yes. Can you fax me the copies? Oh, email is fine. Yes. Thank you." Satisfied, he hung up. Perhaps this would be a good starting point.

*

The email actually came later that day, proof that money and influence really could move someone up the BS list. He counted seventeen checks, most written to cash. He printed them out, separated the bills, and laid them out along the desk. Two were from December, after Eshan's death. He moved those out. January through April seemed okay. That left seven. He studied them as an archaeologist might a bone fragment, looking for clues, smears, changes, anything.

After an hour of scrutiny, he noticed one discrepancy. A check, made to cash, but spelled *CAsh*. A glance at the back of it showed Mack had cashed it. Not too unusual, since Ashton would periodically write his former step-brother checks to pay for stable expenses, and Mack had the liberty of placing deposits of one thousand dollars down on good horseflesh until Ashton could see the prospect for himself.

The memo said "deposit on colt," and sure enough, the log book showed a receipt for the same amount to a horse farm in Texas. One he never got to see, because of the court summons on the accident, but completely legit. He felt confident a voided check or deposit for the money would be easily found in his check register, since the colt had not been purchased.

Still...

He called the bank again. "Hi. I'd like to know where this one check was cashed. You can tell from the stamp on back, right?" He gave them his account information and the validation imprint number.

Center Road Branch. At Cliff Run Way.

Shit.

He'd have to try to get hold of that young mom again—what was her name? Hermosa. Daughter of Vicenta Santiago. Housecleaning First Floor, morning shift. No-show two days in a row now.

The phone rang, jarring him from his slow boil. "Yeah?"

"Ashton?" It was Raylie.

He grinned. "Hey, hi. What's up?"

She sighed. "Ashton, we have to talk."

Chapter 40

Raylie cradled the phone, feeling tears squeeze out. The papers in her hand blurred as she stared at them.

Ashton careened around the corner in the white convertible she still loved. The evening humane society parking lot remained empty except for a few stragglers still finalizing their adoptions before leaving with their new charges. But her hallway, back in the office area, remained dark as death, the only beacon of light her office, where just perchance Ashton could help.

She pushed the bar to open the security door for him, and after taking one look at her, he gathered her close. Stroking her hair, he rocked her and kissed her crown for a full minute before asking what happened.

His arms strengthened her. Somehow she managed, "It's the Golden, Ashton. She took a turn for the worse."

He led her to her office, waited while she sat at her desk, then he pulled up a chair. "What happened?"

The tears wouldn't stop. "She started wheezing, so they heartworm-tested her. She's positive." She pounded her desk.

The frown on his face told her he'd never heard of it, so she expounded. "Parasites that infect the heart. Untreated, it's fatal."

At that, he shrugged. "So we'll treat her."

He didn't know, and that alone tore her apart. If she had only checked on this asshole owner, none of this would have happened. Damn it, damn it, *damn it.* "The treatment is as bad as the disease. She needs constant crating, Ashton. We're talking twenty-four/ seven for two months. With three leashed potty breaks a day. While the medicine kills the heartworms, pieces float free and lodge in the bloodstream, where they can cause an embolism." Guilt made her head lower. "Any exercise and the dog can die."

With a frown, Ashton asked, "Embolism?"

"A lodged clot."

He continued to frown, so Raylie let him formulate his words. "She's crated now, in the hospital, right?"

"Yeah, but her case is going to end in two weeks. The shelter won't pay for treatment, because it's too expensive."

"How much?"

"Seven hundred."

He shrugged. "I'll pay it."

"We don't adopt out heartworm-positive dogs." She punched air. "And unless someone is willing to pay for treatment and foster them, they don't stand a chance." *Damn it.* She gripped her hair and leaned on her elbows. "This is all my fault." And since she had the kittens for four more weeks, she couldn't take the Golden. Tears slipped down her cheeks. "I don't want her to die, Ashton. I can't lose her. Not after all this."

"You can't take her?"

She shook her head. "Shelter policy limits fostering to one case at a time."

His knee pumped up and down and he was silent for a moment. "You know, since I'm rebuilding the burned-out section of the barn, I had the contractor divide a stall into two small ones, as an ICU for foals, complete with climate control. You know, heat lamps and A/C. If it'll hold a newborn foal, it'll hold her. I could keep her while you treat her."

Sweet joyous words, but it wouldn't work. She slumped back in her chair. "You're a suspect, Ashton. My boss would never go for it."

To that, he leaned back. "You still think I'm a suspect?" He jabbed a finger at his wrapped shoulder. "Even after this?"

He had a point. "No. No, I don't. We have a suspect now, but no motive."

He leaned forward and his gentle fingers wiped away her tears. God bless him, he leaned closer and brushed his lips to hers.

"Between your official report and Doc's character witness, we shouldn't have any problems." He smiled encouragingly at her. "But if we do, I'll have Ed sign up for fostering her."

Deflated, she looked up and shook her head. "He works for you."

But Ashton only grinned. "Technically, he is employed by Photo Finish Industries, an affiliate." He pulled her to her feet and held her close. "I know how much she means to you, honey, and I'll do everything I can to maintain her safety. Okay?"

A whole new world seemed to be blossoming open before her. She leaned back in his arms to look up at him, feeling awed and humbled and tremendously honored with his thoughtfulness. "Yeah. For the first time, I think things really are going to be okay."

Chapter 41

She spun. And spun. And spun. Waited for the phone in her hand to ring. The unknown driver had taken her to the state line of Oklahoma, where he left her at a BP gas station for further directions.

She hadn't wanted to shoot *Señor* Lyre. As Vicenta widened her path to a pace, she found her hands clenching her phone over and over.

It was no use calling him again. Mack only returned calls when it suited him. No matter that she shot a man and fled the state. No matter she had only the clothes on her back, that she walked foot patrol seven hundred miles from home, waiting for her employer to get here before the incoming storm claimed the land.

No, none of that mattered.

Only Mack.

Mack and his stupid revenge.

An empty water bottle needed a good kicking, so Vicenta complied. Next she leaned back hard against the wall between the boarded-up restrooms. She glanced at her phone. Two hours. Two hours she waited for him.

Clouds moved in swift over the vast landscape, darkening the sky to an ill green. Lightning flashed, and an evil wind raced across the asphalt, sending garbage rolling down the street.

Shaking her fist at the sky, she yelled out, "Damn you, *Señor* Mack!"

But the boom of thunder dulled her voice.

When she moved to the door to escape the giant pelting drops of rain, the station attendant shook his head. He pointed to the NO LOITERING sign and crossed his arms.

"To the devil with you," she spat as she pressed herself under the meager overhang. But no amount of leaning would protect her from this sudden downpour.

A car pulled up. The back door opened. Through the curtain of rain, she saw Mack's and Brittany's faces. "Get in."

Even sprinting into the warm interior did not prevent her from getting soaked. Giant water droplets stained the seat, and more dripped down the car door onto the handle. "*Gracias, Señor, Señora.* I was about to get very wet."

Only Mack's eyes flicked to hers in the rearview. "You weren't supposed to come here. If anything went wrong, you were supposed to go back home."

Wiping off her drenched hair, Vicenta said, "But my grandson is American. I cannot go back when he belongs here."

Dark silence settled over the car, a stark contrast to the torrent battering them from without.

Needing to fill the void, she said, "I shot him for you, *Señor*. With the gun you gave me." Fiddling with her cell could not erase the feeling of the gun's recoil in her hands.

A brief glimpse of panic lit his eyes as he looked back at her. "You did?"

"*Sí, Señor.* In the arm."

He looked at Brittany, who only looked back. Angry, he said, "That was my only gun. Where is it now?"

"In the garbage, *Señor*. I got scared. I wrapped it in paper and threw it away."

The car took a sudden swing left over a curb and onto a bumpy gravel road. Lights disappeared on both sides, to be replaced with what looked like a cornfield. Then he slammed the car to a halt.

"Blew a tire," he mumbled as he popped the trunk and got out.

Brittany made no move.

The oppressive silence made Vicenta roll her cell over and over in her hands. "You look very pretty today, *Señora.*"

Only a twitch of her lips told Vicenta that she heard.

The trunk slammed shut. Her door opened, and Mack tugged her out into the onslaught, the sudden jerking making her phone slip from her wet hands.

"Your services are no longer required."

And in the next flash of lightning, Vicenta saw the crowbar in his hands.

Chapter 42

An easy day, for a change. Raylie actually had time to catch up on filing and clean her desk—a daunting chore. But when she finished, it was almost lunchtime.

She paused, stared at the clock. Picked up the phone and dialed Lexington Critical Care. A few questions later and she determined the Golden should be settled into her new foster home at Starstruck.

Wouldn't hurt to make sure she was okay.

Leann grabbed her purse, and Raylie took out her Bronco keys. "Going out for lunch. Call me if you need me."

To which Leann called over her shoulder, "You're the one with needs, darlin'."

No retort came to her, but Raylie grinned and headed toward Ashton's, noting how the drive seemed shorter every day.

The guards no longer asked for her ID. She drove up the driveway toward his mansion, but faltered at the fork. Turning right, she headed for the barn.

It seemed weird being here without Ashton, but not lonely. Stable hands came and went, horses followed obediently on their white cotton ropes, dogs bounded after each other. All in all, a normal productive working stable.

With lots of horses.

Her foal had to be here somewhere, along with the Golden. So, squaring her shoulders, Raylie forced a march into the long aisles, looking for Mystic Thyme.

And her rescue dog, of course.

A glass office door dominated the left corner, immaculately clean inside. She smiled and kept going. Soon she found the mare and foal, nearing the section that had burned. The sign on the door read, "Mystic Thyme, Foal TBD."

Missy stepped near and blew out on Raylie's offered hand; a friendly equine greeting. "Sorry, girl. No treats here." Warmth filled her as she realized how far she had come already. Facing a horse, letting it sniff her, with no fear. Almost as if Derrick had never died.

"Want to see him?"

Raylie turned to watch Ashton saunter near, and the smile she sent him made him falter, which only made her laugh. Feeling brave now, willing to push herself to heal, she asked, "Will Missy let me?"

"She'll let me." He eased past, opened the stall door and slipped a lead rope off his shoulders and around the colt's neck. With little ado, the baby stepped into the aisle.

"He's just so darned cute," Raylie said, taking in an eyeful. A big head topped a thin neck and stick legs. All his dark brown fur now fell into place, and his bottlebrush tail flicked back and forth.

"Go ahead, Raylie. Pet him."

Remembering those strong little hooves in her hands fortified her, and those brown eyes beckoned her. "Come here, boy." When he didn't move, she stretched out her fingers to stroke him. "Wow, he's soft." After a minute, she stepped closer and buried her fingers into his wool-like mane. Soon both her hands roamed all over him.

Missy nosed her shoulder, and after bracing, Raylie reached up a tentative hand to the mare and stroked her nose. A long equine sigh tossed the hairs on her arm, and Missy's near eye held hers.

It's like she knows I can ride bareback, Raylie thought, and found herself mesmerized by the soft chocolate gaze. If horses could read a person's soul, Missy was a librarian.

"He needs a name, Raylie."

She looked up, smiling. "Fear—"

"*Señor, Señor* Lyre, I need you."

"Hermosa. I have some questions for you, too."

But she waved him off. "*Señor*, I called my *Mamá* from your phone. I'm sorry, I don't have my own phone to use. But a man answered."

Significance lost, they both shrugged and waited.

"'H' found my *Mamá's* cell phone in his cornfield. In Oklahoma."

Chapter 43

It couldn't be. Not Oklahoma. Ashton fiddled with the push latch on the stall door as he listened to Hermosa talk in half-Spanish, half-English.

Finally Raylie touched his elbow. "Ashton?"

He shook his head, slid the bolt in and out of the bracket. "It can't be."

Her voice dropped; she stepped closer. "Can't be what?"

"Brittany. Mack and Brittany."

"Your ex-girlfriend and stable master?"

In, out, up down. In, out, up, down. "Yeah."

"The one who got the Lexus?"

"Yeah."

She studied him for a moment, but he couldn't meet her eyes. "What aren't you telling me?"

The bolt slid home. "He's my step-brother."

Her arms flew in the air. "How could you not tell me that? That makes all the difference in the world, Ashton. Call the police, we've got our perp and motive now." To Hermosa, she said, "Your mom had another boss, right?"

She fidgeted. "*Sí.*" She looked down and shrank.

"Was it Mack?"

"Jesus." Ashton yanked his fingers through his hair. "He asked me to hire her last fall."

"A week after Eshan died," Hermosa whispered.

Raylie continued barking orders to him. "And tell them to contact Oklahoma PD ASAP."

"But what's the motive?" he asked, frustrated he couldn't see what was so clear to Raylie.

"When it's family, Ashton, it all boils down to one thing—money."

Chapter 44

"Shit. Shit, shit, shit, shit, shit." Mack slammed his ball cap to the floor of his motel room and ignored Brittany sprawled out on the bed.

"Come on, Mack. You don't think—"

"I *do* think." He whirled on her. "I thought this whole thing through. No records of the hired foreign kid. False deposit slip on the horse. Cash only transactions. Take the horse at night after you broke up with him, when I knew he'd be as mopey as a winter bear." He paced by the TV and turned off Oprah. "But the damn kid had to go crash and die."

Brittany rolled off the bed and unbuttoned her blouse, paying him no attention as she said, "The kid wasn't nearly as much trouble as the woman. I told you she was screwy, Mack. Didn't I tell you she was screwy? She was one crazy Mexican."

"Chilean," he corrected, then frowned. "If Ashton finds that gun…"

"Stupid bitch. She almost ruined everything." A wicked grin followed that comment.

Mack turned away, feeling a knot shove into his stomach. "Ain't never killed no one before."

"Come off it, Mack." His admission made her clomp near in her high heels and bouncing bra. "We talked about this. Planned it out. It was her or us. You got it? Her or us." She jabbed him in the chest. "Two million dollars worth of us, free and clear."

"Not if anyone finds the gun."

"Coyotes should take care of the body."

Images of Vicenta's broken face assailed him just then. No such thing as free and clear, even for two million dollars. A Swiss bank account was set up and waiting. All he had to do was deliver a horse to his cousin in Texas. Not just any horse—High Eminence. A colt whose looks and lineage replicated Jubilation's so closely that they could pass for twins. Born only days apart, with four white hairs over their left eyes and two white ones on the left fetlocks. Their dams were sisters, one year apart.

Only problem was, Jubilation died in his field under a toppled tree, and when Frank called with the bad news, a plan had formed. *Tell no one,* Mack said. *Give me twenty-four hours and I'll make all our dreams come true.*

Ashton had lived a charmed life. Too charmed. Once his stepmother Karen left, all hell broke loose. Of course, Ashton never got to experience the beatings, the drunken fights, the impossible side of the man Mack called "father." No, Ashton and Aunt Karen disappeared after fifth grade, and suddenly this skinny little punk owned the largest horse-racing farm in Kentucky.

Yeah, he had changed his name, but for all Mack knew, he went back to his birth name. Until he found him in high school.

Frank never would have invested in racing if Mack hadn't steered him that way. Even a successful dumpster operation wouldn't keep the Feds from sniffing out Frank's drug deals. But a nice, respectable racehorse? Hell, he could retire and live on stud fees. So Frank had agreed, and Mack had tasted the flavor of his own death if he didn't come up with a replacement.

Soon.

Like, last November.

Time raced from him. Frank had run out of excuses as to why he couldn't show, stud or race Jubilation. He needed High Eminence. Now. So in order to distract and confuse Ashton and the staff, Mack had instructed Vicenta to poison some apples for the horses until he could orchestrate High Eminence's fake death.

He had the anesthetics. He had the flat bed. He had even procured a blank receipt from a burial service to claim proper disposition of the body.

But the only horse vet in the area was Doc Schneible.

Ashton's goddamned character witness at the trial.

His cell rang, and he grumbled as he flipped it open. "Hey, Frank." Wiped a hand down his face. "Yeah. No, Galveston. I know. I *know*." Frustration dogged his every move these days. "The goddamned horse won't trailer, coz. Ever since the accident, he won't load. I've canceled two halter shows, three jogs and an auction so far this year because of it." He paused. "No, no, I'm not auctioning him off. I just wanted to get him seen, get his name out there, and thought being trailered with other horses might help him load."

Frank's voice rose, so Mack said, "I won't." But when his cousin's anger spilled over, Mack yelled, "Look, I'll do my job when you get a new vet in here. Schneible won't be bought off. They're pals, okay? Get a young schmuck who can be bought off and we'll be back in business."

Frank still ranted, but Mack clicked off the phone. To Brittany, he said, "Pack your bags. Get dressed. We're leaving."

Frowning, Brittany reached for the blouse she just hung. "But we just got here. Where we going?"

Sending her a look cold enough to freeze marble, he said, "Back to Louisville. I need to get me a horse."

Chapter 45

Raylie's assumption about Mack really irked. Really, with all he had taken from Ashton, and all Ashton had done to maintain his comfort while employed here, why would Mack turn so toxic?

Aunt Karen had been kind to the boy, but Mack's father—Uncle Bruce—didn't want her "breaking his balls" over his unrestrained actions—his "boys will be boys" bullying behavior.

So Aunt Karen had protected Ashton from his step-brother/cousin as much as she could, until the bruises and locked-in-closets episodes turned into a weekly event. It wasn't until high school they crossed paths again, by which time Ashton had sprouted a foot and had lots of friends—too many for Mack to mess with.

Even though Ashton had been a scrawny little computer geek.

Computer.

While Raylie sat in front of the Golden's door, waiting for the police to show up, Ashton marched into his office, a new clue surfacing. On the top shelf of his closet, covered in straw dust, sat the laptop that Mack always used.

Hmmm.

He unpacked it and booted it up, then searched for his keystroke monitoring program and loaded that. It took a few minutes to narrow the search, but he decided September through December, up to and after Eshan's death.

"Oh, man." The screen looked like alphabet soup vomited all over it. A head shake and resigned sigh helped Ashton focus. Luckily, Mack hadn't used the computer to surf, only to correspond, so it didn't take Ashton long to determine that Mack had been up to no good.

"You rat bastard," he whispered, then read, "*I got your application and I think you'll be perfect for the job. Where in Italy are you coming from?*" The typing left much to be desired, with as many typos as correct letters, but the damning evidence remained.

Raylie's head poked in the room. "Whacha doing?"

"Come here." When she stepped near, he drew her into his lap and read the decoded verse.

"What is this, some terrorist spy program?"

"Keystroke logger. Installed on all my computers."

Eyeing him, she said, "Paranoid, Ashton?"

He grinned and crunched her to his side. "I protect what's mine." He highlighted and printed the whole screen. "Can we get subpoenas on his emails?"

"Sure. Just ask my good friend Chuck. He's in the barn with Hermosa."

"Great," he moaned. Nuzzling her ear, he whispered, "How's Brandy doing?"

"She's fine. Bored, I guess, I bought her a bo—wait. You named her Brandy?"

"For you." He hugged her tight. "I never want you to lose another animal from loss of finance. She's here, she's safe, and she's going to live a good long life."

After a moment of silence, he noticed her hands clenching convulsively on her lap.

"Honey?"

She turned to face him, her eyes bright with unshed tears. "That's the nicest thing anyone's ever said to me." And when she threw herself into his arms, he knew the truth of her words, the depth of her sorrows. She kissed him ravenously, with a recklessness he never dreamed to behold.

Somehow, by sheer luck, he hoped, prayed—*believed*—he had managed to make Raylie fall madly in love with him.

Chapter 46

Friday. Tonight would lead to his big date tomorrow morning with Raylie, and he hadn't even told her a word about it: helicopter ride to a seaplane headed for the Ozark Mountains, where an untouched pond—complete with lush island—would hold their tent for two days.

The one damning check copy sat before him, as did Mack's favorite laptop. No clues remained regarding the strange spelling of *CAsh*, but his best guess was Brittany. The capital A seemed to have her telltale curl, so perhaps she had started to write the check to Ashton and decided to change it to *CAsh*.

Damn. He always suspected he couldn't trust her.

This would certainly clinch it.

He looked at his watch. Raylie should be here shortly, and with any luck they would dine on the veranda and watch the sun set. He felt himself harden. After her reckless kiss yesterday, he truly hoped their intimacy could resume.

The missing servant's cell phone number still sat on his desk. Oklahoma PD had been alerted, so there really was no reason for him to call.

So he picked up the phone and dialed Chuck. "Hey, it's Ashton. Any news on my missing housecleaner?"

Chuck made a grumbling noise and said, "Yeah, it's a crime scene, all right. We got some dogs on it, looks like blood. Got her cell phone and let me tell you, these two had some contact. I've run the dates, and looks like they chatted the night before each one of your horses died."

The check crunched in Ashton's hand before he realized he did it. "Really."

"Nothing really before that, but the other link is the area code. Her phone was activated in Oklahoma. Can't really see a woman with no ride hopping a bus just to buy a phone out-of-state."

"Good point." He shifted. "Hey, I got her daughter here with some proof that Mack was behind all this. I'd like to know if you can subpoena his emails," he paused, "and perhaps even reopen the case."

"Emails, huh? She write to Mack?"

"No, her husband did. I got it all on my keystroke logger. I printed it up as long as I had his old laptop going."

"Yeah, keep it. I'll be down for it soon. And I'll need the laptop as evidence, too."

"No problem. I'll show you how to load the program."

A few seconds of silence followed. Chuck cleared his throat. "So, yeah, if Oklahoma PD finds them, we'll extradite. Or, if we get a body, we'll call."

Disheartened, Ashton said, "Okay."

Chuck hung up the phone.

Only one thing could change this mood, and even the thought made him smile. He picked up the phone and dialed Raylie. When she answered, he beamed. "Hey, honey. I just talked to Chuck." He took a minute to update her on the case, all the while feeling more and more responsible for Vicenta's death.

She must have sensed it, for Raylie said, "Ashton? You aren't to blame for any of this."

His chest squeezed in on him. "I know, it's just that—"

"No, you're not. I'm not going to let you beat yourself up over what Mack did. We are not responsible for the actions of other people, remember?"

He smiled. "You're right. Thanks for reminding me."

"My pleasure."

He hummed. "Just remember, I'm taking you away for the weekend, starting Saturday at nine a.m."

"Where we going?"

"It's a surprise. But I'll tell you this; it's beautiful."

Then she shocked the hell out of him when she said, "Baby, let's start it tonight."

Chapter 47

The kittens seemed to like their new daily excursions to Marta's office, but after today, Raylie had little strength left for the transporting of them.

"Oh, good, you brought them again," Marta said with a warm smile. "I must say, our appointments are my favorite time of day."

"That's only 'cause you get to go home after me."

They shared a laugh. "That's not true."

Grinning, Raylie bent over and opened the carrier. "I feel like Pandora," she said as they spilled out. Sure enough, Mischief, Mayhem and Chaos raced around the room, while Curiosity tipped over the trash.

"Please, have a seat." Marta's arm moved graciously about the room, where Raylie noticed the same blue saddle pad folded innocuously on one chair.

Her heart raced, but she slowed it down with a few deep breaths, unable to look away.

Until two kittens raced over her sandaled feet, their nails like a meat tenderizer on her toes. "Ow, brats."

"I noticed your reaction to the blanket again. Care to talk about it?" Marta sat in the chair beside it and draped one hand on the patterned top.

One toe bled as she looked down. "It's identical to the one they covered Derrick with when he died."

"The blanket didn't cause his death, Raylie."

"I know that. Don't you think I know that?" She sat down and applied pressure to her cut. "It's a trigger, that's all." The video wanted to replay, step by step, but Raylie refused to watch Derrick fall this time, focusing instead on her scratch, the kittens, Marta, and seeing the blanket as a hunk of thread and dye.

Still…

"Can you put it away, please? For, like, a half hour?"

Marta nodded and tossed it in a drawer.

Feeling a need to demonstrate progress, Raylie sat up and said, "I'm getting better, Marta, really, I am. I went and petted my foal, and let his mama sniff me, and I petted her and didn't have any anxiety. I wasn't afraid." She laughed. "The baby was, though, when a girl ran up."

"Does Ashton like the name you chose?"

"He…" she stopped. "Oh. I never got to tell him. That girl interrupted us. Her mama disappeared, and it turns out that's the woman who shot Ashton. She's working for his stepbrother or something. So I think I've solved the case. We just have to get Oklahoma PD on it and bring his brother in for questioning."

"So, you think his brother did it?"

"Step. Ex-step, actually. Yeah."

"Why?"

Raylie shrugged. "Money. Ashton's rich. It's family." She looked down. "Dad always said when Mom died, her family picked through the house and took everything not nailed down. They were like vultures. Just because they were owed money."

"So, this is kind of painful to you? A little too personal?"

"It's not personal. It's human nature. People are inherently corpse-pickers. Cash, pins, clothes, whatever. The dead can't use 'em."

"Kind of harsh, Raylie." Head tipped, Marta studied her. "What brought this on?"

It took three attempts to collect a kitten, but soon Raylie cradled one in her hands. "I don't know. Fear?"

"Of what?"

Losing Ashton, but she wasn't ready to say it. "What if Ashton's only keeping me around until I solve his case? What if all of this is a lie?"

"What if it's not?" Confused, Marta leaned forward. "Where… why…how does Ashton fit into this picture?"

Now or never. Stroking the kitten with her fingertips, Raylie took a deep breath. "Because…I'm falling in love with him."

Chapter 48

Raylie felt a foot taller as she bopped around her house, rummaging through closets for clothes and makeup she had long since abandoned, eager to give them a new life. A flirty top and long, flowing skirt made her test her twirling abilities before her bedroom mirror. Satisfied, she focused on her blush and mascara, taking time to make sure she looked her best.

Perhaps tonight she could modify her motto: jump 'em, pump 'em, pump 'em, pump 'em…

She couldn't apply lipstick over her smile.

No horses had died all week. Jim confided in her that their boss would name her Monday as their next field chief, Marta finished their week of desensitization at a stable, where Raylie petted and groomed an old gelding, and now Ashton reminded her he would be taking her away for the weekend on a mystery mini-vacation.

She lengthened her lashes.

Life was good, love even better. Nothing would go wrong tonight.

She tucked a foil packet into her bra, eager for Ashton to find it tonight, more so for him to use it. She stuffed another one in her thong and tossed a handful more into her duffle bag before leaving.

At the door, Raylie took down Cheddar's leash and Doggles— dog goggles. He spun in happy circles, yipping.

"Sit."

He plunked down, tongue lolling stupidly out the side of his mouth—the melted-cheddar side. She clipped his leash, and as she slid the Doggles over his eyes, he made the highest, most excited whine.

"Ready to go play with Snot?"

He nearly vibrated with readiness.

She yanked open the door and he flew out to her Bronco while she locked up. A string of barks trailed from him. And when it seemed locking up took too long, he raced back and forth between his personal chauffeur and limo, his long leash flapping in his wake.

"Hey, I only got two feet, all right?" She opened the passenger door and he hopped in as she rolled down the window.

She dropped her duffle bag in back next to Cheddar's, his filled with everything a dog could need for a weekend of pet sitting: dishes, food, chew bone and emergency tennis ball. Leann jumped at the chance to dog-sit while Raylie and Ashton went away. Ditto with Marta, who offered to take Pandora's lot until Monday.

Weatherman said sunshine all weekend.

Perfect.

Cheddar already had his head out the window by the time she started the car. When they got to the main road, his pert ears and tongue flapped in the wind like a kite tail, one of them leaving a spray of spittle on the window behind.

She hoped they'd take Ashton's car.

Leann and Snort waited in the front yard, and Cheddar bolted over when freed, earning a firm correction from the Pug.

"Darlin', you're gonna melt that man's heart," Leann said with a fond embrace.

"Turnabout's fair play," Raylie responded with a grin. "I know he melted mine. Over Chinese dumplings."

They laughed.

"Any word on that girl's mama?"

A head shake. "Dogs found blood at the scene. Chuck just called, Mack's house looks deserted."

"Great," she murmured. "Girl, you be careful."

"Always."

"Where's your gun?"

Instinctively, Raylie patted her hip. "Oh. I left it home. Vacation equals no gun."

A look of worry and rue crossed Leann's face. "You keep that man at your side, darlin', and leave first thing in the morning. There's an evil moon out tonight."

Indeed, it sat low and large and orange on the twilight horizon. "I will."

"Even if you don't sleep at all tonight."

Laughing, Raylie said, "Well, that's kind of the plan."

Grabbing her hands, Leann spread her arms wide. "Looking like this, he'll have no choice."

Snort's throaty growl made them look over. In his eternal puppydom, Cheddar had solicited play from Snort, who had rolled him over and now pinned him to the ground, his tiny Pug paws restraining Cheddar's massive barrel chest.

"Your dog's a big mean bully. Come here, Ched."

Cheddar bolted to his feet, sending Snort rolling. She squatted down to scrub his head. "Good bye, boy. Behave." She stood up and hugged Leann. "Thanks a bunch. See ya Monday."

"Bye."

She felt as if she flew down the highway. Starstruck's gates seemed more welcoming than ever, and the guard pointed north and gave her directions to the track.

Intrigued, she followed the single paved lane to the long circular well-lit racetrack and got out.

A cloud of dust indicated the action, and she maneuvered toward a man with a stopwatch.

"You must be Officer McPherson. I'm Ed."

She shook his hand. "Raylie, yes. Nice to finally meet you."

He pointed to the sulky clearly in the lead. "That's Ashton in the lead, with High Eminence." He smiled. "Look at him go." He bounced in time to the ticking of the second hand.

"Is he fast?"

"Like a rocket."

"But he won't load."

Ed's face clouded. "Yup. The fatal flaw."

The brown horse's even pace eased him around the bend, and Ed started jumping up and down. When they blasted past, five lengths in the lead, Ed pushed the button, his hands fisted in the air.

It took another few minutes for the horses to finish their cool-down circuit, but Raylie watched, intrigued, as Ashton came rolling to a stop before them.

"How'd we do?" he asked, all business in his red and white gingham racing silks as he got off the sulky.

"The half in sixty-one."

Awe filled Ashton's face as he tipped back his head. "Oh my God."

"That fast?" Raylie asked.

"The half-mile in a minute? *Very.*" He smiled down at her, then yanked off his helmet and leaned forward for a kiss. "Help the others, will you, Ed? We got him." He unhooked the jog cart and head poles from the colt and looked at her. "Think you can lead the horse?"

"Yup." Feeling a surge of confidence, Raylie stepped near and looped the horse's fourteen feet of reins in her hands. Tired from his race, High Eminence blew out his lips and lowered his head to follow.

"It's like you've been doing this all along."

"I have been, Ashton. For years." She clucked to him, and the horse stepped up his pace, not showing any fear at all for the two-wheeled cart rolling along beside him.

"He trusts you. Being followed is a great compliment."

"You're sweet. But I know he's just too tired to argue."

They laughed and chatted as they walked the horse back to the stables for a rubdown. Once cleaned and dried, Ashton turned him out to pasture overnight, then ducked into his office to exchange his racing checkers for his normal jeans and polo.

Raylie couldn't help but grin at his more casual attire. "I think I prefer you in jeans over silks."

"Hardly the comment one would expect of an aristocrat."

One loud laugh burst from her. "Is that what I am?"

He grinned, wrapped his arms around her waist and kissed her nose. "Apparently not."

She jabbed him on the shoulder. "What can I say? I like my cowboys in jeans. Shows off the tight buns."

His eyes darkened. "I like my cowgirls *out* of their jeans." He glanced down. "Or skirts, as the case may be."

"Soon," she whispered, then, "Where's my foal?"

He jostled her, rubbed his hips against hers. "Your foal, huh?" He grinned. "Name him yet?"

She nodded and touched his strong chin. "Fearsome Time." She looked up at him. "Like it?"

"Like it? It's perfect." Ashton stopped and pulled her closer, his lips sealing over hers in a knee-bending kiss. Arched backward like this, it was all she could do to hang on.

Completely aroused, Raylie did her best to focus and remember why she brought him here. Taking one step away, she said, "Come on. I want to show you something."

So he kept pace down the lit aisles, and Raylie proudly opened Missy's stall door and stepped in. Little Fearsome peeked between his mama's legs, then came over. She patted both of them.

Beaming like a proud papa, Ashton said, "In her day, Missy could give High Eminence a run for his money. But she's been such a good brood mare I'd stopped racing her."

Caught in another world, Raylie merely nestled her fingers into the matching brown manes, listening to the strings of "goodbyes" as his staff wrapped up for the night. "For eighteen months I avoided horses, seeing them only as the source of Derrick's end." Her fingers braided Missy's long brown mane, glad she had come this far, this fast. "When his aneurism killed him while we were riding, I wanted nothing to do with them, always associating them with death."

"But with Fearsome and Missy, it's now with life."

Those whispered words made Raylie look up at him. "Yeah. I guess now it does." She studied him. "You knew that, though, didn't you?"

"I've seen the look, Raylie. I've seen hundreds of kids scared to death of horses, and knew I had to do something to get you over that. Especially since I had the feeling you'd ridden before."

"You said that before. How did you know?"

"First time we met. You called Ralphie a 'leaner.'"

She nodded, familiar with the term, her fingers still tugging Missy's mane into braids. "Lean forward. Over the knee. An old horse."

"Oh, I knew what you meant. But only someone well versed in horses would have pulled out that term. Fifteen years I've never heard Doc spout that one." He stepped close and brushed his lips to her cheek. "Will you ever go riding again?"

Fearsome nuzzled her shoe strap, then tugged. She pulled her foot away. "Yeah, I guess I will. Someday."

"Tonight?" Hope shimmered in his eyes.

"I have better things planned for tonight." To prove it, her fingertips nestled into the top of his jeans.

Lust burgeoned in his eyes. "Careful, baby. This stallion's a little on the wild side tonight." He undid his button and waited.

Such opportunities deserved to be explored, and Raylie took advantage of the deserted stable. One hand unzipped his fly while the other reached down to stroke his swelling flesh.

"Raylie," he whispered. "I want you. Now."

"Let's go back inside." His hot flesh throbbed as she gripped him, but the blasted house seemed so far away. She didn't want to let go.

"I have an idea." He closed his eyes while she caressed him, then he jerked back. "Come on. Follow me."

"Where we going?"

"To the loft." He headed toward the end of the aisle holding her Golden.

In the hay? "You're kidding, right?"

"Nope." He reached up and grabbed a white rope hanging from the ceiling, and tugging on it brought the ladder sliding down with a series of loud clacking. She had passed by it numerous times and never seen it before. Smoldering eyes held hers. "We pull the string up with us, no one can see us or get in. Our own little private escape." He drew her close, rubbing her back as his tongue probed her mouth.

"Race you up," Raylie sighed.

But Ashton took a full two minutes to explore her lips and tongue, and his free hand slipped under her shirt to tease the wire of her bra.

"You go first," he whispered. "I like the view."

She climbed up and felt for the light, taking a full second to flash him from the top.

"It's on the right," he said, his voice sounding choked.

When she turned it on, soft yellow light bathed the bales, the turnout rugs, the chairs and blankets in welcoming piles. "Looks like this place was made for sex-capades." She stepped inside and waited.

"Perhaps." He waggled his brows. "Care to find out?"

"Oh yeah." She toyed with her top button.

A wolfish grin answered hers, and Ashton drew up the ladder, going around to pull up the string before locking them in. The ladder looked like it was stacked on the floor. "There. Now, where were we?"

"You sure we're safe up here?"

He unbuttoned his shirt as he advanced on her. "Yup."

"No one's going to hear us?"

He shrugged. "No one's here."

"Good point."

He stepped closer, and when Raylie went to tear off his shirt, he stopped her hands. "Last time I went too fast."

Sucking on his neck, Raylie managed to say, "No you didn't."

But he held her at arm's length. "Tonight, Raylie, is about pleasuring you."

A flood of moisture made her achingly uncomfortable. "Then let's get busy."

"After I've heard you scream my name." He dipped her backward in another spine-melting kiss, and everything in Raylie went limp.

He collected her in his arms and strode to a pile of blankets to lay her down.

"We're not leaving until you've writhed in ecstasy."

"Then you better begin."

He moved agonizingly slow. Light fingers trailed up her forearms as his lips moved down her throat. Rough knuckles dragged across her chest, teasing her nipples through the width of her bra. When she went to unclip it, Ashton stayed her hand.

"In time."

"I'm horny now."

"In time." His lips nuzzled her throat, the V over her buttons. Eternity passed before he slid one free, then his tongue dragged a damp trail down her chest as he undid the rest.

He slid lower, to her abdomen, and his tongue danced around her naval before nipping her there. She bucked, shocked at the sensation, making him chuckle. Then he tugged on her skirt with his teeth, and the elastic made it easy for him to slide it off.

A foil packet peeked out from her thong, and she saw he

noticed it. The smile disappeared to a hooded gaze as his tongue traced the string of her panties.

"Ashton."

He worked his way back up, kissing her flesh and making her quiver with the contact. His hands slid behind her back, and soon her breasts fell free of their restraint. He chuckled as another foil packet emerged, this one stuck to her skin. "I'm going to use both of these quite soon," he whispered, making her squirm with anticipation.

He fanned her shirt out and sat back on his heels to gaze at her. "You're so beautiful, Raylie. So beautiful. I'm so glad you came into my life."

His words choked her, made her want to share too much. *No.* Opening her mouth right now would only spoil the mood, make it seemed forced. Worse, she might weep when she told him how important he had become to her.

"You were delivered into my life at a time when I most needed an ally. I couldn't imagine going through this with anyone else, Raylie." He met her eyes. "I really can't."

Her resolve shattered, she could only hold his gaze. "I… I feel the same way. I needed to deal with my fears, but didn't know how. And I was getting to the point where I gave all the horse cases to Matt. But with the promotion," she looked up at him, knowing he would see where her thoughts went, "I knew I had to get better."

He almost smiled. "So you could arrest me. But if you tossed me in jail, I couldn't do this." He peeled off her panties and knelt between her legs, hooked her knees and drew her bottom closer to him. Bracing her buttocks, he lifted her up and plunged his tongue into her cleft.

She cried out with pleasure, arching into his hot mouth and needing to drape a leg or two over his strong shoulders. His tongue plunged and licked and teased as his lips and teeth roamed over her clitoris. She gripped the blanket, desperate for anything to cling to as her hips arched higher in the air.

He lowered her to his lap, and she felt him thrust inside her for a few welcoming strokes. Then he laid her down and reclined alongside her, his fingers dipping into her swollen flesh.

"Oh, Ashton."

She reached down to stroke him as well and was rewarded by a low groan and hip thrust. "Oh, baby, that feels so good."

Her fingers roamed, wanting him to feel as much as she did, but he rolled on top of her and kissed her deeply.

Legs spread, all Raylie wanted was for him to plunge inside, to ride her like a wild mare, but his fingers continued to tease and titillate. He rapped them along the inside of her thigh, along her nipples, across her lips. "Oh, Ashton."

"I want you to experience more pleasure than you've ever known, Raylie. I want you to explode."

"I want you in me."

"In due time." He flipped her to her stomach and lightly stroked her back. His relaxing touch only aroused her more. Then he worked down her thighs, caressing and massaging her buttocks and nestling his fingers into her damp curls.

When she could no longer take it, Raylie rolled over and tried to push him onto his back, needing to take control of her urges. "My turn."

"Oh no." He eased her back down. "You're going to come in my hand or mouth first, my love. I was far too aggressive with you last time."

"But I like it that way."

He met her eyes. "Perhaps that's because it's the only way you've ever known."

His gentle gaze seemed to sweep right through her, and she fell back into the blanket. "Perhaps."

No comment, only a thorough nipple-sucking in conjunction

with his skilled fingers stroking over her thighs.

She sniffed out a laugh. "When I helped you deliver Fearsome, I wanted so much to be that foal, feeling your hands roaming on me."

"There is no flesh in the world I'd rather touch than yours, Raylie." He claimed her entire breast in his mouth, making her gasp. "You've been steadfast for me. You know that?"

Images swirled in her mind as his tongue caressed her flesh over and over. "It's…it's my job."

"Racing over here daily is your job? Meeting me for dinner is your job?" He leaned back to eye her, then stroked her sensitive nub with his thumb. "Is getting naked with me your job, too?"

She grinned and purred. "Thought I had learned once not to mix business and pleasure."

"I'm not Derrick, Raylie. I would never cut you down or hurt you."

And there stood the truth. As she gazed at him, it all made perfect sense. "You know, you've been more a friend to me than Derrick ever was."

His fingers plunged in and out with promising strength. His crooked grin tugged on her heart. "Is that what we are? Friends?"

"A relationship is nothing without friendship, Ashton. I've learned to rely on you when I'd stopped relying on anyone."

"Me too," he whispered. "I couldn't see myself trusting anyone but you." A pale shadow crossed his visage, but it vanished like smoke when he kissed her.

His fingers stroked and played and nestled until her hips began rocking to a rhythm she couldn't deny.

"Come in my hand, Raylie."

He sucked her nipple harder, thumbed her nub as his fingers stretched her sensitive skin.

"Come for me."

She couldn't deny him. Her hips arched high in the air, and her hand clutched his arm in her passion. "Oh, Ashton." All sensation boiled down to a tiny knot somewhere in her center, until her very existence focused there, waiting, waiting, and then her world exploded into a thousand tiny pieces, blasting out into the empty loft. She squeezed her legs together, holding him in, holding in the rush of fluid, the waves of pleasure emanating from her woman's core.

"That's my girl," he whispered.

When her breathing slowed, shock made Raylie open her eyes. "I am, you know," she whispered to him.

"What? My girl?"

Mute with the realization, she could only nod.

He lowered himself beside her. "And I'm your man, Raylie. Always. I hope you know that."

She felt tears gather, but knew the truth of his words when she heard them.

He nosed her cheek, licked her earlobe. "What if I didn't wear a condom? Just, what if?"

She felt herself swallow. "I…I don't know if I can have kids. We once tried, but… "

He covered her, stroking her cheeks, contemplating her words for a moment. "Do you believe animals need to feel secure before they can breed? Have offspring?"

She considered his words. Bird nests, rodent hidey-holes, dog dens… "Sure. Yeah, I guess. They would have to be able to protect their babies."

"Do you think you ever felt safe enough, in the past, to offer that?"

She looked down. "I…I don't know."

"Maybe, Raylie, it wasn't that you couldn't, but that you *shouldn't*. At least, not then. You said your mother-in-law was dying. Maybe it was too much stress."

She licked her lips, still surprised at how easily Ashton could read her, know her. She held her thoughts for a moment, wondering how he would handle this bit of news.

In for a penny.

"When Angie had…suggested…that she would love to hold a grandchild before she died…it was on the tail end of Derrick hearing about a bit of news I had just learned." She searched his face, seeing only curiosity. Feeling braver, she inhaled and continued. "He had really become such an asshole. I had just found out that my mom had a drinking problem. She was driving drunk, and sped through a check-point, killing a cop. Derrick held *me* responsible for that, even though I was only two at the time, and home with my dad." She looked away. "He kept calling me a cop-killer."

"What a prick."

Even pinned under his impressive weight, she felt lighter than she had in years. Giddiness filled her, made her feel happy in a way she no longer thought she could. Raylie smiled and wiggled underneath him. "Speaking of, shouldn't we be putting yours to good use, and not wasting time talking about people who act like one?"

He grinned. "I'm just saying." He slid into her again, *au naturel,* and both of them groaned at the complete sensation of skin on skin.

He pulled out with effort. "Well, let's find those foil packets, shall we, and then I'll really make you mine."

Chapter 49

For a second, the barking dog seemed like background music to a dream—a dream in which she and Ashton danced on clouds to the music of their souls. But then the beat turned to the rapid-fire warning of *intruder*, and Raylie snapped open her eyes.

The Golden's urgent bark made Raylie reach for her gun in the nightstand, but all she touched was straw. *Oh.* Feeling heavy and logy from their lovemaking, she eased her hand to the warmth at her back. "Ashton."

He moaned, cuddled her closer. "Again?"

"Ashton, someone's in the barn."

She sensed him straighten up. Then he turned on the light and got dressed. "Stay here. I'll go check it out."

"But…" she reached for her skirt. "I'm an officer."

"An unarmed officer."

"You're not armed either," she hissed, as she yanked on her top and stepped into her panties and skirt.

"But I have a gun in my office." The look he gave her brooked no argument. "Turn off the light. I'm lowering the ladder. I want you to pull it up when I'm gone."

She hated this plan, but shut off the light. "Fine." Brandy's barking covered the clickety-click of the ladder, but the sound of horses stirring made the barn a noisy place anyway. Ashton shimmied down and ducked around the corner as she pulled it halfway up and turned the light back on.

Voices, and Raylie heard the clatter of hooves on tile. One of the horses had been freed of its stall or had broken out. More yelling, and a solid *thunk* made her envision a shovel striking flesh.

Unarmed, Raylie hesitated for a second. She might get clobbered, but Ashton had already been shot once. So she lowered the ladder again and backed down.

A man on horseback raced toward her down the dark hallway. As he entered her pool of light, she saw his arm extended out from his side. His fist caught her square in the stomach—a veritable jousting move from knights of yore—and knocked her five feet away from the ladder. All breath left her as the midnight thief plowed past on the tacked Standardbred.

It hurt to breathe, but Raylie forced herself upright. Another horse raced near, this one mounted by Ashton. A smear of blood ran from both his brow and mouth. "Stay here," he snarled as he blasted past. Once outside the barn, she heard him yell, "Mack, get your ass back here."

Mack. His stepbrother. Step-cousin. Whatever he was. "No." She backed up, straight into a stall door, clutching her stomach. Damn, that hurt. Ambient light filtered through the long dashes of windows as the first brush of morning touched the sky.

The horse behind her whickered. Raylie turned to face Mystic Thyme. The large soft brown eye held hers, and even Fearsome Time looked up at her and waited.

Her fingers shook as she undid the latch, but Missy didn't notice or care. She stepped into the aisle, giving Raylie the look of patience that only a loving mare could accomplish.

Hooves thundered along the central causeway as Raylie placed her hands on Missy's back. "I can't do this." It was no longer Derrick's death she feared, but Ashton's. A man she loved more than she ever thought possible. What if something were to happen to him?

The last time she rode, her fiancé died.

If she did nothing, a man she loved fiercely would die.

Three, four seconds ticked by, their hooves growing softer in the distance.

Missy nudged her and stomped a foot, then pricked her ears toward the two men charging headlong across the field.

Ashton needed her.

Hell, she needed Ashton.

A guard raced in, eyes wide as he surveyed the barn.

"Call the cops. Ashton's just been robbed."

He nodded, radioed the home base for backup, and Raylie still stood there with her hands on Missy's back.

"In for a penny," she said as she grabbed hold of the mane and swung onto the barebacked horse despite her painful stomach, arranging the long skirt until she could properly sit. She took a deep breath and held her stomach once more. It wasn't the first time she'd been sucker-punched, but this time would be the last. The round barrel felt like a long-missed home to her thighs, and Missy's mane felt like nylon strings being twisted in her hands. The lump in her throat swelled until it felt larger than an apple sitting there. "I must be crazy," she whispered, but she realized the truth of her desire. *She would protect what was hers.* As impossible as it seemed, Starstruck was her home, more so than the residence where she hung her hat. Her bare heels kicked the brown ribs, and she heard herself yell, "Yah!"

Missy took off like a rocket, with baby Fearsome right at her flank. Down the stable lanes and across the dewy fields they ran, following the crushed wet path as easily as if it were paved.

She crested a hillock and saw Mack riding a horse that tossed its neck and fought the reins. Behind him came Ashton, his lighter weight and greater skill putting him only a length or two behind.

A dozen lengths separated them, and Raylie feared her mare would slow down too much for her foal, but Missy's head only dipped down, asking baby Fearsome to run harder.

Mack and Ashton curved around a tree, and a litany of curses strong enough to make Raylie blush issued forth from Ashton's mouth. Hesitant, she followed, eased between two fence posts missing their slats. Clever, Raylie thought, for the thick tree's shadow hid the escape route from any patrolling guards' eyes.

Down the dirt deer path and onto the asphalt they went,

clattering along at almost forty mph. Ashton reached out time and again, but Mack evaded him or swatted him away. Soon houses crowded the streets, and the smell of oleander filled the air from the decorative hedgerows on the sidewalk.

Ahead, the yawning mouth of a horse trailer dominated the street.

Someone revved the engine, and taillights glowed like evil eyes in the still air. This time Ashton managed to grab the horse's bridle, but Mack still aimed the horse for the trailer.

Just then Mack's horse reared up screaming, pulling Ashton to the ground and tossing Mack straight into the hedgerows.

Raylie caught up, slowed Missy down with her seat. "Are you okay?"

Ashton groaned and tucked his hand into his stomach, holding onto the reins of a panicked horse with all his might. "I think I broke a finger."

The trailer pulled away fast, the loading ramp sending up a shower of sparks in its wake.

Mack groaned, cried out at a branch sticking through his arm, and Raylie eased near and hopped down. Mack's horse still spooked, even with Ashton holding onto him.

"Take off your shirt." Raylie grabbed the reins and bridle on the off side as he stripped, then she took his clothing and wrapped it over the colt's eyes. Immediately the horse settled. Next she unclipped a rein.

"What are you doing?"

With six feet at her disposal, Raylie grinned and snapped the leather between her stretched arms. "Tying up my suspect. And the case."

Mack groaned as he tried to extricate himself from the impaling branches. "I don't feel so good."

"The thought of prison does that to a man," Raylie informed him, deadpan.

"No," he whimpered as she yanked his leg off a small stake. "Sick."

"Oh. Well, you did land in oleander."

"Oleander?" Now he struggled with vigor. "Get it off me!"

A sauntering Ashton stopped before him. "Why, Mack? Why'd you do it?"

But Mack only swore and spat. "You're nothin' but a rich prick."

When Ashton stormed toward Mack, his intent to fight obvious, Raylie put up a hand. "He'll be dead in an hour if we just leave him here."

That stopped him. "No. No. Don't leave me."

"What about the driver?" With his chin, Ashton indicated the empty road.

"Cops will get him."

"Her."

In disbelief, Raylie asked, "Her? You mean Brittany?"

Ashton's jaw squared; Mack looked away. Apparently that was all the admission of guilt Ashton needed; his face hardened and he yanked Mack's arm off the one-inch shard protruding through his limb, then stripped a piece of the torn shirt to bind the wound. "Why'd you do it?" she heard him whisper.

"Money," Raylie quipped. "You are a rich prick, you know."

Mack cussed her a blue stream, and Ashton punched him dead in the face. Her suspect fell limp into the bushes again.

"Well, we might as well tie him up." She bound his wrists and feet and helped Ashton drag him to the curb.

Those self-same appraising eyes scanned her for flaws. "You rode. Bareback. At a gallop, nonetheless. I'm impressed."

Feeling elated and terrified and victorious and a hundred other nameless emotions, she managed, "Missy's got a smooth gait."

"But you're the one with the balance." He grinned at her. "Really, Raylie, I'm impressed." He stepped near, one hand on her hip.

"The baby kept up, too."

Ashton's eyebrows flew high. "Hmm. Our next contender."

A trail of blood marred his handsome visage. Raylie found herself wiping off the dried evidence. "I'm glad you're okay."

His forehead lowered to touch hers. "You solved your case, Officer McPherson."

She scoffed. "Who cares? I got my *real* man right here." And she looped her hands behind his neck and pulled him down for a long kiss.

A siren whooped; they looked over. Chuck merely studied them. "He need a ride to the hospital?" He jabbed a thumb at Raylie's hog-tied prize.

"In an hour or so. Oleander needs a little time to work."

Chuck cracked a grin and got out. "Help me load him in. I'll question him once he's awake." He laced his fingers and flexed until they all cracked. Then he crushed each fist until they cracked again.

Raylie pointed after the disappearing trailer. "Get your boys out looking for Starstruck's gooseneck. Brittany's driving off in it."

Chuck cracked another grin at that, brows high. "Yeah? Can't wait to hear that songbird sing." He picked up his hand piece to radio in for backup.

Raylie laughed. "Give them hell, Chuck." They grabbed Mack and flopped him into the squad car.

Chuck paused for a moment, studying the two of them. "Nice job, Raylie." To Ashton he said, "She's a good girl. She deserves a good man. Take care of her." Then he booted the rest of Mack into the backseat and drove away.

"Wow." Raylie watched him turn the corner. "Can you pinch me?"

"Gladly." He tweaked her bottom.

She yelped and swatted him. "Brat."

"Why the pinch?"

Shaking her head, she whispered, "Chuck complimented me."

Ashton crushed her to his side, planting a kiss on her head. "You are a good girl. A great one, actually." Soft eyes smiled down at her. "And I can't wait to spend my life taking care of you."

This time his gentle kiss eased hot tears from Raylie's eyes. She sniffled and clutched him close, knowing now all that she had missed those long years trapped with Derrick. Soon his fingertips brushed her jaw, and Raylie's hands wrapped around his neck and into his hair, trying to collect all of him close as the kiss lingered on.

Ashton pulled gently away, his fingers erasing the damp tearstains on her cheeks. He indicated the mare. "Shall we head back?"

Dawn now illuminated the horizon, sending wavy orange lines through the clear sky. "Why not?" Raylie walked up to Missy, and Ashton gave her a leg-up. Once mounted, he stroked her calf. "I really wanted to see you on a stallion."

His wolfish grin made Raylie laugh. "I'll mount a stallion tonight, Ashton. When we're alone."

He bellowed out a laugh filled with promise. His shirt he reclaimed from the panicked horse, now calm, and he took the single rein to lead the horse to his own. As he mounted his steed, Raylie pointed to the one Mack stole. "Let me guess, High Eminence?"

"Yup."

She took a deep breath. "I'm sure Chuck will get us a reason soon."

"Yup. Probably right."

They stood there, silent and mounted, overlooking the pink-tinged street two miles from the stable. Fearsome Time stepped near, nuzzling his mother's flank before slurping down a meal.

"I agree," Raylie said as she watched him. "I could go for some breakfast myself."

Birdsong erupted from the nearby trees, heralding a bright new day.

"Let's take the long way home," Ashton said, appraising her with a soft look. "After all, I did promise you one free ride."

Unable to control her smile, Raylie urged her horse forward into the buoyant morning air.

Chapter 50

"Do your chefs ever sleep?" Raylie asked as she perused the endless assortment of breakfast foods that greeted Ashton every single morning when he came in here. Silver trays held cooked varieties of eggs, bacon, sausage, pancakes, waffles, fruits, bagels, French and regular toasts, even steak. "I don't even know where to begin."

Proud of his staff and the impression they made on her, Ashton puffed out his chest. "I suggest the multiple course approach. Usually by your third trip, you know what you want."

She laughed and plucked some waffles and an omelet to her plate. "Everything looks wonderful."

"Tastes even better." Glad he could surprise her, he dropped an apple onto her tray. "They're Empire."

"New York apples?" Her eyes said she couldn't believe it.

"Just for you," he winked.

Juice and coffee completed their trays, and they settled into the cafeteria-style seats. One bite later, Ashton's cell rang. Groaning, he managed to answer it with a bandaged finger. "Hey Chuck." He waved Raylie to his side, and together they listened.

"Yeah, that Brittany, she's a piece of work. A real turncoat. Sang like a goddamned warbler when I told her Mack spilled the beans. 'Course, she don't know he's still in ICU, all juiced up and strapped down." He laughed. "But here's what I got. Your horse is identical to some horse in Texas. Your main stud there bred two sisters?"

Ashton looked up and thought back. "Yeah. Flight-N-Fancy is full sister to Dare to Dream. Ralphie bred both of them his last stud season."

"Well, your horse, High Eminence, is a dead ringer to this Texas horse, who by the way is dead. Fallen branch crushed it. Identical right down to the four white hairs over the left eye. Mack was offered two million to steal High Eminence to fill in."

Ashton groaned. "Half-brothers. Identical half-brothers that are almost cousins. Mack could forge the name on the certificate, but the bloodline would ring true. Ralphie's get are all winners. People would pay a fortune, and the lineage would be exact."

Chuck kept going. "And the kid who died last winter, well, they paid him in cash, with the intent of killing him upon delivering the horse and taking back the dough. The kid, of course, thought he was on the up and up. Was told he'd get ten grand at delivery, when all they planned to give him was a gaping chest wound. They got all pissed when he crashed. Mack was getting some pressure from his cousin, Frank, who needed the replacement ASAP. Texas PD is giving Frank a once-over."

Chuck took a deep breath. "So he found this South American import and had you hire her with the intent of killing off your horses until he could work out a back-up plan. Had her filling apples with oleander after the boy died, walking a mile or so from the stable to collect the leaves. 'Crazy old lady,' Brittany called her, said she left weird shit everywhere."

"Apples," Raylie whispered, then added, "I dreamed of apples."

Chuck's words made Ashton rub his eyes. "Like a soap dispenser pump left in a horse stall?"

"Yeah, stuff like that. Oh, yeah, and he's got false certificates on six different methods of getting that horse away from you. Of course, he won't trailer, which thwarted him every time."

"Yeah, well, Emin's career is ruined if I can't get him to the tracks. He's like a bullet afraid of the gun."

Chuck had more, though. "Going after Mack on murder one for the Spanish woman. Man, they liked their foreigners. Easy to prey on, hard to trace. We found her blood all over his crowbar, along with his prints. Brittany said they dumped her in a field. Cadaver dogs are working on recovering the body. She have kin?"

Raylie bowed her head. Ashton tucked her close and closed his eyes. "Yeah. I'll take care of it."

Another deep breath over the phone. "All in all, seems like your problems are solved." They could practically hear Chuck's grin.

"Thanks, pal," Ashton sighed. "Nice work."

"What is it?" Chuck barked out, then told them, "Got to go. Mack's waking up. Gonna go have me a little chat." The phone clicked off.

"Wow." Ashton tucked his phone away, but he looked down.

Raylie touched his arm. "I can help with Emin, you know. With his fear. I'm practically an expert at desensitization now." She grinned. "I had a cruelty case where we had seventeen starved horses that we had to trailer, and they were feral. I was pretty good at it. Now, I think I'd be even better, with all the help Marta's been giving me." Her fingers felt warm as he pressed them to his skin.

She studied him in his profound silence. "What's wrong?"

"Nothing."

She shrugged and attacked her waffles. "All right." After a few bites, she moaned. "Oh, Ashton, these are *good*."

He whirled on her. "Not *all* my problems."

Mid-chew, Raylie stopped. "Beg pardon?"

"I have one *big* problem left unsolved." God, his throat swelled just admitting it.

She chewed slowly. "What is it?"

Glancing around for eavesdroppers, Ashton leaned close. "There's something I haven't told you. You see..." He took a deep breath. "Raylie, I found out about two weeks ago that..." He met her eyes, then looked away, ashamed. His voice dropped. "That... my aunt...stole money from a casino. Lots of money. Enough to buy Ralphie and change our last names." He couldn't swallow, but his throat worked convulsively.

She studied him, and although he braced for anger or disgust or outrage, he felt more like a piece of abstract art she tried to understand. "She hid the fact well enough. Lyre, liar. Pants on fire." She winked.

Ashton looked down. "I've been eaten up with guilt, Raylie. What if someone learns how I got started?" Fearful, he held her eyes. His words barely registered as a whisper. "Raylie, I could be ruined. From the deaths, to a scandal…" He felt his eyes mist up. "I've lost not only horses, but a handful of boarders have left, and even some of my good students have transferred. If this continues…" Terror clenched his chest, and he felt his breathing come fast and shallow. Raylie just had to understand, or all would be lost.

Thoughtful, Raylie sipped her coffee. "Ash, how many waffles are on your plate?"

She must be cracking. He looked down. "None, why?"

"And how many glasses are on our table?"

He figured she'd flipped, but he counted anyway. "Four."

"How many days since we've first met?"

He almost laughed, and he leaned back to study her as he thought back. "Twelve?"

"Feel better?"

He grinned. "Actually, yes. What just happened?"

She gave him a cheeky grin of her own and went back to her omelet. Without looking up, she asked, "Why don't you just pay it back?"

"What?" It sounded too simple.

But she shrugged. "Pay it back. With interest, if you'd like. Write them a letter stating you just learned of your aunt's misdeeds and you'd like to rectify the situation. And if they have any further questions they can contact your attorney."

"*Attorneys*," Ashton stressed.

"Even better," she grinned.

He hacked off some bacon to chew, needing to digest something alongside her words. "I guess the best answers are sometimes the simplest ones." He brushed her lips with a kiss.

"Did you love her?" Her eyes probed his, and he knew who the "her" was.

"No. I never loved Brittany. It was more like…" he looked off into the cavities of his mind. "Like taking in a wild mustang. Yeah, you can offer them safety, and food, and protect them from their environment, but sometimes, they're just too unruly. They *like* the danger, the hunger, the raw elements. Sometimes it's best to just let them go." He collected her fingers and planted a kiss on her knuckles. "Does that make sense?"

She grinned. "Gonna toss me back to the waters?"

"Never." They shared a smile.

Motion along the wall caught his eye, and Ashton looked up to see Hermosa balancing a tray with one hand and her baby with the other. The way she kept looking over her shoulder, he figured she feared discovery. "Excuse me." He walked over and touched her shoulder.

She paled. "*Señor*! I'm so sorry. I have no food. My baby is hungry. I didn't mean to—"

He collected her tray for her. "I'm not mad. I don't care that you're eating here. Come. Come sit down with me." He led her back to their table.

"What is wrong?" she asked, bouncing her baby and staring between the plate and his face.

He indicated her tray, and she dove in. "Well," Ashton sawed into his own pancakes, "We just got some bad news. It turns out Eshan was hired by Mack, my former stable master, under false pretenses."

Eyes wide with fear, she ceased nibbling her slice of cantaloupe. "What does that mean?"

"It means he was lied to. Mack promised him a lot of money but had no intention of ever paying him. In fact, they were going to kill him as soon as he delivered my horse to Texas."

Tears filled Hermosa's eyes, and she turned to mash a kiss on Noe's ear.

"I have worse news." Ashton dropped his utensils and leaned forward, hands folded. "Hermosa, your mama is dead. Mack killed her." He took a deep breath. "They got a confession and the weapon."

Her face screwed up.

"I'm so very sorry."

One long elegant hand covered Hermosa's mouth, but her agony still showed around it.

Ashton leaned back. "Since Eshan was lied to and hired unjustly by my own former stable master, I'd like to make amends. I'll give you the ten grand he was promised, and I'd like to hire you. It seems I have a vacant housecleaning position these days, first floor."

Hermosa burst into tears. "I have no place to live, *Señor*. My apartment kicked me out. And Maria says all the servant's rooms are full. She's been letting me sleep on her floor."

Ashton's hand reached out to her. "I'll help you pay for your apartment. Or find you a new one. Ten thousand will get you and your baby on your feet."

"Speaking of simple," Raylie stood and pulled out her keychain, finally seeing a way to unload years of agony and help an innocent victim in the process. "I'm getting a new house on Monday, with my promotion." She peeled two keys off the ring and slammed them to the table in front of Hermosa, then took a pen out of her purse and scrawled the address on a napkin. "Hope you like pink." She plopped hard into her chair and resumed eating.

Ashton's mouth dropped open, but then he smiled. "Does this mean you're not going to be my first on-staff Peace Officer?"

She grinned, delighting in how badly he wanted her with him. "Yup. I got a job to do. There's a whole lot of helpless animals out there needing me."

His hand squeezed her knee. "I need you, too." He glanced at his watch. "In fact, we need to wrap up and get going. It's almost nine a.m."

Hermosa kept watching them, alternating between relief and disbelief and gratitude and shock as she ate with confidence that her food would be there again in three hours. "*Señor*, you are so good to me." Fresh tears ran down her cheeks.

"You protected my horses and thus my livelihood by telling me the truth. It was a brave thing you did, and the least I can do is watch out for someone who watched out for me."

Hermosa's face mashed up with tears. "*Gracias, Señor.*"

"*Gracias, señorita.*" He bowed to her, then took Raylie's hand. "Come. Our bags are waiting for us."

"Where?"

Grinning, he led her through the house, down a long hallway, through a heavy metal door and then up onto the flat roof. When the pilot saw them, he started up the helicopter, the blades tossing their hair every which way.

"Your chariot awaits, my lady." With his help, Raylie strapped herself in, and together they lifted off into a crystal blue sky.

Epilogue

One year later

Raylie couldn't believe how big and strong her little foal had grown, but here he was, all long and lean and muscular, lunging on a white cotton line in the training pen with a kiddie saddle strapped to his back, looking for all the world as if he'd been doing this for two years and not two days.

She clucked to him, and he stepped up his pace from a walk to a trot, his gait as smooth and even as his mother's. Ed had been great about letting her train him, and she suspected Ashton had slipped a bit of wisdom into his ear about letting her train as part of her recovery. She couldn't prove it, but she didn't mind.

Everyone had baggage.

A familiar white and green van rounded the corner, and Raylie smiled when Matt got out, his red freckles even more pronounced with all the time he'd been spending outside here in the sun. She waved wide for him, and he came over.

Raylie called out "Whoa," and Timmy shook out his growing mane and plodded close.

"Hey, Ray," Matt said in greeting as he reached for the colt, who obediently came over for a nose rub.

"How's it going?" He looked good, like the extra income from her open position suited him well. Or maybe it was the added responsibility he had chosen to undertake. Either way, Matt had come into his own over the past year.

"Great. I thought I'd take my lady out to lunch."

"A great idea," Ashton said as he came up behind Raylie. The two men shook hands, then Ashton jabbed Matt in the shoulder. "So glad I introduced you two."

"*Excuse* me?" Raylie turned to face him, impassive. "Really."

He grinned, knowing he had gotten her goat, but continuing as if he were right. "At your promotion/case-closed party. I introduced them."

She gasped in mock outrage and poked him in the chest. "*I* introduced them. *You* were too busy schmoozing new clients."

It was his turn to act affronted. "Well, I never."

She smirked. "That's right. Because *I* introduced them."

Across the fields came Hermosa, baby Noe toddling at her side. Matt beamed like a proud papa at the sight of them. As she neared, seeing everyone watching her, she faltered. "Why does everyone look at me?"

Ashton chuckled and sauntered over. "I was just reminding them how I introduced you and Matt."

She frowned, opened her mouth and pointed toward Raylie. "But, it was—"

They all burst out laughing. Raylie jumped on Ashton and covered his mouth. "Stop the lies, mister, or else."

He wiggled out of her grip. "You'll turn me in?"

"To a toad."

Noe squealed with joy and toddled his way to the fence, where Timmy reached down to nose him. The baby fell on his bottom, laughing, and grabbed onto the halter and pulled himself back up.

Raylie squatted down and clapped her hands, and Noe ambled over to her. She scooped him up and placed him on the colt's back.

Ashton took a protective step closer. "Don't—"

"He's fine," Raylie said with a smile. "Noe's been riding Timmy for two days now."

"Really."

Hermosa eased through the fence, the dirt leaving a small smear on her white uniform. She brushed it off and came to the colt's side. "Noe loves him, *Señor*. And Timmy loves Noe."

"Timmy?" He looked at Raylie.

She shrugged. "A better call name than Fearsome. Timmy just sounds so…friendly."

Noe laughed and giggled and held on to the saddle while Hermosa walked with the horse in a few wide circles. Then she gathered her son and said goodbye as she and Matt took their lunch break together.

"Ahh, young love," Ashton sighed as he scooped her from behind.

She spun in his arms to hug him. "Oh, I don't know. I think I like the more mature kind, the type that comes with shared experiences and trust."

He bumped his nose to hers. "I like the passionate kind."

Raylie pressed her forehead to his. "Maybe we could have all three."

"That's what I was thinking." He kissed her. "You ready?"

"For what?"

"Lunch."

She looked at her wrist and saw only skin. "My wrist says it doesn't know what time it is."

A secretive smile tooled around on Ashton's lips as he gathered the lunge line from her hands. "Mine says it's time to spend time with your man."

"Cool." She cocked her hands on her hips and looked around the paddock. "When's he getting here?"

"Ha ha." He grinned at her, then indicated the barn.

He seemed a bit off, like he really did have a secret, and on some level she wondered if he knew she had one as well. "I had my staff ready our horses," he said as he handed Timmy over to a stable hand.

"What's going on?" When he only gave her that secretive smile again, Raylie tucked her fingers into his elbow. "Can we bring Brandy? She would love a trail ride."

"Sure."

Inside the stables, High Eminence and Mystic Time were both saddled and ready for their riders, and Brandy and Cheddar bounced at their feet. Raylie mounted Missy and Ashton hopped on to Emin after patting the stallion's neck. "I figure after he got second place at Saratoga Springs that he deserved a nice trail ride."

Missy stepped into a walk when Raylie urged her with her seat. Brandy barked once and raced out the door, sniffing the grass and running circles around them, with Cheddar bowing and whining and doing all within his power to make her play with him. "Glad he's finally able to earn his keep," Raylie said.

Soon the sounds of two horses clomping through the stables offered a backdrop to their words. "Yeah. You did well, teaching him to trailer."

"About that." Raylie pretended to be abashed. "I, um, may have promised him that every time he trailered, he'd be coming right back home afterward. If you sell him, you'd be going back on your word."

"Not *my* word. *You* made the promise." He eyed her, and Emin made a low whicker, like a warning that he would brook no lies. To the left, Brandy barked aggressively at a rock. Cheddar stepped near, wondering what threat it posed.

Raylie licked her lips, not sure if she overstepped her boundaries. "I know, I understand. I just, well…"

"You like him. You saved his life. I know. I get it."

"And he's a money-maker. I know you'll want to sell him." She nestled her fingers into Missy's mane, feeling foolish for wanting to be sentimental. She had no business interfering in Ashton's livelihood. She yelled, "Brandy, leave the rock alone." The dog barked once more at it, then bounded over, leaving Cheddar to sniff it for intruders.

She felt Ashton watching her, and knew she was being ridiculous. "I'm sorry, I shouldn't have—"

"Raylie, I have no intention of selling Emin."

"What?" She stared at him, rocking along with the bump and sway of her horse. "You don't?"

"No." He shook his head gently and smiled at her. "These three horses, Emin, Missy, Fear—uh, Timmy…they are important to you. They helped you heal. They got you to where you are today. Selling them would only bring you pain, and I swore to you when we first started dating that I would never do *anything* to cause you pain. I meant it then, and I mean it now."

Damn, he still knew her cover to cover. Opened her up, read her like a book, retained every word on every page, set her down, then picked her up to read again. Her throat tightened. "You amaze me."

"My pleasure." He tipped his hat, making her laugh.

Brandy found another rock to bark at, this time circling it and really telling it who was boss. "*Dain bramage*," Raylie sighed, then wobbled a smile. "The price of heatstroke, I guess."

"Better rocks than horses. At least they don't spook."

"Most of them," she nodded.

He took off his Stetson and wiped down his brow. "Is she always going to bark at rocks?"

"No." Raylie faced him, wide-eyed. "Sometimes she barks at stones and boulders, too."

He slapped his hat back on and hung his head, making Raylie laugh. "She alerted us to Mack's presence, and I couldn't ask for more."

"I'm not complaining." He tugged the reins and hopped down. "It's over that hill." He looped the reins over Emin's head and draped them on a tree branch.

Raylie dismounted and tied up Missy to another log. "Where are we going?"

"Here." He took her hand and crested a small hillock, and there she saw a blanket spread out, with a picnic basket and a bucket that she assumed held wine. Brandy loped over, nosed the blanket, then bounded off.

"*Oh.*" She melted at his thoughtfulness and fell into his arms.

His strong fingers brushed a wisp of her long brown hair off her brow and pulled it back into a ponytail. "We met a year ago today, and my life has never been the same."

The strength of his arms, the strength of his love, the strength of his belief in her was more than she ever felt possible. She stood there, dumbfounded, simply staring up at him as every emotion she ever felt for this man burbled up inside her.

"I love you too, babe." He dipped his lips to kiss her, and Raylie choked out a sob.

"I do love you, Ashton. I love you so much." She pressed her lips to his with all the passion she could muster, and Ashton groaned into her mouth.

"I'm glad you finally said it," he told her around the kiss.

"Me, too." She relaxed in his arms, feeling her last barrier crumble. Ashton had been saying it for months now, and she had felt it ever since they began dating, and saying it just now, well, it was high time.

He nuzzled her neck. "Say it again."

She laughed, exposing her throat to him. "Only if you make me moan."

He sucked on her skin, and she purred. "I love you, Ashton Lyre. I thought you were the most handsome man I had ever met, one year ago today, and now I think you are the most amazingly perfect man I have ever met."

"Do you love me?"

She smiled, enjoying how good it felt to say it. "I love you, damn it. Now kiss me."

He did, thoroughly, and Raylie wondered if they were going to make love right here, right now. She submitted in his arms, and Ashton slowly eased back. "Keep your eyes closed."

"With pleasure." It was much easier to enjoy the aftermath of his passion if she didn't ruin it by opening her eyes. She heard a rustle near her feet.

"Raylie?"

She opened her eyes, dragged them down to Ashton, who knelt at her feet. A small blue velvet box he presented to her, and as he opened it he asked, "Will you do me the honor of being my wife?"

Every instinct in her screamed *yes,* but she squelched them down for a moment. She had been dreaming of pink clouds, pink rainbows, pink puppies, pink shoes. She dropped to her knees before him and said, "If you want to marry me, we better do it soon."

He cocked a brow.

"Before your daughter is born. I'd hate to have little illegitimate Lyres running around here. What would the neighbors think?"

He frowned at her. "Are you saying…?"

She nodded. "You're going to be a papa, Ashton. And yes, if the offer still stands, I will marry you."

He collected her close and kissed her senseless. "Really? You are? A girl? You sure? When do you want to get married? Want to elope? Do you have names? When did you find out? Were you going to tell me?"

"I suspected two weeks ago, and the doctor just confirmed it yesterday."

"I thought you looked, well…" Ashton's voice cut off, and she thought he looked a little abashed, like he overstepped a boundary.

She challenged with, "I looked like what?"

He chewed his lip. "Gravid. Maternal. I don't know. I've seen it so long on the mares, I thought I saw it reflected there, on you."

She grinned. "Turns out you were right."

He eased her down to the blanket. "I planned on wine, dine, and sixty-nine, but…"

Raylie touched his lips. "I'll pass on the wine, but my OB says that sex actually exercises the baby." She gave him a jaunty look. "I'm ready when you are."

He flicked off his hat and eased himself onto her. Then he

reached off to the side and collected the ring, which he reverently placed on her finger. "I get a wife and family in one fell swoop."

Raylie looped an arm around his neck. "Don't forget lover," she said as she drew him close.

"Oh, no," he murmured against her lips, "I would never forget to be that."

ABOUT THE AUTHOR

Dorothy Callahan lives in New York with her wonderful husband, a pride of demanding cats, and two loyal dogs, all rescued from shelters (not the husband). When she is not writing, she enjoys shopping for antiques and renovating their pre-Civil War house. Please visit her at *www.dorothycallahan.com*, *dorothycallahanauthor@gmail.com*, or friend her on Facebook under Dorothy Callahan Author.

In the mood for more Crimson Romance? Check out *Power Play* by Nan Comargue at CrimsonRomance.com.

www.ingramcontent.com/pod-product-compliance
Lightning Source LLC
Chambersburg PA
CBHW010635100726
47900CB00011B/2839